Casa loma Ballroom

AND THE

BOOK

OF

DREAMS

Tom

Obermeier

ISBN: 1460971027
ISBN-13: 9781460971024

CHAPTER SIXTEEN

Jamal Taylor stuck his nine year old head around the corner of his great grandmother's house. He could hear the sound of his mother's voice from the front of the house as she called out his name.

"Jamal. Jamal, you better not be hiding from me, Jamal Taylor. I know you know it's time for you to get ready for services, **Jamal.**" Gloria, Jamal's mother, called to him, taking heavy, determined steps through their old home.

Jamal heard the back door shudder as it always did before allowing anyone through. The old house had sunk and shifted more than once over the years, leaving cracks in the walls, creaking floorboards, and doors that had to be shaken loose from their frames before opening.

Jamal didn't wait to hear the outer screen door. He ran as fast as his little legs could take him to the front of the house and scurried under the wide porch through several broken trellises, sliding to a quick stop.

"You know Mama's gonna find you, Jamal, and the longer it takes, the more trouble you're gonna be in." Marchand, Jamal's seventeen year old brother, was in black dress pants, white shirt and tie. He was waiting outside on the porch for the rest of his family to go to service, including his little brother, who was hiding right under his feet.

Jamal stuck his head out from the 1 ½ story brick house. It was a style of house that was popular in 1918 when it and many of the homes in the surrounding city were built.

"You ain't gonna give me up, is you, Neon?"

Neon was Marchand's nickname which was given to him when he was a young gang banger at the age of twelve. They called him Neon because his temper could go on like a light if provoked.

"I don't have to. Mama's gonna find you soon enough without any help from me."

Marchand's mother had named him after something she had seen on television during her pregnancy. She was up late one night watching a British film on the TCM network when she saw the name 'Marchand' in the movie credits. She liked the sound of it, saying the name aloud as she read it off the rolling credits. It was strong yet cultured. She wanted so much for her son and wanted to do the right thing by him. She hoped that picking a French sounding name would be a good start, never knowing the movie credit was for a female actress.

"Not if I can hide here long enough," Jamal argued. "Mama will have to leave to git to services on time."

"Oh, yea, that's a good plan. Then you'll be in even more trouble when she gets back."

"At least I'll miss services," Jamal said.

"What's so bad about going to church services? You'll see some of your friends there…and they got some really good singers now."

"What's that you say, Neon? Are you tellin' me you like to go to services now? Is that where you is?"

Neon thought a moment before answering. "That's where I am, little brother."

"Well, that ain't me," Jamal rejected the idea. "Ain't no gang banger go to services and that's why I ain't goin'. Cause I'm gonna be a 'Utah 32' playah. Jus like you were, Neon."

"Don't you even say that," Neon's temper switched to 'on'. **"You don't know what you're sayin'. Now get out from under this porch and go inside…and stop trying to sound like some gang bangin punk, which you ain't."**

"What's all this yelling going on?" Their mother, Gloria, came out the front door to see what all the commotion was about. "Who are you talkin' to, Neon? Is Jamal out here somewhere?"

"He's right here under the porch, Moms."

"You said you wouldn't tell," Jamal's small voice came from under where the two were standing.

"Jamal, is that you? Get your little butt up in this house and get ready for services. **I mean now, Jamal."**

Reluctantly young Jamal dragged himself out from under the porch and up the front steps. On his way in he paused long enough to eyeball his older brother. Neon did not flinch in the stare he returned to the younger Jamal, he was resolved to keep him safe and out of the street gangs.

"That boy is getting more stubborn every day," Gloria said, shaking her head and still looking in the direction of the house where Jamal had gone. "You two sounded like you were fighting out here. Is everything alright with you, Neon?" She stroked her son's head fondly; her voice was soft and concerned.

"Everything's fine, Mom," Neon held his mother.

Gloria never gave up on her son and it had not been easy. At thirteen years old, Neon was running drugs for the Utah 32's. His young age and innocent appearance kept him under the police radar. Gloria knew something was going on but didn't want to admit her little son was involved in anything criminal. When he started wearing expensive clothes and jewelry and staying out late at night, the signs were too obvious to ignore. She yelled and pleaded, then begged and screamed for him to change his life around before it was too late but her words fell on deaf ears. The street gangs had become his family and the house he grew up in on the corner of Utah and California had become a stopping place on his way to bigger and better things.

It all came to a dramatic conclusion when he was caught with small amounts of crystal meth and arrested for possession with the intent to distribute. Neon had been on his way to meet his fellow gang bangers and was picked up by the police.

His home boy and mentor, seventeen year old Martel Johnson, had gotten in a fight with a rival gang member on the same night. Martel was out-matched against a bigger adversary, but Martel had a gun, and in the heat of battle he shot his opponent dead. While Neon was sentenced to two years probation, his friend got 25 to life.

Neon came home after the trial to find out his girl friend, Janeakwa, was pregnant and Neon was about to become a father at the tender age of fifteen. His mother sat him down that evening and laid it all out for him. She told him that his father, who was Jamal's father as well, had abandoned them right after Jamal was born. Just like her father had abandoned her. Neon's father lived not more than a 40 minute ride from where they were. She said that she would give him the address if he wanted but it wouldn't do him any good to go there since he was now married with two daughters and wanted nothing to do with them. This was the legacy Neon had inherited and now it was the legacy he was almost surely to leave behind if he didn't change his ways and give his own son a chance.

Whatever the words she used, or whatever way she said them, Gloria had gotten through to Neon. He went to church services that next Sunday and accepted Jesus as his savior in a torrent of remorse and tears. He was determined to change his life, to be a good father to his son, and make his mother proud, but it wouldn't be easy. Janeakwa did not want to give up her baby and wanted nothing to do with any church going crusader. She wanted a playa, a gang banger, with money and style, and now that Neon had left the gangs, he had nothing; no money, and no job. He was a high school drop out with no future and no friends, but he was determined to get his son away from Janeakwa and those gang banger influences. He found a job stripping floors at night and studied to get his GED during the day.

"Does Mr. Waterman got work for you this week, son?" Gloria asked.

George Waterman had been the one big break in Neon's life, besides his family and the birth of his son. George was the one who had given this young man on probation a chance to prove himself. After two years of hard work and consistent service, Neon had become one of George's best employees.

"Not until Wednesday night. I'm meeting him over at that Casa Loma place on Iowa. You know, it's just around the corner."

"You mean that place where white people go to dance?"

"Yea, that place."

"Welllll, maybe my son can learn to dance?"

"Those people do ballroom dancin', Mom's," Neon informed her. "Besides, I'll just be there to do the floors."

Standing on the 60 year old floor of the Casa Loma Ballroom, Rita, Klaus, Monica and Pat Donovan were discussing the upcoming Frankie Manning workshop.

"We expect the number to be right around 50 couples by the end of next week," Rita told Pat.

"Fifty couples at $85.00 per person, you should do alright with this thing," Pat nodded approvingly. "Plane fare for Frankie Manning and that other instructor…"

"Erin Stevens," Klaus spoke up.

"And you're getting this place for a song." Pat continued. He was concerned whether the Vintage Dance Federation, being new, had the organizational ability to host this kind of event, especially since they were using the Casa Loma Ballroom as their venue. "Are you going to put them up in a fancy hotel while they're here?"

"Rhonda Fleming is providing a nice 'home stay' for them," Monica answered. "She's a nurse at Barnes Jewish, and since Frankie is like 85 years old, we thought her skills might come in handy, just in case." She wrinkled her nose as if Frankie's advanced age were an uncomfortable subject.

"So you should come out lookin' pretty good on this deal?" Pat arched his eyebrows and cut to the chase.

Rita nodded and smiled back. "Hopefully the Federation will be able to continue to bring in talented instructors like Frankie and Erin and be able to host more of these kinds of events."

"Well, good for you guys. It's nice to see people doing well." A big smile of congratulations spread across Pat's face. "I gotta warn you though, if you do decide to use the Casa Loma Ballroom again, I won't be letting you get off so easy. This was a onetime deal. I'm only doing this to help you get started."

"And we appreciate all your help, Pat," Rita told him. "I'm sure the Casa Loma Ballroom and the Vintage Swing Federation will have a long relationship."

"Yea, well, I need someone with an official title to sign the contract that's in my office. Who would that be?"

Rita gently shook Klaus's shoulder. "I think that could be one of your responsibilities Mr. Treasurer."

Klaus fell in step behind Pat. "I'll be right back."

"Ok, dear," Rita gave him a quick smile.

Monica put her arm around her friend. "Bringing in Frankie Manning is going to be the biggest thing yet for the Federation. It's so cool."

"Oh, this is nice, but it's nothing compared to Harvest Moon Swing Out in beautiful...Pasadena...California." Rita stretched out the name of the location as she strolled across the hardwood dance floor, accenting the weekend trip she and Klaus were planning.

"Oh, I hate you," Monica joked. "But I wouldn't if I was going there with you? I mean, if the Federation needed a 'photographer' to record the event." Monica looked at her friend from over her shoulder.

"That would be so much fun," Rita agreed. "But we have to get Klaus to go along with it."

"That would be your department, girl friend. Shhhh, here they come." Noises coming from the halls of Pat's office stalled the girls' planning.

"When will you have a final count on the number?" Pat asked Rita, as he and Klaus walked out to meet the two girls.

"Probably not till the day of," Rita told him.

A ring from Klaus's cell phone prompted him to look at the caller ID.

"Excuse me a minute, I think this is someone who wants to register," Klaus put the phone to his ear. "Jerry Russell. How are you doing, my friend?"

I was watching an instructional video when I remembered to call Klaus and make sure Ann and I still had time to register for the workshop next weekend. The video I was watching had a German couple who were painstakingly teaching the basic steps of the Lindy 'swing out'. I forced myself to sit and listen to the technique they were describing to get a better feel for the step. I was motivated to learn as much as I could and get it right from the beginning. This vintage stuff was like a breath of fresh air. It was another chance to bring dancing back into my life without the constraints and conditions I was under when I taught dance to earn a living. With my experience I was a little bit ahead of the game; I could do this and have fun with it.

When I stopped to call Klaus, I pressed 'pause' on the video I was watching and walked over to the sunlight streaming in through the front window of Ann's house in Dogtown, St. Louis. I hung up the phone and looked out into the neighborhood. It was a beautiful Sunday afternoon and I was considering what kind of outdoor activities Ann and I could do when my cell phone rang.

"Dancin' Don, how are you doing?" I wondered how Don had gotten my cell phone number, and why he would be calling me.

"I'm fine, thanks, Jerry. How are you doin'?"

"I'm good."

"You're probably wondering why I called you. Uh, well, I'll get right to the point. I heard that the Federation is going to have a Lindy Hop swing dance contest. Do you know anything about that?"

"As a matter of fact I was just on the phone with Klaus. He said something about it in passing last night and I'd say it's a possibility at best. But how did you find out so fast and, not that I mind, but, how did you get my phone number?"

"I was just talking to Bob about the competition and your name came up. We're interested in your opinion since you're new on the scene and still have some objectivity and, knowing your professional dance background, well, we wanted to know what you thought our chances would be in that kind of contest. Or really, if you think we should even be entering a competition at all? Of course, that's saying there is going to be a competition."

It was amazing how much thought and discussion about a 'potential' dance competition had fired the wireless phones this early in the day. I shouldn't have been too surprised at how self-conscious people were about their dancing though. There are more than enough stories about people who vomit before performances and competitions, and dancers who freeze once the music starts to fill volumes of anecdotal books. But the idea of a competition, on the other hand, is something else all together. People, especially men, are always sizing themselves up against others, assessing who would come out on top, whether in actual physical combat or who is the better dressed, or better looking, or who is just better in some way. The chance to validate those assessments and even be judged the best in some way by an 'impartial body' is almost too appealing for any ego to pass up. We thrill and obsess at the idea of winning - anything.

"Please don't overemphasize my limited experience as a beginning ballroom dance teacher," I told Don, "especially as it concerns my knowledge of vintage swing, which is even more limited. But if you're asking me if I think you're qualified to compete in a dance competition, I would say yes. Having said that, I would also say that anybody who is willing to compete is qualified to be in a dance competition; winning that competition is anybody's guess."

"Oh…," he said, and after a moment's pause, pressed me further. "All that's true of course, but what we are looking for, Bob and I that is, is more of an analysis of our dancing." Don went right into enumerating the potential talent. "You know Klaus and Rita would be in there somewhere, they have to be the odds on favorite. Then there's Joe and Jennifer, they've been getting better each day, and then Wally and Fran, and Janice and Dave, and of course you and Ann look pretty good out there, too. And then there's a whole bunch of good dancers who don't have regular partners like me and Monica and the rest. To put it plainly, Jerry, would we be making fools of ourselves if we got into the Federation's swing contest?"

"Listen, really, I don't know that there is even going to be a Federation swing contest, but no, Don, I don't think you'll make fools of yourselves if there is one. I think you guys would look fine and could have fun in a competition. Just remember, it's not always the best dancers who win, it's the ones who dance the best that evening. The most important thing, of course, is to have a good time, and you don't have to win to have a good time."

"Yea, that's good advice, Jerry."

"Anytime," I told him.

I wasn't sure that competitions were the best thing for the vintage swing crowd. They seemed to be divisive enough as it was. But like I told Dancin' Don, as far as I knew, there was no competition.

Monday and Tuesday came and went with a few dance practices in Ann's living room. Bob and Sheila joined us Tuesday night and, though Bob said nothing to me about Don's phone call, I could tell he was looking for me to comment on his moves as we practiced. Whenever he did ask about how he looked, I never went into too many specifics, knowing how your words can come back to haunt you, especially when repeated and passed from one person to the next. It's different when somebody pays you to critique their dancing. You are the teacher, they are the student and they expect some criticism, but when you're just another dancer, any negative comments are seldom met with any approval, or more importantly, acceptance.

When Wednesday came around, I was ready to start my work week. I didn't know how long I would be willing to balance two different work places with two different pricing structures but I was willing to give it a try, at least for a few weeks. One thing was for sure, as I went up the cement stairs to the ballroom, I was a lot more relaxed going to work at Casa Loma than any day at The Boa Constrictor.

Terry Strahan was waiting for me at the bar. He reached out his hand and greeted me like a patron, "Hey, Jerry, how are you doing? Are you ready to get started?"

"Ready as I'll ever be, I guess."

"Great, come on back and I'll show you around. You'll be working with Anna tonight unless it gets really busy and we have to open up the side bar. If you have any questions, just ask Anna. She knows this place as well as anyone."

It was different in the big hall without the usual collection of voices and music playing. The sound of our single conversation accentuated the vastness and emptiness of the room. It was like there was a holding space for a three story elephant that was right in front of me.

After Terry showed me how to operate the manual register and gave me a price list for the drinks, he left me alone to look around and discover what was back there. I went about opening the drawers and pillaging through them just out of idle curiosity. I hoped to find some old, hand written notes about famous bands and musicians but there was nothing that dated back any further than a couple of years, along with some blank paper, a few pencils and a flashlight. Disappointed and bored, and my curiosity getting the better of me, I progressed to sticking my head inside the lower cabinets and shelves with the flashlight to see what I could find. I brushed away several cobwebs, squeezing my shoulders deeper into the little space so I could maneuver the light, when I saw some writing scratched on the back wall. '*Lord, keep and protect all....*' was all I could see. There was more scribbling, but it was blocked by a string of electrical conduit that was hanging down. I could see the last part that ended '*Jack Buckmueller and the Book of Dreams, 11/5/41*'. I had almost half of my body stuck inside the cabinet with my ass sticking out when I heard the sound of someone at the bar.

"Yea, just a second," I called out from under the woodwork of the back bar. I knew how I must look to whoever it was. "I'll be right there." I pushed and wriggled and bumped my shoulder and then my head as I extracted myself from the bleak space, and when I got to my knees and looked up, I felt a rush of blood go straight to my brain causing the room to spin and making me feel a little queasy.

Through the haze that was in my head I thought I saw a thick man with black hair combed straight back wearing a white shirt and black tie walking away from the bar, but once my head started to clear I was not able to spot my unknown guest. "What can I get for……?" There was no one. Once I got to my feet and I looked around, I realized that nobody was demanding anything from me. I looked to the right and to the left and leaned over the edge of the bar to see behind the popcorn machine. I was sure I heard something, so I called out once more. "Is anyone there?" But there was nothing. I had been offering service to an empty room.

In less than a minute I had my head and shoulders shoved back under that filthy crawl space behind the back bar. Armed with pencil and paper I was ready to find out what the rest of the message said. Who was Jack Buckmueller and what did he have to do with the Casa Loma Ballroom? I continued my archeological expedition under the cabinets and metal shelves of Casa Loma's darker regions with renewed vigor. I had almost my entire body wedged under the dark woodwork with only my feet dangling outside. When I pointed the flashlight up, the rest of the message showed clear. It read,

> '*Lord, keep and protect all who enter this building.*
> *May their hearts have rhythm and their soul a song,*
> *Clap hands and dance their whole life long.*
> *Jack Buckmueller and the Book of Dreams 11/5/40*

I wanted more but was thrilled to have found this much. I took out a pencil and paper and wrote it down and shoved it in my pocket. It wasn't a map to a treasure or lyrics to an unpublished song but it was something, and I felt linked to the past, a connection to a different time when all this was still new and wonderful. I couldn't wait to tell someone.

"Uh, Jerry, what the hell are you doing under there?" I recognized Pat's voice.

"Just a second, Pat," I answered from behind the wooden structure. "I'll be right out in just a second," I promised. But it wasn't a just a second or a minute, it was five minutes and only after Pat had come round the bar and grabbed me by my ankles, pulling my wedged shoulders out from the narrow opening.

"I'm not positive here, Jerry, but I'm pretty sure you're the first bartender to get stuck under the back bar here at Casa Loma."

"Yea, thanks for your help," I was trying to come up with the right words to explain myself when Pat spoke first.

"Ok….I'll bite, how did you get stuck behind that God awful place?"

When I told him about the message, his face lighted up like the neon Budweiser light glowing in the window.

"Message? There's a message down there?"

"Oh, yea, it's back there scribbled on the wall." And before I could say anything else Pat was on his hands and knees burrowing his head deep into the crevasses of the back bar cabinet, holding the very flashlight I had used earlier. He had thrown caution to the wind, not worrying whether someone might come along and find him in such a compromised position, or that he was shoving his head across decades of grit, grease, and grime.

Ten minutes later his enthusiasm began to diminish considerably.

"How big were the letters? Were they good size or really small?" he called back to me.

"Pretty good size," I told him. "You should be right in front of it." I knocked on the wood next to the frozen drink machine. "Right about here. Do you see anything at all?"

"No," was his solitary answer.

"Maybe you rubbed it off with your shoulder."

"No, I couldn't get my shoulders in far enough to reach the wall if my life depended on it….I'm comin' out."

With a fair amount of effort he wriggled out and pulled himself up. Standing in front of me I could see small handfuls of dust clusters wedged in various parts of his blonde hair and smudges of dirt on his face and forehead and all over his shirt. His eyes were dark and staring me down.

"This better not be one of Strahan's practical jokes."

"Pat, I swear," I put my open palm up in the air.

Pat shook his head and left without saying another word. As soon as he left, I got my head back under the back bar to take another look, but just like Pat had said, the wall was blank.

"Can I get a pitcher of water and three cups?" a voice asked. It was time to take my Indiana Jones hat off and put the bartender hat back on. The voice that asked for a pitcher of water belonged to a large young man in his early twenties. He was stocky, probably carrying 200 pounds with his six foot and an inch or more height, and when I looked up, I could see a boyish face topped with a short haircut. There were two girls standing next to him. I would later find out their names were Michelle and Elizabeth and the big guy was Marty. The girl to Marty's immediate right had brown, straight hair that hung along the sides of her face. She wore bib overalls and a turquoise top with puffy sleeves. I noticed these details only because I had to force my stare from Michelle, the girl next to Elizabeth, to keep from being too obvious. Michelle stood out so much it was as if she was the only one standing in the room. Of all the vintage clothes I had seen in the short time I had been going to the Casa Loma Ballroom, only Vanessa's outfits had come close to the look Michelle gave to the ensemble she was wearing. She wore a light blue denim dress with a hem that ended just above her knees. There were two straps that came over her shoulders and buttoned at the waist. She wore a white shirt that was dotted with little red strawberries and underneath it all was a curving figure that spoke volumes in support of tight fitting clothes. She was the kind of girl you had to ask yourself if she would be worth the trouble that it would take to keep all the other guys away, if you were lucky enough to get your hands on her in the first place.

When I handed over the pitcher of water, I was still looking at her like she was something in a store window. I realized the three of them were watching me watch her, and it was then that I finally managed to get my mouth open and form words.

"N'nice outfit," I stammered.

"Thanks," she said, and in spite of the little bit of drool that was forming at the corner of my mouth, she rewarded my meager compliment with a smile so big it could have warmed the entire cast of C-span. Michelle's two friends retrieved the cups and pitcher of water without any signs of criticism. They must have understood my reaction because of similar reactions in the past. Still, I couldn't get over the feeling that I was left standing there with egg on my face.

The night wore on and customers stepped out from the staircase like a slow drizzle but with enough frequency to fill up a good size group class. The floor was almost completely empty with the exception of two couples who were doing what they could to remember what they had learned in the class the previous week. When the teacher, Sherry Martin, announced that the class was starting, a random collection of timid and shy, want-to-be swing dancers came out from the shadows and up from the chairs and tables that circled the dance floor. While I watched and listened to the lesson from my spot behind the bar, I wondered how many times a teacher could say 'slow, slow, quick-quick' before those words came back to haunt them in their dreams like a possessed spirit.

Neon and his employer, George Waterman, walked up the cement steps to the Casa Loma Ballroom, and like every other person who had come up that staircase for the first time, craned their necks toward the walls and ceilings as if someone or something were about to jump out at any moment. The tiny cage at the first flight of stairs where Louise Brinkmann was usually stationed was empty. Louise was getting on in years and would occasionally take a night off for health reasons.

Once they got to the top of the stairs they met Terry Strahan, who was taking the entry money for Louise. He pointed them in the direction of Pat Brannon who was standing a few feet away from my bar. Pat introduced me to George and George introduced his assistant, Neon, to Pat and me. After we exchanged greetings and introductions, Pat took them over to the edge of the dance floor and got down to the reason they were there.

"It'll take at least four days to do this job properly." George looked at Pat's reaction to see if that was more time than Pat was willing to give. "I could probably do it in less, but it would be pushin' it. We have to strip the floor completely and then allow time for the dust to settle; then clean the floor before we put any protective seal on it." George explained the process as Pat responded with an occasional 'Uh, huh', mostly just to let George know he was listening.

"Of course, if we have to do it in less time, that means I'll have to bring in more workers and that means more money?" George gave Pat a sympathetic raise of his eyebrows.

"How much money," Pat asked right away?

"I'd have to say……with the size of this floor…….it would be another five hundred." George waited only a few seconds for the shock to sink in before going on. "Now if it's just Neon and me," George motioned to Neon standing behind him who was trans-fixed at the sight of the group class that was going on behind them, "then we can do it for a lot less, but it's going to take more **time,**" George emphasized the word.

Pat said nothing. He wanted to think of something other than the cost of re-doing the 5,000 square foot dance floor and allowed himself to be distracted by Neon who was being distracted by the group class.

"Ever see any swing dancing before, Neon?" Pat asked him.

Neon turned his attention away from the rotating females. "Is that what they're doing?"

"That's right," Pat said proudly. "That's what we do here, mostly; swing dancing, and a few other ballroom dances, but mostly just swing."

"You know, Pat," George mentioned for some unknown rea-son, "Neon lives right around the corner and down the street."

"Is that right?"

"Yes sir," Neon confirmed, looking about the large interior. "Lived there all my life, and my mother too, and this is the first time I've been inside here…first one in the family to be on the inside of this place, I think."

"Why don't you take a look around?" Pat suggested. "You can't get lost. The place is just one big bowl with the floor and stage as the center of everything."

"Thank you, sir," Neon turned to George. "Is that alright, George?"

"Yea, go ahead. Give yourself the nickel tour. I'll find you when it's time to leave."

Neon walked around the outside of the circle of the group class. He was more interested in the pretty girls then the history of the old building, but after receiving several dubious looks, he made his way upstairs so he could watch without bringing any unwarranted attention to himself. He found a spot at the railing across from the ladies restroom where he could look down unnoticed, which he did until he was interrupted by a pretty voice.

"Why only watch when you could be down there dancing? We can always use a good lead."

Neon jumped a little at the sound of the pretty blonde. He hadn't heard or noticed her come up behind him.

"I know, you're probably too advanced to be in any 'beginner' group classes," she said.

"Oh no, that ain't it. Ya see, from up here I can watch without bein' seen," Neon was doing his best to be cool and not look directly at the girl. She was fine, even in that strange get up, anyone could see that, but he knew if he let himself stare at her, his eyes would write checks his body had no way of cashing. "I don't even know how to do any of that swing stuff. Besides, I'm with Mr. Waterman. We're only here to give Mr. Brannon a quote on strippin' the floors."

"Oh, I see. Well, I'm, Michelle," she held out her hand.

"Nice to meet you, Michelle," Neon took her hand and as soon as his eyes met hers, he immediately dropped them back to the floor. "I'm Neon. That's what everybody calls me anyway."

Michelle was taken by the young man's shyness, "Nice to meet you, Neon."

Neon looked up for another moment and met her smile with his, then looked back to the dance floor right away.

"You know this dance was originated in Harlem back in the 1920's by African Americans. It seems a shame that more African Americans aren't dancing it now."

Neon dropped his smile. Maybe it was the way she kept saying 'African American's like it was the first time she used that word to refer to black people. More often than not, Neon and his gang banger buddy's had referred to themselves as 'nigger this' or 'nigger that' and he only guessed that white people did the same thing when they were not around blacks. Although they better not say it to a black man's face; and that's for damn sure. Or maybe it was all her talk about swing dancing coming from Harlem in the twenties, like she really knew something about black people that turned him the wrong way. Whatever it was, it caught him off guard.

"Uh, I don't know about any of that.....do **you** do that swing dance stuff?"

"I've been learning. I'm interested in anything vintage," she said, "like my outfit. Do you like vintage clothes?" she held on to her skirt and twirled.

"I gotta say, I like it," he said smiling. "But I think you'd look good in most anything you put on."

"Thanks," she beamed. "Listen, I should be getting back to my friends but you should come to the Frankie Manning workshop this weekend."

"What workshop? And who is Frankie Mannin?"

"It's Manning, Frankie Manning," Michelle corrected. "He's one of the people who helped create swing dancing, and it's his workshop."

"Oh...so it's how to swing dance, lessons; the stuff that you like?"

"That's right."

"Is it expensive?"

"It's eighty five dollars," she said solemnly.

Neon moved away from the railing and took his hand away as if it was about to shoot fire through him and out various orifices. "I can't afford that."

"Ok, Ok, then," she calmed him. "You could go to the party afterwards. It's at Our Lady of Hope on Washington." Michelle turned to head down the stairs and back to her friends. "Listen,

I have to go, but if you're serious about learning to swing dance, there will be plenty of people at the party to show you."

"Will you be there?" Neon asked her.

"I'll be there."

"Then I'll be there, too," he said, and watched as Michelle bounced down the curving staircase.

It took about a half hour after the group class was over before the 'experienced' swing dancers started to come up the stairs from the street.

"You look like you belong back there, Jerry," Klaus reached across the bar and shook my hand.

"Congratulations on your new job," Rita added.

"Thanks, but it's only temporary, until they can get someone permanent. How's the workshop going?"

"Great," Rita answered without hesitation. "We should have a big turnout. Have you and Ann decided about going?"

I held out an envelope with our check inside. "Yes we have, and here's the check with our registration money, even if you don't need it."

"Oh, we need it, and we need people like you and Ann to attend," Klaus added.

"You know, Jerry," Rita started her sales pitch, "Federation members get a ten dollar discount, and it's not too late to join. You see with the annual membership fee, you'll not only get the ten dollars right back from the Frankie Manning workshop, but you'll be eligible to get discounts on all our other promotions, like our dances, and lessons, and you'll get e-mails prior to all the events so you will have first option on attendance in case we sell out."

"Well, you're quite a salesperson, Rita," I said it like it was a compliment but I was thinking anything but. I recognized her pitch line and red flags went up in my head. I knew they were getting more than they were giving no matter how good the offer sounded, though I wasn't exactly sure of what.

"But…."? Klaus noticed I was hesitant for some reason.

I decided to tell him the plain truth. "Well to be honest, I heard some unsettling things about the Federation, and Ann and I have some reservations."

"What things have you heard?" he asked without being defensive.

"Nothing specific; a lot of it sounds like the usual amount of unsatisfied customers that everybody gets." I didn't want to get into a 'he said, she said' discussion so I brought up an incident I knew about first hand. "I will tell you this though, I didn't care for the way the Federation tried to blackball Vanessa Saturday night. If that's the kind of thing the Federation does, then I can tell you right now, it's not for us." I knew I could speak for Ann.

"Oh, that," Klaus exclaimed, and gave a knowing look at Rita then back at me. "That was not the Federation. That was someone else's idea of what the Federation should be doing."

"You mean Monica?" I guessed.

Rita blushed as if she were just as guilty. "I apologize for that. It was a mistake and probably as much my fault as it was Monica's. You see, we were just talking about how guys can be turned off swing dancing when they get turned down over and over again, and maybe even give up on dancing altogether. We were watching Vanessa at the time and I guess her name got mentioned and…. well, Monica tends to take things on her own sometimes. Please believe me, we are not the kind of organization that is exclusionary in any way. As soon as I see Vanessa I will apologize to her myself, and I promise that won't happen again."

Her explanation seemed sincere. "Well, I appreciate the help you and Klaus have given me, and I can see how a friend might get overzealous," I told them. "Go ahead and take this check for now. I'll plan on getting a discount on the next promotion which, from what I hear on the grapevine, will be a dance competition."

"Dance competition? Where did you hear that?" both Klaus and Rita were tickled by the idea.

"From you," I said.

"Me?"

"You told me the other night that someone suggested the Federation should hold a swing dance competition. I told Ann, Ann told Sheila, Sheila told Bob, and Bob told Dancin' Don, who called me Sunday afternoon wanting to know what I thought his chances were of winning the Federation's upcoming dance competition."

"Cause and effect," Klaus chuckled, surprised at how fast the grapevine could work.

"One ripple in a small pond and everyone in the pond feels that ripple," I intoned.

"And this is one small pond," Rita remarked and turned to Klaus. "Well, I guess that means we should be getting this dance competition under way."

"Are you sure you want to do that?" I countered. "I mean, this is a new scene, as everybody puts it, and a lot of the dancers are just getting to know each other. Couldn't a competition be a little divisive among this young group?"

"You've got a good point there," Rita acknowledged.

"Especially when you consider how critical people can be when they talk about other people's dance skills," I added.

Klaus seemed to agree with me as well. "If we held the thing and no one entered, the federation would look stupid, and if a lot of people entered, then a lot of people might walk away feeling like losers."

"You can only have one winner in a competition," I pointed out.

"Let's keep our plans for a dance competition where they are now…non-existent," Rita decided. "And we'll watch and see how this thing evolves."

I thought then that there was more going on in that head of Rita's than knowing how to turn.

"Jerry Russell, as I live and breathe," and there, standing next to Pat and Terry, was Detective Robert Towning. We reached across the bar and shook hands. "I thought you were working over at that yuppie place on Washington?"

"I'm still there, two nights a week and two nights here; keeps me off the streets. How are you doing, Detective?"

"I'm good, I'm good."

Both Pat and Terry stood quietly behind Detective Towning without expression. I was putting together pieces of a puzzle that could only come out spelling trouble; trouble for me, trouble for Ann, and trouble for everyone at the Casa Loma Ballroom."

"Can I get you something?" I asked him.

"No, thank you, I'm here in an official capacity."

"Don't tell me," I said.

"It looks like a girl's gone missing, Jerry," Terry spoke up.

"She was a regular with this swing crowd and she was last seen here Saturday night," Pat added.

"Was it Vanessa?" I asked.

"Vanessa Billings, and please don't tell me you know something about this?" Detective Towning asked.

"We may have been the last ones to see her, Ann and Sheila and myself," I said it straight out.

"Not again?" the Detective exclaimed.

"Ann thought she saw something strange."

"What did Ann see?" he asked, his mood changing from warm and pleasant to upset and impatient.

"She thought she saw someone with a broad brimmed, fedora hat stop Vanessa's car at the parking lot exit, then go around to the driver's side, get in, and drive off." I told the story quickly in an avalanche of words.

"Did any of you hear any screams or see signs of struggle from the car?"

"No, none of that," I said. "I don't think Ann did either but you'll have to ask her yourself."

"Of course you didn't consider alerting anyone, like the police?"

"As you may remember, we don't have a rich and warm relationship with the St. Louis police force. Besides, we were in a car on the other side of the parking lot at night, and saw no struggle. As far as we were concerned, there was nothing to report."

"Other than having a fedora hat, what else did this person look like?"

"Well, I can't say, it was Ann who saw him. By the time Sheila and I looked up, the car was driving away."

"Yea, it started with Ann the last time, didn't it?" The detective had his notebook out.

"You can't think we are guilty of anything here?" I asked in defense of myself and Ann.

"I was just making an observation."

He turned his attention to Pat and Terry, including them in the conversation. "Look, right now all we have is a missing person. She may show up tonight and everything will be much to do about nothing. These kinds of things often turn out like that." The detective had put away his notebook and was now addressing Pat and Terry as well as me. "Vanessa is a single girl who lives alone and didn't return her mother's cell phone calls, so her mother calls where she works and they haven't seen her either, so she calls us and here I am. Could be the girl went off on a romantic trip to the Bahamas's and doesn't want to be contacted. Could be she's staying with a boyfriend and lost her cell phone, could be a lot of things, but until we have anything else to go on, it's just another missing person. We've got about a hundred files like that and some of them never get solved. My advice is to say nothing about this to anyone or you'll only spread unnecessary panic and fear and that won't do anyone any good." Detective Towning turned to address Pat specifically. "Mr. Brannon, it looks like you've got a real nice place here and this community needs businesses like yours to keep it alive. I'm going to get a statement from Ann Brill and this Sheila person and we'll go from there. Tell those security people of yours to keep an eye out for someone wearing a fedora hat or anything else that might be suspicious and I'll see if we can't get a better description of this guy after I've had a chance to talk to Ann."

"Thank you, Detective," Terry and Pat took turns shaking hands with Robert Towning. "If there is anything you need from us, just let us know. One of us, either Terry or I, is always here and you can call me anytime on that number I gave you." Pat and Terry walked away in different directions exchanging a wave and a nod as they went about the normal operations of the ballroom.

"What is it about you and nice places, Jerry? You know, you could get a very bad reputation?"

"Tell me about it," I agreed.

"How about that drunk factory you work at on Washington? Do they have any suspicious characters I should know about?"

"The Boa Constrictor…only a couple hundred or so," I told him. "By the way, I thought you were a homicide detective. There isn't a murder investigation you're not telling me about is there?"

"They disbanded the missing person's department…..cut backs. We all take turns picking up any missing persons reports that come in. The fact that I got this one was just the luck of the draw."

"A coincidence," I questioned?

"If you believe in coincidences," he answered.

"I'm guessing you don't believe in coincidence then, Robert."

"Nope," he said decisively.

"So what does a homicide detective believe in, if I'm not getting too personal?"

He waited a long moment before answering. "I believe that the hardest thing in life is to live with someone and get along with them. I believe we all have dreams of some kind or another and if you're not sharing your dream then you're probably taking someone else's dream from them." He stopped when he saw my surprised and curious expression at his reflective candor and tried to give me a better answer. "I'd say 75% of all the calls that come into the department are some kind of domestic disturbance. I wouldn't call that coincidence. I'd call that predictable."

When Ann came in with Bob and Sheila, she immediately left them and headed in my direction. She took one step and stopped dead in her tracks when she saw Detective Towning standing there across the bar from me, shock registering in her face.

"Hello, Ann, nice to see you again," the Detective reached out to greet her.

"Hello, Detective," she shook his hand and looked at me. "Jerry, what's this about?"

"It's Vanessa," I said softy and reached for her hand. "Listen, honey, please don't get upset but, it looks like she's gone missing."

Ann put her hand to her chest and her whole body deflated. **"Huh,"** was all she said and I could see her collapse as her knees began to buckle. Detective Towning caught her by her shoulders and I quickly ran out from behind the bar to get to her and the two of us helped her to a nearby table. I didn't realize until that moment how strongly Ann had felt about what she had seen Saturday night in Casa Loma's parking lot. Terry Stahan saw what was going on from his spot at the door and came right over to offer assistance. Ann was having trouble breathing and I went back to get a damp towel for her forehead from behind the bar. By the time I got back to Ann, Pat had shown up to console her for reasons he could only guess. A crowd had started to gather and Terry told everyone not to worry, that Ann was only out of breath and needed some air. He went about turning one of the big fans in her direction and told everyone to let her alone and allow her to get her breath back.

Pat took me by the arm and whispered that he would take over working the door while Terry watched the bar until Anna Shlemmer got there, which should be any minute.

The small crowd that had gathered began to disperse with the exception of Sheila and Bob. Sheila had recognized Detective Towning and was looking from him to Ann while asking her what was wrong. Ann just waved her off.

"I'm only guessing here, but are you Sheila?" the Detective addressed her.

"That's right, Detective," she said looking up. "We've never met, but I know who you are. Ann and I have been friends for a long time."

Detective Towning allowed Bob to stay; cautioning him to keep their conversation private. He got both girls accounting of what happened that night in fairly quick order. When he finished writing down his notes, he put his writing pad in his jacket pocket and asked Ann one more question.

"Ann, you reacted pretty strongly when you found out that Vanessa was missing. Were you two close, or had you known each other before you started coming to this place?"

"No, Detective. I've never said a word to her; in fact, we've never really met," she looked right at him from across the table. "But I had such a strange feeling that night, and now…" it wasn't clear whether Ann was correcting what she was about to say, or continuing what she was saying,

"…now I feel so bad that I didn't say something, or do something, you know?" she spoke to him like he was a priest, with sincere contrition, and her honesty was not lost on the detective.

"Look, Ann, if I were the dispatcher that night and someone called this in because they had a 'strange feeling', I probably would have just forgotten the call completely. With all the little gang bangers out there selling drugs and fighting with each other with guns and knives…shoot, this just sounds like two people hookin' up." He looked around the table, "of course now, with hindsight, we can second guess ourselves, but that's all it would be, just second guessing. You're not the bad guy, Ann, however this thing turns out. Remember that, Ok?"

Ann dropped her eyes to the table. "Ok, Detective."

It was clear that his words, though reassuring and comforting as they were, had little effect.

He said his good-byes and told all of us to call him if we remembered anything else.

Anna Schlemmer, the top bartender at Casa Loma, had arrived and was now working the bar. I didn't want to take advantage and shirk off my duties on my first night, but I wanted to make sure Ann was alright before getting back behind the bar.

"Ann, are you going to be Ok? I can stay here with you for a while if you want."

Sheila put her arm around Ann. "We can take you home if that's what you want?"

"No, no, I'll be fine. I'll just sit here for a minute and probably stand by the bar for a while. I may even get on the dance floor before the nights over, who knows. Don't worry about me, Jerry. And you need to go back to work. After all it's your first night on the job. I'll be fine, just go," she shooed me away with the backs of her hands.

I went back to the bar while Sheila and Bob sat with Ann for a while longer. The room had about 50 couples scattered about the large dance floor with the sounds of Ella Mae Morse emanating from the DJ's speakers.

In the next hour Ann left the table she was sitting at to stand at the bar and talk to me. It was getting busier but it was mostly pitchers of water and since Anna was happier working than standing around, I had plenty of time to talk to Ann. She was becoming more at ease and I was able to get her to smile and even laugh after a time. It wasn't long before Bob walked over and got her on the dance floor which I was glad to see.

Just after they disappeared between the tables, I noticed Monica at the bar a little to my right. She was there with a pitcher of water in one hand and had several plastic cups in the other and was moving out of the way of others as she slid down the bar to be in front of me.

"We were a little worried about your girlfriend, Jerry. What's her name…..? Is she gonna be alright?" her words were hurried and curious.

"Ann, her name's Ann, and yes, she'll be fine, thanks for asking. She's more embarrassed than anything, just got a little out of breath, that's all." I wanted a reason not to talk to her as I looked for something to do or someone to wait on, but there was no one, and Monica wasn't going anywhere.

"Who was that man you guys were talking to? He looked like a cop."

"He's an old friend and was concerned about Ann," I lied a little and hoped it wouldn't come back to haunt me.

"Oh, don't mind me; I'm just nosy, if you haven't noticed," she justified herself and went right on without skipping a beat. "Anyway that's not why I came over here. I wanted to apologize for telling everyone they shouldn't dance with Vanessa Saturday night, not that anyone listens to me anyway. I think she danced more Saturday night than any other night she's been here." She laughed a full and rich laugh, the way some people do in case no one else laughs at what they say, then their laugh can hide the awkward silence. "I just want this to be so special for everyone that sometimes I go overboard, know what I mean?"

I wondered how the hierarchy of command went that got her over here to apologize. Had Klaus told her or had Rita.

"Yea, I know what you mean. Say," I said, changing the subject, "this is the first time I haven't seen Dancin' Don here. Where's he at tonight?"

"I don't know," she said, surprised at my question. "He's such a strange bird, who knows where he is."

"He seems Ok to me. Doesn't he live close to here?"

"Oh you should see his little place. It's right around the corner above a coffee shop. He doesn't even own a car," she was more than ready to dish the dirt on poor Don and I was more than ready to defend the guy.

"I heard he taught himself to dance….from watching old movies. That's pretty impressive."

"Yea, well, when you dance with Klaus you can see the difference."

"That doesn't make him strange, that he doesn't lead as well as Klaus. I can't imagine how many times he had to hit rewind and play before he got a step right? I admire anyone who is dedicated enough to work that hard at something."

"Oh, it's not his dancing; he's actually a pretty good lead. It's all that religious crap that weird people out. Whatever you do, don't get him started on religion. He'll quote you Bible chapter and verse from cover to cover if you let him."

"I haven't noticed that about him," I said, and thinking what it would be like having a conversation with someone like that.

"Well, that's why he and Vanessa broke up."

"Dancin' Don and Vanessa were a couple?" I asked.

"Can ya' believe it? Her with all her sexy vintage dresses and him quoting the Bible at her. Oh, boy, there must have been a big disconnection somewhere…." there was that laugh again. "But if you saw them standing next to each other, they looked like they were out of a page in history with all those vintage get ups. The problem with Vanessa is, it doesn't matter how good you look in the clothes, eventually you've got to get up on the dance floor, and then all the clothes in the world, no matter how good they look, won't help you dance."

Monica reached out across the bar and tapped my hand to get my attention. "Anyway, I just wanted to come over here and let you know we're not bad people at the Federation. And…. well… .I'm… sorry for telling people not to dance with Vanessa….OK?" the words did not come easy for her.

"That's Ok, Monica. I appreciate you saying that," I felt sorry for her at first. Then I wondered how someone could become so full of themselves that those few words came out with such difficulty. Were the feelings of others that insignificant to her that she never had any practice apologizing? Surely those two simple words 'I'm sorry' should fall out of anyone's mouth, easily and comfortably.

She gave me half a laugh and shook off the whole thing in the time it took to do so. When Monica left, there was a vacuum in the air that was complimented by the off- beat music I was now hearing.

One of the advantages to having a DJ versus a live band is the wide selection of music, and one of the disadvantages to having a DJ is the DJ having the opportunity to play anything from that wide selection. The once crowded dance floor was empty as people stood around listening to one such selection from his archives. The problem, of course, is communicating to him that his song selection stinks…in a nice way. A DJ's feelings are just as easily hurt when you criticize his music as a dancer is when you criticize their dancing. It is not difficult to convince yourself that the one or two or even three complaints do not reflect the collective audience's more positive experience. You can even justify an empty dance floor as the price your audience must pay to hear alternative types of music. In fact it is the duty of every good DJ to broaden the minds of those who are uninformed and less experienced. To most people however, it is an issue of whether it has a good beat and is easy to dance to.

"Well, how'd Jerry do on his first night?" I knew Pat's question to Anna was more rhetorical than anything. It was a chance for her to sing my praises and let me feel accepted. Unfortunately, Anna did not pick up on Pat's lead.

"Well, he didn't have to do very much. I did most of the work. Hell, we weren't that busy, Pat; mostly just pitchers of water with these kids." She turned to me to confirm her assessment. "I don't think you made more than one mixed drink while I was here. Just a few beer orders and those damned pitchers of water."

Pat was trying to think of what to say next while Terry Strahan, who was standing at the end of the bar, enjoyed the missed intentions. "Yea, but he did a good job getting those beers, didn't he, Anna?"

"Well, how can you screw up a beer order?" Anna was not getting any of the passes that were being thrown her way until the silence that ensued compelled her to say something nice about me.

"But he's not bad. People seem to like him."

Pat could tell this was possibly the high note of Anna's praises for the night. "Well, first in, first out, Jerry. Anna will stay and close and you can get a couple of dances in before the nights over. You can stay and help Anna count the tip money if you want or wait to get it on Saturday."

"Thanks, Pat," I dropped the bar towel on the edge of the sink and faced Anna. "I'm Ok with leaving them with you, if that's Ok?"

"Sure, go ahead and have some fun," she told me.

When I found Ann, she was standing with Sheila and Bob. They were still talking about Vanessa.

Bob was still trying to comfort her but with little success. "We don't know for sure that anything bad happened to Vanessa,"

"I know," she said angrily, "and I could have done something about it. **We** could have done something about it."

"Yes, we could have, but what did we have to tell them?" I jumped right in. "There were no screams, no visible signs of struggle, and besides, even Detective Towning said they would have had very little to go on."

"I still wish we would have tried," she pouted.

"I do to, honey," I tried to comfort her.

"We still don't know that anything happened to her," Bob insisted. "We don't know very much at all, except that she's missing."

"Well, what do we know?" Sheila asked.

"We know that she's not answering her cell phone when her mother calls her," I said.

"Maybe she doesn't want to speak to her mother. Has anyone else tried to call her?" Sheila suggested. There was a quick exchange of looks among the four of us. It was then that Bob dropped a small bomb when he pulled out his cell phone.

"I'll try her now." he volunteered. And when he walked over to the outer edge of the ballroom we assumed, or hoped, it was to hear better and not to hide any of his conversation.

Having Vanessa's cell phone number did not necessarily mean anything. Many of the people in the swing scene knew each other's phone numbers. But looking at Sheila standing there with sunken shoulders and faint smile, whatever consideration we might have given Bob, was all but lost on her. It was obvious to all of us that there had been something between Bob and Vanessa. The long minutes before Bob came back to report his findings were spent in either merciful or merciless silence; only Sheila knew the difference.

"No answer. I got nothing." Bob read the looks on our faces. "We went out, **briefly**," he emphasized to Sheila, who responded without expression.

Anxious to let the two have some privacy, I turned to Ann, "Can we get one dance in before we go?" I said.

"Yes," she said quickly, jumping at the opportunity.

We left Casa Loma right after that dance. When we got into the car, I put in a Benny Goodman CD and turned the sound to a level that was conducive to both listening and conversation. I wanted Ann to have the opportunity to decide what she wanted to talk about, if anything at all, before I started babbling about the little insignificant things that had happened to me.

"How was your first night?" we had driven little more than a mile when Ann broke the silence.

"Probably not as eventful as yours," I paused a moment and then went on. "I was a little spooked at how you reacted to the news of Vanessa. You had me worried, honey."

"It was more than a little spooky," she said.

"You know it's my fault more than anyone's if something has happened to Vanessa. You wanted to go to the police and I…."

"She's dead," she stopped me in mid sentence. "She's dead and I know it."

It wasn't so much the dire and drastic outcome that she was declaring as much as it was the finality of the way she was saying it. There was a certainty in her voice that left no room for argument. I dodged a broken edge of pavement on the right shoulder of the exit ramp from 40/64 to Hampton and I shifted my thinking. We were no longer talking in 'if's' or 'maybe's' any longer.

"How do you know that?" I asked.

She was facing the windshield but she wasn't seeing anything. She was transfixed on an image in her mind and was only half listening to me.

I looked from the road to Ann and back to the road and saw her slowly turn her head to face me, taking time before answering my question. Her strange actions and slow response made me worry all that much more for her, this person I loved so much.

"I knew it as soon as Detective Towning mentioned Vanessa's name. I could see it. I can still see it," she said staring at me. "Her body is lying on a couch, with a bloody, star-shaped, glass ashtray next to her," Ann described her macabre vision but the addition of a couch, and a large, star shaped, glass ash tray was curious. I could tell by Ann's furrowed brow that she was as surprised as I was at the incongruous details. "She's wearing a sheer night gown that goes from her feet to her shoulders and underneath is a black leather bustier. She's tall…" Ann hesitated. The details she was describing were inconsistent if not completely strange. "Her head and face are bashed to a bloody pulp by that glass ash tray." Ann buried her head in her hands and fiercely shook her head from side to side. "Aaaaaaaaaahhhh, I don't want to see this. Why am I seeing this?" she cried.

I reached across and put my hand on hers as I pulled into the driveway of her house. Once I was able to put the car in park, I reached across and put my arms around her.

"You're distraught, Ann. You need rest and you need to put this out of your mind."

"I know it doesn't sound like Vanessa, but at the same time I know it is Vanessa. I know I must sound like an idiot but I'm telling you the truth. I don't want to see it but I can't get it out of my head. You believe me, don't you?"

"Honey, I believe you see something, but even you say it doesn't sound like its Vanessa that you're seeing. I mean, who has large, star shaped, glass ashtrays in their homes anymore? And whose home are you describing…. And that outfit, with a long sheer nightgown and leather bustier, it sounds like a cheap detective magazine from the 1940's."

Ann dropped her head slightly in acknowledgement of the facts at hand.

"It could be that all of this vintage stuff we've immersed ourselves in has your mind playing tricks on you."

"But that's not it, Jerry," Ann reasserted her convictions. "Forget what I said about the ashtray and her clothes. I'm telling you now; I know in my heart that Vanessa is dead. You've gotta believe me, I just know it."

I took her in my arms again. "I believe you honey, always."

CHAPTER SEVENTEEN

A good night's sleep can make a world of difference, especially when you get to bed at a decent hour. I have the DNA of my hunter-gatherer ancestors and their habits of sleeping at night and waking in the daylight. That was my natural, biological clock, but I had been working against that clock with my graveyard work routine at the Boa Constrictor night club.

Graveyard shift, how accurately those words succeeded at describing my work as a bartender. It's an expression taken from the 19th century when there was a problem of accidentally burying those unfortunates who were misdiagnosed as dead, and would suddenly 'wake up' inside of their coffins. Those poor victims would scratch and claw in a desperate attempt to get out of their death chambers. To prevent this from happening, as the story goes, caskets were equipped with bell-ringing devices to notify the world that they were no longer dead. The attendant who remained vigilant through the night was said to work the 'graveyard shift'. The idea that anyone could open their eyes inside of a darkened space only to discover that darkness to be the inside of a sealed coffin several feet underground, was one that I did not want to dwell on for any length of time. Yet, realizing that it was now 3:00 am and I was just finishing my Thursday night shift at the Boa Constrictor, was a reality that added stress to my already aching back.

"It's all that bendin' over we do." Rob saw me arching back with my hand supporting my lower lumbar regions as he loaded bottles of beer into the cooler. "Sometimes I get these muscle quivers in my side and I can see it pulse in and out. Feels really weird, man."

"Yea, I get those sometimes, too." I agreed, while I twisted from side to side. When I did I caught a glimpse of Marissa sucking in a big gulp of her cigarette. She was at her usual table where she counted the collected tip money. I could see her from around the corner of the island in the back of my bar, but she did not see me. She was looking up from all the cash in front of her, and with each drag of her cigarette and every drink of her Long Island Tea, made it look as if the torturous duty of counting money was more than a soul should bear. Then I saw something else happening that no one else could see as she took those little breaks. It was when she looked up and smoked or brought her glass to her mouth and sucked that straw that she checked to see if anyone was watching before dropping a ten or twenty dollar bill into her clutch purse that was wedged neatly between her legs.

"I got her," I announced, with way too much enthusiasm, and marched straight to Reggie's office.

I walked in his open door to find him counting the cash drawers from the collected registers and, curiously enough, he too had a drink in front of him and a cigarette burning in an ashtray.

"Yea?" was his one word 'hello' and 'what the hell do you want' greeting.

"Reggie, we got a problem," I was still way too eager.

"Yea?" he repeated only this time he took a second to look up to see who it was that was bringing him a problem.

"Look, I know you don't want to hear this, and I'm sure you don't need any more problems…but…"

"But?" if Reggie was as economical with the bar's money as he was with his words, the business was destined for greatness.

In my excitement I had not given enough consideration to the relationship between Reggie and Marissa and had not prepared myself with appropriate words.

"Well…I know you and Marissa are close….so…"

"So, well, but, com' on, man, you got somethin' to say, say it."

"I just saw Marissa put some money in her purse from the stack of tip money that she's counting."

I said it, knowing there was no good way to say it and half expected the very large, powerful man behind the desk to get up and physically remove me from the building; but he didn't. In fact, I could only describe his reaction as calm and unruffled.

"Ok, go tell Marissa I want to talk to her in my office."

I was guardedly relieved. I was both glad that he did not harm me and at the same time suspicious that he did not harm me.

Marissa did not want to leave. She didn't want to leave her drink, the money, or her purse; so I got Johnny, one of the other bartenders, to sit and watch the money while Marissa collected her drink, her cigarette and her purse, and the two of us went, without another word, into Reggie's office.

"What the hell is this all about? I'm in the middle of counting the goddamn tip money when, asshole here, says I gotta drop everything and go to your office. So what the hell is this?"

Reggie was sitting back in his chair when he got all fatherly on us. "Just settle down a minute Marissa, and we'll get this settled quickly. Jerry, close that door, please."

I didn't like the sound of that but I did what he asked.

"Why don't you tell Marissa what you told me?"

"I saw you putting money in your purse from the tip pile when you were taking a drink or a drag on your cigarette."

"Bullshit," Marissa spit her words at me and the smell of tobacco and Long Island liquors splashed across my face.

"I want to hear what Jerry has to say first. Then you'll have your chance, Marissa."

"How many times did you see her do this?"

"A couple," I told him

"Only a couple of times, or was it two times or more?"

"Only a couple," I held firm.

"And you're sure it was money?"

"I'm sure," again, firm.

"How much, was it ten, twenty."

"I couldn't tell how much, but I could tell it was money."

"You're sure."

"I'm sure."

"Ok, Marissa, what's your side of this?"

"He's an asshole. I don't know what he thinks he saw, but I didn't put anything in my purse. He probably thinks if I get fired he's gonna get more shifts. I know he doesn't like me but I thought we could work together and be professional. I guess that's too much to ask. He's just gotta stir up trouble…wherever he goes."

"Look," I was tired of her attacks and the whole stupid process. "Just look inside her purse and see if she doesn't have a bunch of money. Just look if you don't believe me."

"You want to look inside my purse, you son-of-a-bitch, go ahead and look," she shoved the empty purse in my face. "Is that proof enough for you, ya prick?"

"It's probably in one of those zippers. You gotta open the zippers, too," I demanded.

"I don't gotta do anything you say. My purse is empty."

"Reggie?" I knew in a second he was the wrong person to turn to.

"Thank you, Marissa. That will be enough. Just go back outside."

"Is that it?" I pleaded. "Is that all you're gonna do? But she didn't open up her zippers."

"Don't get weird on me, man. You're in enough trouble."

"**I'm** in trouble. What did **I** do?"

"Listen, Jerry, you've done a pretty good job for me up until now. I was a little bit apprehensive about taking you on when you first came here. You know the last place you worked didn't give you much of a recommendation…but you proved yourself. The problem is we have to work together here and you've just accused a co-worker of stealing."

"But what about the zippers?" my only defense was the mad ramblings of a soon to be out of work bartender.

"What makes you think having money in a girl's purse makes her guilty?" Now he was getting angry and I was running out of arguments. "I know Marissa," he continued, "I've known her a long time and she's a damn good bartender and a dependable employee. She's been with me for years and I don't like hearing anyone slander her name around like I've been allowing you to do.

"Now you've worn out your welcome at the Boa Constrictor and I want you out a here, and I mean right now." He had walked around from behind the desk and was holding the door open.

"But my tips," I asked?

"We'll send them to you."

I walked out with my tail between my legs. I could have said something to him as I went past him, God knows I wanted to. Something like 'I've been fired from better places than this', which wouldn't have been too far from the truth. I could have pointed out that if she was stealing from us, she probably was stealing from him too, but I didn't.

I passed Johnny on my way out. "So you went up against Marissa on your own, pretty ballsy, man."

"I caught her stealing tip money. She's been robbing us."

Johnny looked up and saw Reggie looking down at us from his office. "Look, man, I don't want to get in trouble talking to you, but I'll tell you this. Everybody knows about Marissa, but as long as Reggie is in her corner, she's untouchable. You shoulda known that, man."

"Yea, right," I told him and left the Boa Constrictor for the last time.

The ride along Highway 40/64 at that time of night was quiet and peaceful and a stark contrast to the environment I had just left behind me. There were only a few service type vehicles and misplaced travelers like me with questionable agendas left traveling the roads. With only one car that was a considerable distance ahead of me and one even farther behind me I could view the changing clouds that were blowing across the night sky and ponder my existence without too much risk to anyone's safety. My income had just been reduced to zero and any references from my last two workplaces would amount to about the same. How did I get here and where was I going? What future could I offer Ann at this place in my life? I decided it was too early in the morning and I was too tired to come up with any substantive answers and focused on my quest.

There were no grocery stores operating in the city let alone ones that were open 24 hours so I was making a 20 minute ride to the county Schnuck's Store on Olive Blvd. The inside of the supermarket reflected the same number of assorted night owls, insomniacs, and miscreants that were on the streets and I was able to make my selection and purchases quickly. It was another twenty minutes driving on dark and almost empty roads to get back to Ann's house.

When I got there, I went to the kitchen before shedding my cigarette smoke encrusted work clothes and removed the flowers from their wrappings. As quietly as I could, I cut the stems of, what I thought was an impressive collection of carnations, blue irises, and sunflowers, and put them in the vase that I had bought, then filled it with water. Satisfied that the arrangement was presentable enough to display on the dining room table, I placed them there for Ann's discovery when she shuffled out of the bedroom to get the coffee started only an hour or more from now.

Feeling like I had accomplished more than getting fired from yet another job, I went about my routine of wash and removal before entering Ann's bed.

After my shower I found that I was still a little wired as I walked out of the bathroom and went right to the couch where I planted my tired butt. I found the previous day's newspaper spread out on the floor at the end of the couch and I fished through the pile of pages until I found the unfinished story I had started the day before. After about 10 minutes Ann shuffled out of the bedroom cinching the belt of her white wool robe around her and brushing her hair out of her eyes. The lights were turned off in the dining room and she walked right past the floral display I had set out for her and plopped down on the couch next to me. "What are you doing, honey? Is anything wrong?"

"What woke you? Was it the light?" I had broken my usual routine of turning on the TV and, although I always had the volume so low that I had to sit in front of the screen to hear it so I wouldn't wake Ann, this night I had been sitting in silence, other than the shuffling of the pages of the newspaper.

"I heard you come in but then I didn't hear the TV so I thought I'd come in and see what's up…So, what's up?" It was late, she had no make-up on, and the white wool robe she wore revealed nothing from her ankles to her neck, but she looked very special to me.

"I'll tell you what's up, my lovely. I got canned. Thrown out at the Boa Constrictor," I told her.

"Well, I can't say I'm disappointed, but why? What did you do….or didn't do?"

"You know how I'm always telling you about Marissa and how I'm sure she's stealing from us?"

"I remember."

"Well, I saw her taking bills from the money stack tonight and putting them in her purse."

"Really?"

"Oh yea, so I told Reggie who immediately got Marissa in the office and asked her about it and she immediately denied the whole thing."

"But you saw her. Didn't they search her purse?"

"And what does that prove? That she had money in her purse? That doesn't make you guilty," I was getting more frustrated talking about the incident. "I don't know what I was thinking. Reggie's probably stealing more than anybody, and I went to him for help."

"Aren't Reggie and Marissa…Uh, an item?" Ann was being delicate for no good reason.

"That's the other thing. It's not like he's gonna take my side over the girl he's been bangin' almost every night." I was sick of the whole sordid mess. "I can't believe how every job I get is either totally corrupt, or one of my clientele is a serial killer. What's wrong with me, Ann? Do I attract dishonest people? Am I a backstabber magnet?"

"It's not you, Jerry, it's everybody; and when I say everybody I'm talking about this whole crazy world. You, me, the guy down the street, and the lady who works in the produce section," she hesitated a second to see if she was getting through, and she was. "It's the good politicians and the bad politicians, its social workers and lawyers. It's people, Jerry, all people. Some are good, some are bad, some are good more often than they are bad and some are bad more often than they are good, and some just like to mix it up," Ann's sleep ravaged ramblings were comical to me.

"The lady in the produce section…Really?"

She stared at me while trying to come up with a good comeback but couldn't, so instead we both just laughed at each other.

She brought her legs up under her and shifted closer to me "Now can we go to bed and get some sleep?"

I lead the way down the hall with Ann on my right side, keeping her from seeing the flowers on the table. I wanted her to find them in the light of the new day, a symbol of hope and a new tomorrow. That's how I wanted her to think of me, with hope of a new tomorrow.

I was tired, really tired, but a part of me was wide awake with everything that was happening. I was worried about Ann more than anything that was happening in my life. She was so upset over her vision of Vanessa having been beaten to death with the glass ashtray. I looked at the digital clock by the bed which read 4:55. - Ann was sound asleep. She was so deep in sleep I put my ear to her nose to make sure she was still breathing.

I had had a crazy experience right here in this bed just last week. At the time I thought it as real as anything. Even now I could remember seeing the girl's face looking at me from where Ann's face should have been. And, if I let myself think about it, the look on the girl's face suggested she was….dead. And that smell of wheat, that persistent smell of wheat. What did these visions mean, if anything? Did the girl represent Ann, and did the smell of wheat mean we were going to be broke and Ann would starve to death now that I lost my job at the Boa Constrictor. I shook the idea out of my head. It was stupid; no one was going to starve. I tried to fall asleep as the clock read 5:45 am.

These things all started happening after we began the vintage swing dancing. The image that Ann had seen of the woman with her face crushed sounded like something from the fifties or maybe forties. The girl I saw had make-up like someone from that same time period. Then there was that music that kept playing….what was it, 'Blue and Sentimental' by the Count Basie Band? What did that mean? Were they only strange occurrences, random events that have no other common link than the vintage experience we were all caught up in? The clock read 6:30 am.

There was one other thing. That name I saw under the back bar at Casa Loma. What was it? Jack, I think the name was Jack something. The date was November 5, 1940. *'Bless and protect all who enter here'*, and the rest, whatever that was. It was right around the time when they had the fire. Jack something, it started with a 'B' I think. What was it, Buckman, Buckmiester, Buckingcamp, or something like that? I had it written on a piece of paper in my wallet but I wanted to remember without getting up. Jack Bucking.. ton, no that's not it. Buckmueller…Jack Buckmueller, that was his name. The clock read 6:55. In ten minutes the alarm will go off, I only had to wait ten minutes longer, and then I could talk to Ann who would be waking up and getting ready for work.

"Jerry, wake up, honey. We've got company," it was Ann shaking me out of my deep slumber. With only ten minute left to stay awake, I had fallen asleep.

"What, who is it?"

"It's Detective Towning…..they found Vanessa," her voice was steady and sullen.

"Is she alright?"

"No, honey, she's dead," she finished her answer and turned her head as she tried to stop the tears.

"Oh, damn it," I said, expressing my displeasure at the news, the timing, having fallen asleep and then having to wake up to all of the above.

I fumbled with a shirt and workout pants and tried to wipe the dreariness from my face. I came out of the hallway to see Detective Robert Towning standing next to the dining room table clean, dressed, and ready for the day in stark contrast to my semi-waking state.

"Morning, Jerry. Sorry to get you up so early. I won't be more than a few minutes."

"Good morning, Robert. Please, have a seat," I pointed to a chair and pulled one out for myself.

"Would you like a cup of coffee, Robert?" Ann offered. "I'm making some for us."

"No thanks, Ann. Actually it's you I came to talk to this morning."

"Oh," she said softly. She was almost in the kitchen when she turned around and slowly took a seat on the other side of me.

"Ann tells me you found Vanessa," I said.

Robert leaned back in his chair as he pulled out his small notebook. "You know one day I'm going to come here on a purely a social visit, without any bad news at all."

"That would be nice, Robert," Ann replied. "You could bring your wife. I'd love to meet her."

"It's a date, Ann," he smiled across the table. "Unfortunately, today is not that day. As I told Ann earlier," the detective began to fill me in, "we did find Vanessa's body. She was in her car ten miles down the Mississippi River, and a body that's been in water that long gets pretty bloated and unrecognizable. Which means the cause of death will be difficult to determine," the Detective lifted his arm and checked his watch. "I've arranged a meeting with her mother at the city morgue in about an hour so she can identify the body."

"That poor woman," Ann dropped her head.

"Could it have been an accident?" I suggested, thinking of how this was affecting Ann as well as it would Vanessa's mother.

"Hard to tell without an autopsy.... or any evidence to suggest otherwise," he looked over at Ann. "I'm betting it will end up being listed as an accidental death."

"And when you say, other evidence, are you talking about my statement about a man in a fedora getting into her car that night?" Ann picked up on Robert's not so subtle hint.

Robert was nodding as he answered, "That's right. But I seriously doubt if our captain will think that's enough to warrant an investigation. For now it's just a detail that I need to follow up on. I'll put your statement in the report just as you gave it to me the other night....unless you want to change anything?"

Ann raised her head and looked directly at Detective Towning. "No, it's just as I told you at Casa Loma. I saw a tall man in a broad brimmed, fedora hat get into Vanessa's car from the driver's side and a half a minute later the car drove off."

Robert Towning checked his notes as Ann recounted her statement and, once he was satisfied that both statements were the same, he closed the book and replaced it in his coat pocket.

"That's all I need to know," he stood up from the table. "Like I said, unless we find evidence to suggest otherwise, this will be listed as an accidental death."

I stood up from the table with the Detective and at the last minute said what had been on my mind from the start. "Is there any reason to think it might have been a suicide? I mean we didn't know Vanessa really, but is that a possibility, from what you've seen."

"It's hard to say, but of course it is a possibility. The car's a little banged up but that's going to happen when it drifts down that river a few miles." I felt like the Detective was assessing me and my question. "I'll have to ask the mother as a matter of routine, but we seldom get a yes from them, not initially anyway. No parent wants to believe their child would commit suicide. Why? Do you know any reason why Vanessa would want to kill herself?"

I took a deep breath and looked at Ann. We were already involved in this more than we wanted to be and I didn't want to involve anyone else. "It's probably nothing and I don't even know if I should even mention it. It's just that some of the dancers were telling everyone not to dance with Vanessa that night. She had broken some sort of dance etiquette rule and they were trying to teach her a lesson. We didn't agree with it or go along with the idea, but I thought she looked a little depressed that night."

"Nice bunch of people you've got there, Jerry," he said.

"It wasn't everybody, and she danced as much as she always did, if not more."

"Yea, Ok, whatever; I don't know much about swing dancing but it doesn't seem like something you'd kill yourself over, is it?" the Detective was standing at the doorway.

Ann and I both shifted weight uncomfortably. "Well, you never know," I spoke up when I saw Ann did not want to answer. "Some people take their dancing pretty seriously."

"I'll make a note of it, but I don't think that will make much of a difference. I'll let you know what happens, if anything."

We said our goodbyes to Detective Towning. As soon as the Detective left I took her in my arms. "I'm sorry about Vanessa, honey. Are you alright?"

"I'm alright," she held me a moment longer and then pushed away to look at me.

"I told you she was dead. This was no surprise to me."

"Yes, and in your vision you said she was murdered."

"I still think that, but I'm not going to tell that to the Detective. I'd sound like a crazy woman."

"But you did tell him about the man in the fedora hat getting into Vanessa's car?"

"That was not a vision, I saw that man as clear as I see you now." She pushed herself completely out of my arms. "Listen, I want to talk to you about all of this but I've got to get ready for work. Can we talk about all this later?"

"Sure, honey," I said.

Ann left for work and I went back to bed. I dragged myself up at around noon, and by the time I had showered, shaved, got dressed and eaten, it was a little after 1:00 pm. I was thinking about putting in the instructional video when Bob called from his job and wanted to know if he and Sheila could come over later and work on their swing steps with my help. I told Bob about our visit from the police and how they had found Vanessa's body in her car in the river. Even though he tried to hide it, I could tell the news was a shock. I told him that he and Sheila should come by anyway since we could all use the company during such a time.

I had not known Bob for very long but he looked as if he was pretty serious about this swing dancing. He had a M.A. in psychology and made a fairly good income with full benefits from the State Correctional Institution. He and Sheila had become an item almost as soon as they met each other and since Bob wanted to be a big time swing dancer, Sheila did, too.

After brooding on the subject of Vanessa for a short while, we decided we should use the dancing as a kind of therapy but it wasn't long before emotions began to express themselves.

"You've got to stop pulling on me," Bob informed Sheila.

"I'm sorry. I didn't know I was pulling on you."

"I can't do my steps if I'm constantly being pulled off balance by you. Try using your body to dance sometimes, you'd find it a lot easier." Bob walked into the kitchen as if to escape his frustrations.

"I'm sorry," she said again, calling after him.

My first impressions of Bob were that he seemed to have a pretty good handle on things, but this was a side of his personality that was unpleasant to see.

"We're all a little on edge with this terrible news about Vanessa," I offered as an excuse.

Bob came right back from the kitchen when he heard me. "It's not because of Vanessa," he said emphatically, "it's having to tell her over and over again not to pull on me and to listen," he pointed dramatically to his ear. "Listen to the music. We're never going to win a competition dancing like this."

"There is no competition," I reminded him. "It was only a rumor."

Bob was unwilling to back off his tirade. "Doesn't matter, if we're going to dance together she has to learn her part."

Sheila stood silently in the center of the living room, humbled and hurt. She was one of those people who are never truly appreciated by their partner. Her mistakes were criticized with overly dramatic expressions like 'constantly being pulled' and sarcastic remarks like 'try using your body to dance'. I'd known people like Bob, who are so immersed in their own little dance experience that they have a hard time seeing beyond the immediacy of their personal needs, especially when it's so easy to blame someone else for their short comings. And when your partner lets you get away with a brow beating or two, you begin to believe it actually is them that's holding you back, holding you back from your dreams, whatever those dreams are, even if they are as humble as being a big time swing dancer.

It was easy to see that Sheila cared very much for Bob and that Bob was proving himself more and more unworthy of her affections with each rant.

"You're early, Sheila, you're always early." Bob threw up his hand in disgust.

"But there's no music, how do you know I'm early?" Sheila looked at me for help.

"I think we all have to work together to get this thing done," I told them both as diplomatically as possible. "Remember, it's a partnership, nobody can make this happen on their own."

The front door swung open and Ann came in with her purse slung over her shoulder and carrying a pizza box in her hand. I had called earlier to warn her that we would have company when she got home and she had taken it on herself to provide food.

"Hi," she greeted us with reserved enthusiasm.

We all said our hello's and Sheila almost ran to her and helped carry in the pizza. "Are you Ok? I was so worried about you when Bob told me about Vanessa."

"I'm Ok now, I think. I have to admit I was really shaken when I went to the door this morning and I saw Detective Towning standing there. I knew. I knew the second I saw him in the doorway what he was about to say."

"Oh, you poor dear," Sheila said as the two walked to the dining room table and deposited the pizza box. "What did he say?"

They were chattering like sisters, leaving Bob and me standing in the background like the wallpaper. Sheila was getting the explanation I thought I was going to get, but I didn't begrudge her. I could see how much of a tonic it was for Ann to talk to another woman about her experience and was glad to see her get some comfort from it.

I figured the best way to get into the conversation was to invade the now open pizza box and gave a nod to Bob to come join me. We stood around the table listening to Ann recount the mornings events. I was the only one eating pizza.

"Then Jerry asked him if it could have been a suicide, and when the Detective asked him why, he told him about how Vanessa was blackballed by some of the swing dancers." Ann said proudly.

"Good for you, brother," Bob said.

"I didn't mention the Federation or anyone by name."

"Why not, they deserve to be called out for what they did."

I didn't answer but it was clear that Bob would have wanted to name everyone.

"What did the Detective say about it maybe being a suicide?" Sheila asked Ann.

"Well, he said he was meeting with Vanessa's mother to identify the body this morning and that if she wouldn't allow an autopsy then they would probably rule it as an accidental death."

"You know truthfully," I suggested, "even though Vanessa looked a little depressed that night, I find it difficult to believe anyone would kill themselves because nobody would dance with them - unless they were suicidal to begin with."

"Don't tell me you're defending the Federation, now that Klaus and Rita have got their hooks into you?" Bob was half serious and half sarcastic. I was about to answer him when Sheila directed a question at Bob. It was the first thing she had said to him in a while.

"You knew Vanessa, certainly better than any of us. Do you think she was suicidal?"

Bob thought a minute before answering. I was beginning to believe this may have been the first time during this whole afternoon that he was giving Vanessa more thought than his swing dancing or the Federation.

"I think it's possible, and not because of the Federation," he admitted to the surprise of all of us. "Vanessa's problem wasn't about getting into relationships, it was about sustaining them. I blame myself more than her for our break up." Bob looked right at Sheila, "and I think I owe you an apology for the way I've been acting this afternoon. I just want to be good at this thing, ya know? I'm sorry I was such a jerk."

I think we were all a little surprised at his honesty and the sudden humility of his answer. Sheila took the two steps to get to Bob and put her arms around him. Bob returned her embrace for a short time and looked back up at us.

"Vanessa got around alright, but she was never cheap or easy." His eyes watered as he was finally letting it all out. "It was never a one night stand for her. She was always looking for a long term relationship with the right person, that's all."

"Ann," Bob said, changing the subject. "Forgive me for being nosy, and if you don't want to answer, I completely understand. But you still think that someone is responsible for Vanessa's death, don't you? I mean, like that guy you saw getting into her car?"

"All I know for sure is what I saw that night," Ann steadied herself. "There was a tall, thin man, with an old fedora hat that stopped her car as she was leaving the parking lot. He walked around to the driver's side of the car, said a few words, and got in. Then they drove off."

"That's what you saw," Bob pointed out. "But what do you think happened?"

"I think that man killed Vanessa," she said without hesitation. "But that's just my opinion, and you know what they say about opinions."

Now that it was out there for all of us to comment on, the speculations started to fly. Sheila was the first. "Has anybody seen anyone who looks like that guy?"

"No," we all agreed.

Sheila did not want to give up. "Well, who could that be? Who wears a fedora hat that's tall and thin?"

"Maybe he's not a swing dancer at all," I suggested. "Maybe he just wore that hat to make himself look like one of us."

"That could be," Sheila agreed.

"I hate to be the first one to suggest this, and I only mention it because, well it's too obvious not to," Bob spoke up.

"What?" I urged him.

"Ann," Bob asked her, "was the man you saw white or black?"

"I'm pretty sure he was white," Ann said.

"You're not sure?" I asked a bit too sharply. This was the first time I heard Ann express any doubt about what she had seen and I was concerned that maybe there were other details that were just as unsure.

"I'm not sure," Ann repeated, noting the distress in my voice.

The thought was on all our minds. Bob was just honest enough to say it out loud. With Frankie Manning coming the next day we had all become a little overzealous in our defense of minorities, specifically African Americans. We were almost as afraid that the potential assailant might be black as we were it might be one of our fellow swing dancers.

"Sorry, sweetheart," I said to Ann, "but I'm a little surprised you never mentioned it before."

"No one asked me before," she defended.

"Right," I said.

"But you're sure he was tall?" Bob continued.

"I'm surer about that than the other thing; the white or black thing," Ann began to sound apologetic.

"How tall," Bob continued. "Was he as tall as me or taller?"

"Taller I think. He had to stoop down to look into her car," Ann reported.

"That should limit it, if it was someone from Casa Loma," I addressed Bob. "You're what, six one, six two?"

"Six one," Bob answered. "And you think he was taller than me."

Ann nodded. "Maybe a little, and thin," she added.

"That guy would certainly stand out in our crowd," Bob stated.

"Sure would," I agreed.

CHAPTER EIGHTEEN

I was scheduled to close that Friday night so I got to Casa Loma at 9:00 pm. The group class had just ended and everyone was waiting for the band, Hudson and the Hoodoo Cats, to finish setting up and start their first set.

Hudson was one of the swing scene's favorite bands. Their jump, swing, boogie blues a' billy sound covered a range of musical backgrounds and played well with the vintage swing crowd. Hudson Harlan, the leader of the group, wore his usual snap brim fedora hat. Everyone liked the guys in the band mostly because of their relaxed and easy manner. Hudson and the other two members of the band, both male, wore mostly suits and dress shirts that were sometimes with, and sometimes without ties, giving them a look that was a cross between beatniks and Blues Brothers. They were good people, always warm and friendly whether they were on or off stage.

Without any ceremony Hudson and his crew looked once at the audience and then started the night off with 'Little Bird' an easy triple rhythm for most swing dancers.

There were always single dancers who came by themselves, scattered on the edges of the floor, looking for someone to dance with or just...looking for someone. The swing scene, like any other dance scene, was a mix of couples and singles and everyone danced with everyone else without concern. If you were a good dancer and you were familiar with everyone, or if you had a partner, you were likely to do a fair amount of dancing. But if you were new, or a beginning dancer without a lot of experience and were alone, then you were taking your chances. A new dancer, whether male or female, had to get up, get out, and get asking people to dance. If you didn't, then you often found yourself standing off on the sidelines a lot. An unskilled dancer who was a little shy and self-conscious could be seen off the floor more often than on. These dancers often had trouble learning, or had no money or time for lessons, and were too proud to admit any or all of the above. You could see their yearning to get up and be on the dance floor when a really good dance song came on. They would look in one direction and then another, get up off their chair, or take a few steps to see if they could find that person who had said 'yes' to them once or twice in the past. Maybe they would chance to ask someone they didn't know, and if for one reason or another they were turned down or came up empty handed they would then have to make that long walk back to the place where they were standing or sitting, alone and by themselves. The scene could look communal and convivial when you were on the dance floor, but if you were looking at it from the outside, it could be a harsh reminder that you came by yourself and were probably going to leave that way, and all the music and all the dance lessons were not going to change that hard truth.

Marty Long was the big guy who had come in with Michelle Torence and her friend, Elizabeth on Wednesday, my first night bartending at the Casa Loma. Marty had paid more than a few dollars for dance lessons from a cute, petite brunette at a local Arthur Murray studio on whom Marty had developed a slight crush. She got him dancing not only swing, but waltz, tango, foxtrot and some Latin dances as well. He didn't get many chances to use the other dances outside of the studio where he took lessons but it gave him confidence and, at least in his eyes, an edge over the other more talented swing dancers. He felt that if he knew something they didn't, it put him on their level.

Marty made his living as a computer programmer with a talent for reading computer code, but he was stuck in middle management because of his poor typing skills. His big fingers either punched a wrong key, or two or more keys at the same time, and he would be forced to hunt and peck for the desired character. He made good money at his position at Dynamic Technologies but was frustrated at watching his peers rise up the ladder and pay scale only because they typed faster than he did. He especially hated to see females and minorities advance past him in the company. He was an old world bigot and the only reason anyone put up with his very un-PC attitude was because of his imposing size and in-your-face personality.

His dancing reflected his singular social life. If a girl turned him down for a dance she suddenly became a 'bitch' and if she danced with a minority then their partners were referred to as 'chink', or 'spick' or 'little black monkey'. With Marty's size and height it would have been easy for him to direct his partner from one place to another, but Marty enjoyed the role of 'lead' a little too much. He took to heart the idea that he was in control and his partner's only job was to follow - him. This, however, was certainly not the case when he danced with his female ballroom dance teacher. There was never any question that the demure, brunette haired beauty was always calling the shots.

One of Marty's big problems was trying to make his partner do steps that, either he couldn't lead or she couldn't follow, which he would always blame on her when everything fell apart on the dance floor. There was one step that Marty was famous for screwing up more consistently than any other; the swing out. His was the same problem as was everyone else's, they couldn't do the swing out like Frankie Manning all stretched out like an ironing board. And Marty was the worst. With his size and frame it just looked so unnatural, and with his long legs, his feet were always catching the pants leg or dress of someone around him. But hope springs eternal and nothing is more dangerous than a stubborn male bent on succeeding at something, like trying to punch through a brick wall. Marty's brick wall was the swing out, and at this very moment he was using his dance partner and friend, the lovely Michelle, to punch through.

On stage, Hudson and the Hoodoo Cats were serving up some of their familiar locomotive, driving beat to an appreciative audience. The music's tempo was challenging but attainable - if you were an experienced dancer. From my perch behind the bar I could see Marty and Michelle dancing together. I didn't think there was anything that girl could do and not look like a million dollars doing it, until I watched her dance with Marty. She had a pretty good idea what he was trying to do but couldn't judge his timing or his direction since his arms were flying and flailing throughout the step. It was the Frankie Manning swing out, and

Marty had found some sort of footwork, quite by accident and totally out of proper sequence, that allowed him to stay with the music. He wasn't aware of his misstep or didn't want to focus on the idea that what was working so well for him could be wrong. The only problem, in his mind, was his inexperienced partner, Michelle, who was having trouble keeping up. So, in what Marty considered at the time to be a valiant effort as help for his sorry excuse of a partner to stay with the program, he used more force.

It was like watching one of those centrifuge machines that tests the effects of G-forces. The two started out slowly, and although you knew where the whole thing was going, it was too late to stop. After having made several passes in a circular motion, there was no place left to go but away, and that's exactly what happened to Michelle when Marty's vice like grip lost its hold on her.

The couple she hit initially took most of shock but after she collided and bounced off of them it was the couple to their right that finally stopped her.

Marty rushed over and tried to help but once Michelle got to her feet, she pulled his hands off her, looking very upset, she walked off the dance floor, angry and embarrassed.

"What?" Marty threw up his hands. "It wasn't my fault, she let go." Was his apology to the others standing around, whose dancing had been interrupted as if hit by a meteor - that being the sudden impact of Michelle's heavenly body.

At some level Marty knew he was at fault, but his pride would not let him acknowledge, what had felt so good could have produced such a horrendous result. Avoiding any chastisement or criticism that he might get, especially from the ladies who were less intimidated by him, he went straight to the bar and ordered a beer. I set down his bottle and then a beer glass, which he pushed away in favor of drinking right out of the bottle.

I tried to think of the right words that would indicate to him, in a positive way that throwing your partner around like a rag was what some people called, wrong. I was just about to test some carefully chosen words when Elizabeth, Marty's only remaining friend left in the building, came up on his left side and took him by his sleeve.

"What did you do to Michelle? She's almost in tears over there." Not only was Elizabeth upset with Marty but she was unafraid of expressing it to him.

"What did I do? Why is it always me? Did you even consider that it might be her fault?" Marty was too quick with his defense to give any thought to Michelle. Her well being came only as an afterthought. "She's not hurt, is she?"

"She's very upset and it doesn't matter whose fault you **think** it is, you should be over there apologizing and finding out how she is. You're supposed to pay attention to your partner and not drag her all around. No pulling or pushing, remember? You can't handle my friends like they're a load of bricks."

"Load of bricks?" Marty repeated her strange choice of words.

"Whatever, you know what I mean." She was still very upset. "You need to apologize to Michelle sometime before the night is over - that is if you want anybody to dance with you again." She turned and walked away in a frenzy leaving the poor, dejected Marty to me.

"Fuckin' bitches," he said after taking a big drink of his beer.

I had to say something as he was staring me down, defying any possible dissenting opinion.

"It takes two to get it right, that's for sure," I said. I was counting on him to think of Michelle as the guilty party, initially anyway.

"That's right," he asserted and took another drink of beer.

"That's the thing about this kind of dancing," I went on, "you're only as good as your partner let's you be."

Marty was beginning to guess what I might be suggesting. "And you think it was my fault like everybody else does?" his sneer was returning to his face.

"Hey, I don't know whose fault it was. I'm in the back here." I lied, claiming bartender's immunity. "All I'm saying is when it works, you should take some of the credit and when it doesn't, you should take some of the blame."

"Yeaaa," he started to take another drink, then hesitated a moment, and drank anyway. "Like you said, you didn't see it." He emptied his bottle and pushed it toward me. "Give me another beer."

I busied myself with other customers and cleaned anything I could find behind the bar to keep from having any further discussion with Marty. I would let him think about things a while before breaking the ice that was chilling the end of the bar where he was standing.

When Anna Schlemmer arrived, she took over her usual spot at the bar which happened to be right in front and to the left of Marty, a position which I relinquished without hesitation.

The music and dance floor was in full swing when Ann arrived with Bob and Sheila and they went right to my end of the bar to get their pitchers of water.

"Do you think anybody besides us knows about Vanessa?" Bob said, as soon as we got past the usual 'Hi's' and 'How are you's'.

"Pat told me earlier that Detective Towning called him and filled him in. I know Pat will keep it to himself but it's bound to get out sooner or later."

"I think it best if we let others spread that kind of news," Ann counseled.

"Of course," Bob agreed. "But did Pat mention anything about looking for a tall thin man with a fedora hat?"

"Pat didn't say anything about that, and as far as I know this is not a murder investigation, and until there is proof, we should keep all of that to ourselves," I cautioned. "Having said that, if any of us sees someone who fits that description, I think it would be best to get either Pat or Terry or both before approaching him."

"Sounds like good advice," Sheila said, and we all agreed.

Klaus and Rita stepped up to the bar where Sheila was standing next to Bob with Ann on his other side. I had seen them a couple of seconds before anyone else from my position behind the bar.

"So, are you guys psyched about the workshop?" I spoke up as an announcement of their arrival.

"The Frankie Manning workshop," Bob questioned my sudden change of topics?

"Sure, what other workshop is there?" Rita questioned. She looked curiously in Bob's direction.

"No other," was Bob's two word answer, surprised at their sudden appearance.

Ann diverted Rita's attention. "Have they arrived yet, Rita?"

"Rhonda picked them up at the airport around 5:00 pm and we met them for dinner shortly after.

Frankie is such a wonderful man, always smiling and so gracious." Rita was not shy about letting people know the advantages her position at the Federation afforded her.

"You're going to love Erin Stevens," Klaus interjected. "We saw her last year at the Harvest Moon Workshop in California. She's great."

Sheila spoke up from the other side of Bob. "Frankie's a piece of history, isn't he?"

"A very important piece as far as swing dancing goes," Klaus said. "Even though it was happening on several fronts, some say that Frankie was the catalyst for the whole swing revival."

"How did it happen?" I asked, "The vintage swing revival I mean? Was it just the force of Frankie Manning's personality?"

"Frankie's not a forceful man," Rita corrected me, "although he is a force of good will and a warm spirit."

Bob couldn't keep himself from joining the conversation even if it did include Klaus and Rita. "If you ask me, and I think Frankie would say the same thing, it's the music."

"I'd agree with that," Klaus was Bob's unlikely collaborator. "The music is like Frankie in a way…it's timeless."

"Oh, I totally agree," Rita chimed in with enthusiasm. "The music is incredible. Sometimes I feel like it speaks to me."

Rita's sentiments were charming….anyway I'm sure they were charming to someone, but I wanted to get back to the history of the whole thing. "It's amazing to me how it all caught on so fast in those days when nobody had access to videos or TV. All they had was radio." I set it out for anyone's comment.

"And dance halls like this one," Bob indicated the big room in the background. "That was how the bands got their following, by playing in these enormous ballrooms. They were referred to as 'dance bands' and if they wanted to make a name for themselves and be successful, they had to fill the floors with dancers. The more they could swing, they better they were."

"That's so true," again Klaus expressed his agreement with Bob. "The few ballrooms that are still around from that era, like the Casa Loma, are some of the few physical reminders of what that experience was really like. And a few remaining dance masters like Frankie."

Each of us was anxious to add something of our own. "It must have been a great time to be a swing dancer," Ann noted.

"Sometimes I think I might have been there in a past life," Rita told us. "I think it would have been great to be around back then."

"I don't think you would like it as much as you think." I questioned Rita's statement as being overly nostalgic. "I mean, would you really want to revert back 60 or more years of progress; to a time when women had such a small place in society?" I didn't want to be too much of a kill joy, so I added, "Don't get me wrong, I know it sounds really cool, what with the music and the dancing and all that, but the country had a long way to go in areas like, civil rights, and human rights. The Miranda law wasn't passed until sometime in the sixties, I think."

Bob knew I was right. "Yea and you can throw in all the technological advances you're used to that you wouldn't have like air-conditioning for example, or seat belts, washing machines and clothes dryers."

"And vacuum cleaners," Ann added to the litany.

Klaus took up the cause that Bob and I had started. "Don't forget color television, or any television at all, VCR's, cell phones, personal computers."

Bob picked up the list, "Or any and all kinds of plastics products, and Velcro, or Teflon."

I had time to come up with a few of my own, "The FDA, Social Security, Medicare and Medicaid, and heart surgery."

"Hey, bartender," Marty called from the other side of Anna, who was busy with the cocktail waitresses. He either forgot my name or wanted to make a point that I had forgotten him. "Can I get a drink down here?"

"Sure," I said, moving to get his beer.

Marty was talking to a couple at the other end of the bar with a bellowing voice and it was difficult to keep from hearing what he was saying even if I had wanted to.

"I don't think Clinton went far enough." Marty was referring to the bombing of a plant in Khartoum for being suspected of developing VX gas. "**And**," he emphasized the word, "I think it was George Bush's fault for not going all the way to Bagdad during the Gulf War. We could have marched right in there without any trouble and taken out Saddam Hussein, no problem."

Marty's arguments were so typical the man next to him couldn't help but reply. "But we don't know whether Iraq has any plans to acquire nerve gas or to use it against the United States. I've read that there is evidence this plant was not producing any kind of chemical weapons at all." The man looked to be about the same age as Marty but almost six inches shorter and thin. He was no match for Marty physically, but Marty was no match for him intellectually and the man was trying to be as diplomatic as possible in offering an opposing argument.

"Where did you hear that? On the internet, I'll bet?" Marty's beers were starting to speak for him.

"We read it in the New York Times." The woman standing with the man spoke up. She was very pretty with olive colored skin and very long black hair. She had been trying to stay out of the exchange but couldn't help herself from answering such a ridiculous statement.

"You see, that's what I'm talking about." It was as if Marty was deaf to any opinion other than his. "These leftist, commie publications will print all sorts of lies to further their extremist beliefs. Those guys were developing **VX gas**," Marty stressed. "That's some deadly shit, man; and you damn well know if they're crazy enough to make that stuff, then somebody's sure crazy enough to use it on someone."

"All right, all right, already," on the other end of the bar Rita had thrown up her hands, "I guess what I really mean is, I would want to live back then if I could have all the luxuries and technical advances that I have today."

"That sounds like the present to me," Sheila said, with the vintage music playing as backdrop.

"No, no, I think I know what Rita means," Klaus argued. "She would want to have been there when it was all happening for the first time, with all the great bands and great dancers and music."

"Yea, that's right," Rita welcomed the help.

There were two, unofficial sides being drawn in this argument, with Klaus and Rita on one side, and Bob, Sheila and Ann on the other. I decided I'd stay in the middle.

Bob lead the charge. "But we have all the music from that time, and we have plenty of good dancers with new music now. Wouldn't you rather be a part of what's happening now than go back to what's already been done, especially since you already know the past?"

"That's a good point," I said. "If you are here in the present you are in a position to take what's good from the past and make it better. What's the expression – if you don't learn from your mistakes, you're bound to repeat them."

"That is if you believe history repeats itself, like Rita suggests." Bob's comment was aimed at Rita but got the attention of the rest of us. "I mean what Rita said about a 'past life', which would suggest a cyclical view of history. And anyone who believes in the Judeo/Christian philosophy, which I believe includes all of us, and Rita, too, was brought up to believe that history is linear."

Klaus challenged Bob. "Yes, but just because you believe history is linear doesn't necessarily mean that events and circumstance can't and aren't sometimes repeated with uncanny detail."

"I disagree," Bob shot back. "It's not the details of history that repeats itself but the mistakes of men and women who continue to repeat them."

And Klaus with the return, "I actually had written a college paper on this very subject in support," he looked to acknowledge Rita, "of the theory that, not only does history repeat itself, but that it can contain predictable cycles in specific detail; as is evidenced by the Mayan Calendar and the Bible."

"Well, sure, the Bible is full of predictions." Sheila surprised herself at speaking up in support of Klaus and thereby in opposition to Bob.

"Most of the predictions in the Bible are about the end of the world," I added. "But what you're saying Klaus, is that history, like the vintage swing dancing, and other events, are predictable, even inevitable because history is in some kind of recurring loop."

"Exactly," Klaus said.

"Whatever's old is new again," Rita said in support.

"Sounds a little bit 'out there' to me," Bob doubted. "What about some anecdotal evidence?"

"Ok, check this out and see if it doesn't blow your mind." Klaus was more than ready to defend his statement. "Now I'm doing this from memory so I may forget a detail or two… Consider two, famous American presidents, 100 years apart, Abraham Lincoln and John F. Kennedy.

Lincoln was elected to Congress in 1846; Kennedy was elected to Congress in 1946. Lincoln was elected president in 1860; Kennedy was elected president in 1960. The major social issue during both of their presidencies was Civil Rights. Both of the presidents were elected by less than 50% of the popular vote. Lincoln's opponent, Douglas, was born in 1813. Kennedy's opponent, Nixon, was born in 1913. Both of the presidents lost a child while they were living in the White House. Both of the presidents were shot in the back of the head and both died on a Friday. Both assassins are known by all three of their names: John Wilkes Booth and Lee Harvey Oswald. Both successors to the presidency were Democratic Senators with the last name of Johnson. Andrew Johnson was born in 1808. Lynden Johnson was born in 1908." Klaus paused a second to take a breath.

"Now these are easily documented facts about two famous presidents but there are examples of many other events in history which are recurring with the same, amazing amounts of similar details at this very moment."

I was fascinated by what Bob was saying but was distracted by what was going on to my right.

"I mean it. We should have bombed Bagdad back to the Stone Age when we had the chance," Marty took a big swill of beer to punctuate his point.

"Is that what you call American diplomacy? Killing millions of innocent civilians to solve whatever problem that comes along?" The petite young woman with olive skin spoke up with sudden fervor. Her friend in the middle was trying his best to calm her down.

"Innocent," Marty came right back at her. "Did I hear you say innocent? When those people protest us in the streets by waving banners that say 'death to America' and burning our American flag?"

"That's just Saddam's camera's showing you what he wants you to see. Surely you can see through that?"

"All I see are a bunch of anti-American, uncivilized, towel heads. What makes you think you see anything different?"

"Because I am a towel head; I was born in Iraq," she almost shouted at him. "I lived there and I know, first hand, what it's like to live under the rule of that tyrant. You don't know. You act like you know, but you know nothing, NOTHING," she punctuated.

Marty was getting a verbal ass kicking, and whether he thought he deserved it or not, he knew he didn't like it. Reason and logic had gone out the window for him and were replaced by alcohol and pride. "Yea, well I know Saddam will never see a day of battle. It'll be those 'innocent soldiers' of his shooting at us and you can bet your passport what's gonna' happen when they meet up with United States forces."

"You arrogant prick." If her friend had not started to drag her away she would have attacked Marty right where he stood.

Their shouts had gotten loud enough to stop Anna from making drinks for the waitresses. She looked over at me to do something and I was already on my way.

"Listen, you two," I said, in a level voice that was firm but without being challenging. "A bar is no place to discuss politics or religion. Now if you can't talk to each other in a civil manner while you're in here then you will have to leave."

It was strange how the words just fell out of me without thinking about what I should say. I didn't wait to hear anything Marty might say in response. As far as I was concerned, I had delivered the message he needed to hear and there was no need for further discussion. Impressed, Anna flashed a quick look of approval over her shoulder and I went back to my friends.

"Those are some impressive coincidences, I'll give you that," Bob conceded. "But I'm still not convinced of your theory. I think its people who keep repeating their mistakes, with an amazing amount of consistency, not history acting on its own."

Monica had walked up and was standing behind Rita. She looked a little worried and waited a moment before taking Rita by the arm and whispered something in her ear.

"Really," Rita responded in a loud voice. "Are you sure?"

"What," asked Klaus? "What is it?"

"It's Vanessa; it looks like she's killed herself."

Marty stood quietly by himself at that end of the bar. He stayed there a long time without ordering another beer, and after 30 minutes without anyone saying anything to him, he left the bar and walked out of the Casa Loma Ballroom alone.

The night got busier and busier from then on. I tried to steal glimpses of dancers on the floor but it was difficult to see through the dark shadows that were around the tables and in between me and the dance floor. I looked up from time to time peering in between the bodies at the bar to catch a glimpse of someone I would know.

I was in the middle of pouring water and removing empties off the bar that something on the floor took my attention. At first I thought it might be a pair of professional actors that Pat had hired to get their pictures taken for promotional advertising. Then I recognized Michelle as one of the two and a second later I realized it was Dancin' Don standing there next to her. They looked completely natural together with both of them in their vintage outfits. I was too busy to get a chance to see them dance but I knew that didn't matter. They looked perfect together, so much so that if they were to dance with anyone else it would have lessened either one, no matter how well they danced. The picture of them standing together stayed in my head and a little while later, when Don came up to the bar for an extra cup, I got a chance to say something to him.

"How long have you and Michelle known each other?"

"We just met tonight," he said, looking distracted.

"Really? Well, I gotta tell you, with the outfits you both have on; you two look like you were made for each other."

"Thanks," he threw off my compliment almost as soon as he heard it.

"Everything alright, Don?"

"I just heard some terrible news about Vanessa."

"Yea, I heard it, too." I stopped my busy movements to give him all of my attention. "Someone said you two were – close. I'm sorry, Don."

"Thanks, Jerry. We were close, very close. I'm really gonna miss her." He didn't wait for any response from me and I could see why. His eyes were welling up and I guess he didn't want to be seen shedding tears in public. I thought about how much one person's life could affect so many others in very profound ways.

It never slowed down behind the bar. The new wave of vintage enthusiasts included serious dancers, want to be dancers, curious on-lookers, and semi-serious participants who had spent a few dollars on old clothes and just wanted a place to wear them. Only the serious dancers remained alcohol-free which meant a large part of the crowd were enjoying a variety of drinks from the bar. I remained busy through the night and the time went by quickly.

When the night was over I found a spot at the bar with the tip money spread out in front of me.

About 30 minutes later I heard someone come out of the office and turned around to see Pat heading my way. He was carrying a file in one hand and was moving toward me at a quick pace. The last time we had seen or spoke to each other I had sent him on a wild goose chase down under in the belly of the back bar. We were the only two left in the building.

"Hey, Pat. Pretty good night, huh?"

"It was a very good night and you were a big help. I hear you're gonna have some time on your hands."

"That's right. So, if you'll have me, I'm here to stay."

"Well, that calls for a celebration." He slapped me on the back and hustled back behind the bar.

He seemed to have forgotten about his failed foray through the grit and grim and acted as though all was forgiven.

"Don't get the wrong idea here, Jerry, we don't do this all the time," Pat had his hand on the handle of the cooler door. "What would you like?"

"An Amber Boch sounds good to me, Pat. Thanks," I accepted.

Pat grabbed two of AB's special brews and set one in front of me.

"I'm glad to see you're not upset with me any longer for sending you under the bar the other night." I took a drink, "I swear to you, I saw some writing down there."

He dropped the file in front of him on the bar and leaned forward on his hands which were placed on either side of the file. "I believe you," he said, with a glow in his face. I could see he knew something I didn't and was dying to tell me.

"What?" I looked at the file. "What've you got in there?"

With the deliberate moves of a three card Monte dealer he turned the file around 180 degrees to face me, and using only one finger he flipped it open to expose a 8" by 11" glossy photograph of four guys in white shirts, black ties, and aprons standing behind a bar.

"Second guy from the right," he said quickly.

"Yea," I took the bait.

"Guess what his name is?"

My first guess was so immediate that I doubted myself because of it. I looked at Pat who was almost laughing out loud.

"You're kidding me, right?" My face was breaking out into a smile that was on the verge of joining in Pat's laughter. "You're telling me that this is…Jack Buckmueller?"

He tipped his beer bottle to mine with a congratulatory 'clink'. "He was a bartender here a few years before, and a few years after, the big fire in 1940. I got the picture from Dot."

"So you found the scribbling on the wall?"

"Nope," he said looking just as pleased with himself as if he had seen the writing. "I looked, Strahan looked, we even got Terry's 8 year old nephew scramblin' back there with a neon shop light. Now that was somethin' to see, the back bar was so lit up it looked like Jesus Christ himself was gonna rise up out of it." His face got serious for a moment and his voice lowered several notes, "nobody saw anything back there but you."

"But according to this there was a bartender, this bartender," I pointed at the photo in the folder, "and his name was Jack Buckmueller. So how would I know this guy's name if I hadn't seen it written there behind the bar?"

Pat just looked at me and smiled and shook his head, "I - don't - know. You might have gotten the picture and information from

Dot, but I really doubt that; she's nearly a recluse and only rarely sees visitors. According to Dot, this guy died about 40 years ago without any living relative, so you couldn't be one of his descendants or relatives."

"So?" I wanted an ending to the story.

"So," Pat repeated, "I don't know. It's a mystery."

"A mystery, right," I repeated without any enthusiasm. "You have to take it on faith."

"I guess," was all he said.

I expected more, and wanted more. "Well there's got to be more than that?"

"Like what? You think something supernatural's going on here? Hey, Halloween is only a few weeks away."

"No…I don't know. Maybe there's more to the story and we're just not seeing it. I mean, he wrote that after the fire, right?"

"As a matter of fact, the date you said was written there, November the 5th, 1940, was about right on the day that Casa Loma reopened their doors. Why?"

"Well, the note, it's so solemn and poetic. It sounds more like something a priest would write instead of a bartender. '*Bless and protect all who enter this building.*' And then he ends the thing with, '*the Book of Dreams.*' What's that all about? Bartenders don't write that kind of stuff on the underside of back bars, it's usually things like, '*Jack was here*' or '*always tip the bartender*' that kind of shit."

"Yea, well, people weren't as cynical back then as they are today." Pat had his bottle poised at the point of entry, pausing only long enough to answer. "Besides, what kind of story do you think there might be?" He tipped the bottle while raising one eyebrow in my direction. I didn't have an answer so he answered for me. "There was a fire, the place burned down, and then they built it back up; end of story."

"I know, I know, I just can't help thinking….or maybe wanting, there to be more. I want to know about these people, about what they were thinking, and what they wanted. What they dreamed about."

I must have been sounding a little too touchy feely because Pat answered me with a slap of cold reality. "You want to know what they were thinking about in 1940, I'll tell you what they were thinking. They were thinking how to put food on the table and keep a roof over their heads. They were fighting the depression all the way up to, and through, World War II. That's the story that was going on back then, and it's the same story going on today as it will be tomorrow."

"You know, for a guy who climbed underneath a 60 year old back-bar to see some scribbling on a wall, you sure sound like someone who's really trying not to believe."

Pat chuckled and nodded his agreement. The beer had escalated his oratory and it had gotten the best of him. "That's because," he said quietly, "I want to believe there's something more just as much as you do."

He drained the final swig of his beer and I followed suit. "Com'on," he said, "let's get out of here."

CHAPTER NINETEEN

Neon had gotten up at 8:30 am. This was especially early for him considering he had been working till 3:00 am the night before cleaning office buildings. He left the house quietly, without announcing of his departure. He didn't like the idea of hiding anything from his mother but, for some reason, he was reticent about having to explain that he was going to learn

swing dancing at the white peoples club over on Iowa Street. Bouncing down his family's front porch steps, he stopped in his tracks when he saw Janeakwa dragging their young child, Jackson. His son's little legs bowed out from under him as they made their way along the sidewalk toward Neon. It wasn't a surprise that she was coming to his mother and grandmother's house. It was her normal routine to drop the child off with Neon, or Gloria, or his grandmother from time to time. The surprise was seeing her out of bed and out on the street at such an early hour on a Saturday morning.

"You gotta take him, Neon," she handed him the child. "I just can't handle his goddamn screaming any more. I haven't been able to sleep more than a half hour at a time since I got home. I'm **tired, pissed off**, and **angry,** and I don't want to be responsible for what I might do." She shook the little arm that hung to her with each pronouncement of her sorry position which only caused the little boy to erupt into another bout of crying, scrunching his face to match his running nose.

Neon picked the toddler up in his arms and wiped the little boy's nose with his shirt. "What's the matter my man? Are you tired, or hungry, or do you just want someone to love you? I'll bet that's it, isn't it."

"Now don't you even fuckin' try to tell me how I should raise my own child. I'm not about to take any of that kind a' shit from you. I'm the one who takes care of him, not you. I'm the one the court decided to put him with while you're out all night *cleaning toilets* for white mother fuckers who make real money. Not that you'll ever see any real money, working for the boss man, doing the nigger work like you do….and that's for damn sure." She turned around without giving Neon a chance to answer or say another word. "That boy is just as much you're problem as he is mine. I'm too damn young to be wasting all my time taking care of your cryin', misbehavin', little shit of a monster while you go about with your goddamn, going nowhere plans to be a fuckin' high class janitor."

Neon could hear her venomous complaints as she shouted them to the neighborhood even after she was out of sight and turning onto California Street. It was hard for Neon to remember what Janeakwa was like when he met her. A young, fragile little girl, who was so impressed by his big attitude and his gang banger friends. He could barely remember when they first met. She never used profanity then or said anything hurtful to anyone those few years ago. But that was history now; he had gone his way and she had gone hers. Neon figured it was partly his fault and his bad influence that changed her from a lovely little girl to the thing that just left.

Apparently Janeakwa had slept in the clothes she was wearing the night before and had not taken the time to run a comb across her hair, or wash off the smudged make-up that was hanging on her face. She and her clothes smelled of the alcohol and marijuana from the previous night's celebrating and would stay with her as long as she wore them. It looked to Neon like those clothes were going to stay on her a while longer still, since she was certain to be headed back to her mother's house and the bed she left to deliver little Jackson.

Neon had been clean and drug free for two years, and at the mature age of seventeen he was physically repulsed by the smell of drugs and cigarette smoke on Janeakwa. He was worried for his son, but since he and Jackson were solidly linked to a drug using mother for now, Neon would have to change his plans and spend his Saturday with his son.

Casa Loma had a different feel in the morning. The daylight that snuck in the room helped shake the cobwebs that still lingered in my head despite Starbucks flavor of the day, a Macchiato Mocha Latte. We shuffled in with pullovers and zip up sweat clothes hanging loosely about our bodies as we dragged in back packs slung across shoulders and blue jeans that weighed heavy on our waist. The October sunlight that crept in from the other side of the building illuminated one end of the dance floor. Pat Donovan was turning on some interior lighting and Frankie's assistant was getting ready to address the motley collection of swing devotee's.

"Hello, St. Louis." A random selection of voices returned her greeting. The woman onstage was not much more than 5 foot tall, with dark hair that was done up in pig tails, and a skirt that went to the knees. She had a warm and giving smile that was unafraid if no one smiled back.

Erin Stevens was one of the first to seek out the old swing dancer legends like Al Minns and Frankie Manning. She and her partner brought Frankie Manning out of retirement and vintage swing back to the present day world.

She got us up from sitting our chairs and tables and onto the dance floor. She then got our sleepy bodies awake and moving by teaching us the Shim-Sham, a dance routine that was done without a partner. We needed the movement to get some of our 'up tightness' exorcised so we could relax and move. Erin then got us in formations of couples and then the couples in four lines and explained, in detail, how the rotation would go. The rotation was always an exercise in itself and could prove to be more difficult than the actual dance steps. Bob stood next to me with Sheila and Ann positioned across from us.

When Erin was sure we understood the rotation, she introduced the legend himself, Frankie Manning.

He was eighty five years old. When he walked, you could almost see a slight stoop in his back that seemed to bob with each step that he took, probably from thirty years of carrying a mailbag. The enthusiastic applause that accompanied his introduction was met with Frankie's generous smile and twinkling eyes warmly receiving all the affection and the love that was given him.

We started with a simple, basic step, with emphasis on connection and focus on partnership. The rotation of partners allowed us to meet and dance with people we never had before. The leads (men) stayed where they were, while the follows, (ladies) moved from lead to lead. I watched Ann as she rotated away from me, toward the center of the room and to each partner thereafter. Her rotation took her to the front of the room to Dancin' Don. At my end, Michelle rotated to me. Michelle and Don were the only two people in the room who had dressed in vintage clothes besides Erin Stevens, the teacher.

Michelle had on the same skirt with wide straps that she had worn the first night I'd seen her, but the top was a little different; this one had dolphins instead of strawberries.

"Hi, I'm Jerry," I reached out and introduced myself as I had been doing with each of my different rotating partners.

"You're the bartender here, aren't you?" she took more delight in recognizing me than she should have.

"You have a good memory, and yes, I am one of the bartenders here."

"Well, it's nice to meet you, Jerry. I'm Michelle." She put her hand in mine and gave it a warm squeeze as we were ready to try the step we were learning. I wondered if she did that for all her partners, and after giving my inflated ego time to subside, I admitted that she did.

I was impressed at how easy she was to move. We were only doing basic steps but you can tell a lot about a partner just by the way they stand in front of you in closed position or when you both move through any step whether simple or not. I had the feeling we could do so much more, and was tempted to try, but I resisted and stayed with the steps we were supposed to be doing. When we were done, we thanked each other, again with the smile and handshake, after which she rotated to Bob, who was standing next to me. When the rotation took her away from Bob, he looked over at me and expressed, with a raised eyebrow, that he had noticed her, too.

I was trying to see where Ann and Sheila were from time to time and couldn't help but notice where Michelle was and saw her rotate to the top of the room to Dancin' Don. I was craning my neck to see her when I heard a sort of scratchy voice in front of me.

"Can ya' believe it? They look like they should be on the back side of an old cereal box." It was Monica who rotated in front of me and was talking to Bob who, like me, was also looking at Michelle and Dancin' Don.

"Don and Vanessa used to look like that," Monica continued, "but this one can dance. I guess I shouldn't say that, given what…. well, you know." Her voice trailed off a bit, exposing what must have been a conscience. It lasted all of a few seconds, then, "Maybe Donnie will be able to keep this one."

We stayed with the basics the whole morning, stopping only once for a 15 minute break until twelve noon rolled around and we broke for lunch. I checked my cell phone and found that Detective Towning had left a message for me to call and went upstairs to find a quiet corner before calling him back.

"Vanessa's mother is mad as hell, and she wants an autopsy, A.S.A.P."

I could tell from his voice that things had changed to active mode on his end.

"Not only that, it turns out Vanessa's mother is Deborah Billings. You may remember her late husband, State Senator Allen Billings?"

"Ohhhhh, that was Vanessa's father?" I suddenly understood the importance of the situation.

"But I thought you said she probably would not want an autopsy."

"She didn't yesterday, not till she found Vanessa's diary, neatly tucked away in a back corner of her closet shelf. Now her mother's demanding one. And I'll tell you this, Jerry, I've been reading this diary all morning and it has some interesting stuff about a few of your swing dance friends."

"What kind of stuff?"

"Stuff that sells scandal sheets, or it would if the Senator were still alive and in office," he told me. "But, God rest his soul, since he is in a better place, it's just garden variety gossip stuff; unless this turns out to be a murder investigation and it gets to court, then the headlines will fly."

"I got'cha," I acknowledged. The Detective and I had an unusual relationship and it put me in his confidence. "So what's the juice?"

"It looks like Vanessa believed some of the girls carried a grudge because of her good looks and from looking at a picture of her, I'd say she could be right."

"You should have seen her in person."

"I'll bet. She also talks about all the guys she's dated in specific detail, which, I'm sure you'll understand, I won't mention."

"I understand."

"Now don't get me wrong. I don't want to speak ill of the dead, but after reading this thing for a couple of hours, I've just gotten to the part where she starts going out with her 'swing dance guys'."

"I think I can guess."

"Don't guess; you might incriminate someone who doesn't deserve it, especially since she says more than one of them was stalking her."

"Stalking her?" I said, surprised with the implication.

"That's what it says in here."

"Couldn't all that just be the ramblings of a very lonely girl? I mean, it is just a diary and not a factual document."

"It would never hold up in a court of law, if that's what you mean. The defense would tear it apart. Now listen, you keep all of this under your hat until we get the results from that autopsy report. We've got nothin' but slanderous accusations if all we have to go on is this diary."

"I understand."

"If we don't find anything in the autopsy then we'll let the family bury the poor girl and we can get on with our lives. On the other hand, if it turns out that there is evidence of a violent death, it's a whole new ballgame."

The revelation that any of the guys from the swing scene had been stalking Vanessa distracted me a little from hearing what the detective was saying.

"We want to talk to these people who are mentioned in this diary as part of a preliminary investigation. She talks about a Bob Trentway. Do you know who that is?"

"Oh, yea, he's here."

"And two other guys, one named Klaus and another named 'Dancin' Don. There can't be too many guys with these names running around down there?"

"Klaus, really? Wow. Yea, he's here and Dancin' Don, too."

"And one other person I need to talk to is Rita, Rita Beltman."

"Yea, I don't think they got along at all, and I sure wouldn't lump Rita in with a bunch of love sick stalkers."

"Oh, they got along alright," the detective disagreed without hesitation.

"No, Rita…"

"Jerry, listen to me. If this diary is at all accurate, then Rita and Vanessa got along…all…right."

"OH….REALLY."

"Really," he confirmed. "Remember, not a word of this gets out, clear?"

"Clear," I told him, still with a slight case of shock.

"When do you think they'll all be down at that dance place together?"

"What? Oh, I'm sorry. They're all here, right now, today. We're here at a Frankie Manning workshop."

"Frankie who?" he questioned.

"Frankie Manning……you never heard of Frankie Manning?" I asked.

"Never heard of him," the Detective acknowledged. "But that doesn't matter. Detective Sails and myself will be down there in a little while to conduct some informal inquiries. If there is a bad guy among you, we want to get an early chance at identifying him."

I was thinking about Ann's vision when something the Detective said brought me back. "Did you say Detective Sails is coming with you?"

"I wanted to give you a heads up about that, Jerry. Detective Sails is my new partner since his partner put in for retirement this past June. You remember, Detective Sails?"

"How could I forget?" I told him. I could hear Towning's laughter on the other side of the phone.

"Yea, well, he remembers you, too, but don't sweat it. These are different circumstances and besides, you gained a whole lot of respect from some of the people down here the way you handled yourself with the Stockyard Killer."

"Can't wait to see him again," I made little effort at hiding my sarcasm.

"Like I said, don't sweat it. I'm going to call your boss as soon as I hang up the phone with you and let him know we're on our way there."

"Ok, Detective, I'll see you later."

Neon loved playing with his young son. He had so much hope for little Jackson, so many plans for his future. It would be different for Jackson; Neon would be there for him. He would advise him and counsel him on what to do and what to stay away from, especially the gangs and drugs. He would make sure he got a good education, even college. They would move from his mother and grandmother's house once Neon got enough money together, to someplace in the county, someplace nice. Jackson could grow up without hearing filthy language like the kind of trash that came out of Janeakwa's mouth. Neon knew that one way or another he would have to get Jackson away from Janeakwa and that would take time and money. Neon was determined to make something out of his life, if for no other reason, than for his son. Nothing was more important to Neon than his son, nothing.

The two of them had a great day together. They played in the back yard and went for a walk around the block. Then they got out Jackson's action figures and played with them. After lunch they colored in a picture of Jesus in his mother arms in the coloring book they got from the church. They watched 'The Little Mermaid' then took a nap with both of them curled up on the floor. When Gloria came home and found them lying in front of the TV, she gently picked up Jackson and placed him quietly in the playpen.

"Are you working tonight, son?" she asked Neon, who was stretching out his arms and getting himself up off of his hard wood mattress.

"No, Moms, no work tonight," he dug into the corner of his eye with his knuckle and cleared out the sleep that had settled there.

"You should go out tonight, honey. You haven't gone out in so long. I just hate to see you staying inside every Saturday night with your grandmother and me watching television. Is there anything going on at the church?"

"I don't know, maybe," Noen called to his mother in the kitchen. "I think I'll take a walk up to the church and see what's going on. Maybe I'll go up to the McDonalds and get a soda."

That Saturday afternoon at Casa Loma Ballroom, when the first day of the two day workshop was an hour away from finishing, Detectives Towning and Sails walked up from the cement staircase. Pat Donovan was standing near its entrance and greeted the two men.

Neon had gotten there only minutes before the Detectives and was leaning against the bar with Pat. He explained to Pat that he wanted more information about the party at the church of Our Lady of Good Hope after having gotten an invitation to go when he was there on Wednesday night.

When the two black men in suits walked in, Neon recognized their confident stride right away. Their air and demeanor was such that it was as if they had just taken control of the whole room without saying a word to anyone. Pat went over to them the minute he saw them as if on cue. Something was up, but whatever it was, it was nothing to Neon. All he wanted was directions and maybe a ride from that nice, clean, white girl with the big smile.

The detectives followed Pat to his office in the back making the long loop outside the perimeter on the outside of the dance floor. I was one of a few who paid any attention to the trio and probably was the only one who understood the meaning of their arrival. A minute later I saw Pat come out and walk up to Klaus and, as casually as he could, whisper something in his ear. Klaus excused himself from his partner and followed Pat back to his office.

The questions were general and specific, friendly and confrontational, personal and private, most of them emanating from the details Vanessa had put in her little pink and yellow diary.

"What exactly do you do for the '*Lindy Hop Swing Federation*', Klaus?" Robert Towning was still not comfortable saying the complete name of the organization.

"I'm the treasurer and one of the dance teachers."

"And Rita Beltman is…what?"

"She is the president of the Federation and also my girlfriend."

"How did you know Vanessa Billings?"

"I knew her socially."

"Socially, you only knew her socially?" Towning pressed him. "Her diary says you knew her better than that."

Klaus shifted in his seat after hearing about a diary. "Yes, well, there was one night, when we had a little bit too much to drink. But it was only one night."

"Was that the night you told her," Towning flipped open the pink book in front of him to a specific page. "Wait a minute, how did she put it here? Oh yea, here it is. *Klaus told me he uses the Federation money to pay for their trips to workshops and for out of town lessons'.*

If Klaus was surprised he did not show it. "As teachers, we need to get the most up to date and professional instruction we can get. That is how we promote Lindy Hop, by passing that knowledge on to our member students."

"That's some pretty good bullshit, Klaus," Sails spoke up for the first time. "When you're done with this dance thing you should go into politics."

"Do the members of this Federation know how you're spending their money?" Towning asked.

"We invest the money in many ways, like the workshop you see here today. Most people can see the results for themselves and are happy with how we run the organization."

"In other words, you don't tell them," Towning pinned him down.

"Am I under investigation?"

"Hell, no. You may end up being the mayor some day," Sails spoke up again.

"Klaus," Towning got his attention back. "After you, *knew* Vanessa, she started going out with Bob Trentway. Is that right?"

"That's right."

"And after Bob, she was with this Dancin' Don guy. Is that right?"

"That's right."

"Are you on good terms with these two guys? Would you say you're, friends?"

"We share a love of Lindy hop but we've had some differences in the past."

"Well, they don't have a lot of good things to say about you, according to this diary. In fact Bob says he's down right pissed off because he says you're stealing money."

"I'm sorry to hear that."

"Oh, cut the crap, Klaus," Sails had stretched his patience. "You trusted Vanessa and she went and told everybody what a crook you are. Isn't that what happened?"

Klaus's defenses were still up but were weakening. "Well, that's what it looks like, I guess."

"You guess?" Sails fired back at him.

Towning changed the line of questioning. "When did your girlfriend, Rita, and your girlfriend Vanessa, get tighter, you know, become intimate?"

"That happened a long time ago, before I knew either of them." Towning could see he had hit a nerve.

Sails could see it, too. "You into that kind of thing…two chicks at one time, kind of thing, Klaus?"

"No." Klaus was no longer returning looks from the detectives; his eyes were now looking down at the floor.

Sails attacked, "No? You don't dig that shit. Hell, I dig that kind of shit. You dig that kind of shit, don't you, Robert?" Detective Towning shook his head no.

"Well, I do, and I'm betting Klaus is with me. Right, Klaus? You're just bein' shy here, aren't you?"

"No, I'm not shy," Klaus almost shouted. "It's different when you know that person, when you know who that person is and you care about them. You think it's cool when you see that on television and in the movies, but in real life it's not cool at all." Klaus had stopped Sails' taunts. His voice was calming with his admissions. "When I confessed to Rita that I had been with Vanessa, she confessed to me that she had been with her, too. It was painful for both of us but we got through it and our relationship became stronger." Klaus looked up at Detective Sails, "It's different when you care about the person. It hurts."

Detective Towning had a couple other questions. "One other thing, do you own a broad brimmed fedora hat?"

"Yes…yes, I own a fedora hat. Why?"

"We have our reasons. And where were you the night Vanessa went missing?"

"I was with Rita, all night. You can ask her."

"We will."

"How tall are you?"

"What does that have to do with anything? Why are you asking me about a fedora hat?"

"How tall?" he repeated.

"Five foot, eight."

"That's fine. Now go get your girlfriend and bring her in here."

Rita was standing in front of the stage watching Frankie Manning and Erin Stevens when Klaus walked up and took her by her arm.

"This won't take long, Rita," Towning told her. "You are the president of this Federation?"

"Yes, that's right."

"And you knew Vanessa pretty well, is that right?"

"Yes, I knew Vanessa, but I thought Vanessa's death was a suicide."

"We're still waiting for the autopsy results. How well did you know Vanessa?"

"We went to high school together. A couple of years later I saw her at a club and we…it was one night and it was a stupid mistake, that's all."

"Would it surprise you to know that Vanessa didn't think it was a mistake? According to this diary of hers, she really cared about you."

"Vanessa never had a problem getting anyone into her bed; her problem was keeping them there. I'm truly sorry about what happened to her and if I knew anything that could help you I would tell you, but I don't."

"Where were you on the night that Vanessa disappeared?"

"I was with Klaus…all night."

By the time Klaus tapped Bob's shoulder, some of the crowd had noticed that something was going on. When Bob walked back to Pat's office, he had more than a few eyes watching him.

"What can you tell us about the Lindy Hop Federation?" Towning's first question confused Bob.

"The Federation? I thought this was going to be about Vanessa."

"All right, let's talk about Vanessa. Did you two, or do you and your friends, ever talk about the Lindy Hop Federation?"

"Sure, we all talk about the Federation all the time."

Towning was playing with Vanessa's diary, flicking it with his index finger. The book was no more than three feet from Bob and he could clearly see what it was. "What do you have to say about it? Is it good, bad?"

"Some good and some bad," Bob's face betrayed a worry line.

"Com' on, Bob,' Sails spoke from the side wall he was leaning on. "You despised the Federation, didn't you? Why be ashamed of it? You didn't do anything wrong, did you?"

"No, I didn't," Bob defended himself. "I don't like the way the Federation manipulates people, or the way they lie to people."

"Like what? What did they lie about?" Sails urged him.

"Oh, I don't know anything for sure, just rumors, really. Not enough to accuse anyone of anything specific." Bob pointed to the diary in front of Towning, "I'll bet that diary you have will tell you how they lied? What did she say about the Federation in that book of hers?"

"Why do you say that?" Towning's tone was soft yet curious. "Have you ever read Vanessa's diary?"

"No, no, I didn't even know she had a diary."

"Then it was something Vanessa told you," Towning started to dig. "You were close, weren't you?"

"We were very close."

"So what did she tell you about the Lindy Hop Federation?"

Bob shifted his body uncomfortably in the wooden chair. "She said the officers used the money they got from their members to pay for their trips and workshops around the country and private lessons from time to time."

"Well, that would piss you off," Sails chimed in. "It would sure piss me off."

"Yea, it did. It pissed me off," Bob admitted.

"Did it piss you off that Vanessa and Klaus had been together, been intimate together?"

"Hey, look, some of this stuff is none of your business."

"Ok. You don't have to answer if you don't want to. What else did she tell you that you can tell us?"

"Nothing," Bob answered.

"Nothing?" the Detective questioned.

"Nothing," Bob repeated.

"Did she tell you about her and Rita?"

"That was before we were together, and yes, she told me all about it."

"And after Rita she was with….Klaus, is that right?"

"That's right."

"And then Klaus and Rita were together," Detective Sails jumped in. "Man, that must have been some freaky shit. Did that piss you off, knowing they were all together? It would sure piss me off."

"Vanessa was with me then, and there was no *'freaky shit'*,"

"But it did piss you off, didn't it?"

"No," Bob was getting angry and turned back to Detective Towning. "I had nothing to do with Vanessa's death. I was nowhere near her car when it drove away from Casa Loma that night, you can ask anyone who was there. Just ask Jerry or Ann or Sheila, they'll tell you."

Towning could tell they were getting to Bob. "Was that the last time you saw Vanessa or did you talk to her later that night?"

"That was the last time I saw her."

"Did you follow her?"

"No."

"Did you ever follow her?"

"What?"

"Did you ever follow her?"

"Maybe once or twice," Bob answered.

"Was it once or twice?"

"Twice, I think."

"You think," Detective Sails questioned. "Com' on', Bob, you can't remember whether it was one time or two times that you followed this woman?"

"Alright, it was twice. I followed her home two times."

"You followed her home two times and that was all. Is that what you're saying, only two times?"

"I…I…. she caught me, sitting in my car outside of her house. I was just worried about her. She got mad and told me never to do that again," Bob hung his head.

"So it was Vanessa that broke off the relationship between you two?" Towning asked with a light tone in his voice, making it sound like the answer was unimportant.

"You might say that," Bob looked across the desk from Robert Towning.

"But you wouldn't?" it was Sails turn.

"I think we both knew it wasn't working. It could have been either one of us to say the words."

"You know what she says in her diary?" Towning didn't wait for Bob's answer. "She says your relationship didn't work because she wasn't a good enough dancer for you." Towning's voice trailed off.

"Is that true?" Sails sounded incredulous. "You screwed up a relationship with a hot babe like that because she wasn't a good enough dancer for you?"

Bob sat silently in his hardwood chair.

Sails shook his head in disbelief. "Damn, I thought dancing was a way to get chicks."

After a minute, that seemed like forever, of nothing being said or asked, Bob's voice crackled. "Is that all you want from me?" Bob stood up ready to leave.

"Just one more thing," Towning had let Bob get to the door. "How tall are you?"

"Six, two, and yes, I own a broad brimmed fedora hat. Anything else?"

"Yea, you can send in this 'Dancin' Don' character," Towning answered. "We'll let you know if we need anything else after that."

Dancin' Don's rotational spot was right up in front of the stage and when Bob tapped him to go to the office, almost every head turned to follow.

"So you're Dancin' Don?" Towning made the name sound like a game show host.

"Yes, sir."

"You must be a pretty good dancer?"

"I'm Ok."

"Well, with a name like Dancin' Don I'd guess you'd have to be a good dancer."

"I'm better than some, not as good as others. I'm Ok."

"How good a dancer was Vanessa?"

"Vanessa? Is that what this is about? I thought Vanessa took her own life?"

"We're waiting for the results of the autopsy. This is just a preliminary investigation. Now how about it? How good was Vanessa's dancing?"

"She was a very beginner, but that was OK. I didn't mind, really. She was a good soul and that's all I cared about."

"Did you try to teach her to dance?"

"I tried but she didn't like practicing. She liked to talk about dancing more than she liked dancing, but that didn't bother me. I liked talking about dancing, too, especially about the history. You know, the bands like Duke Ellington, Tommy Dorsey, Count Basie, Artie Shaw and all those guys. And the dancers too, like Frankie Manning out there, still teaching and still swinging. Man, we'd stay up till early in the morning just talkin'."

"So what happened? If it wasn't about the dancing then why'd you let her go?"

"It wasn't my idea, I loved her. I still love her, and I will for a long time. I knew she'd been with a lot of guys, but I didn't care. She was very spiritual, did you know that? I doubt if those other guys knew that. I doubt if they even cared about that. I just wanted to give her some happiness, to put some joy in her life. She was so beautiful and so unhappy at the same time. I wanted to make her happy. I hope I did."

"At least you tried," Detective Sails acknowledged Dancin' Don's story as sincere and it caught Towning off guard. He too had been moved by Don's candid profession of love for a woman who was less than virtuous. He had never known Sails to express sympathy for anyone, till now.

"Do you own a broad brimmed fedora hat?" Towning asked.

Dancin Don considered his wardrobe, "I think I have one back in the closet, but I haven't worn it in a long time."

"That's fine. And how tall are you, Don?"

"Five foot, seven."

"Thanks, you can go…Dancin' Don."

While the questioning was going on in Pat's office those of us who were still interested in the workshop had progressed enough with our step patterns that we were now working with music.

Benny Goodman's 'Jersey Bounce' at 136 beats per minute was a brisk but manageable rhythm and that, plus the execution of our steps, occupied most of our attention. Dancin' Don left Pat Brannon's office largely unnoticed making a big loop behind the collected dancers on the floor so he could make his way back up to the front.

Don hesitated a moment when he reached the center back of the room just in front of the main bar. There was someone that caught his attention.

Neon had been standing in the back for the last hour and was doing his best to mimic the steps that the rest of the group had been working on all day, only by himself and without a partner. Dancin'. Don noticed he was missing a step on count #6 on his left foot which put him out of sync with everybody else. He stopped and gave Neon an encouraging nod and started to go back up to his spot. Then after having a second thought, Don turned and walked back to Neon.

"That's pretty good, but you're missing a step. Can I help you?"

Neon looked up at the short white man and his funny clothes and shrugged his shoulders as if saying 'why not'.

Don was used to helping beginners. After learning to dance by spending hours and hours watching and rewinding old movies from the public library, he vowed he would help anyone who needed it or wanted it, free of charge.

"The timing is single step, single step, then triple step, or three steps, then single step, single step, and then another triple step. It counts to eight, see - one, two, three and four, five, six, seven and eight. You're missing this one with your left foot on count number six. Can you do it with me?"

Dancin Don would regularly break the rule about teaching before being asked, but he did it with a smile on his face and a helping hand and he always asked if he could help first. Don had gotten good at knowing when to offer help and when not to offer.

He stayed with Neon till the final minutes of the group class came to a close never having made it back to his spot in the front of the room. By the time Erin Stevens had called an end to the day's session, Neon succeeded at getting the correct footwork.

"Thanks, that helped," Neon told Don. "Are you one of the teachers here?"

"No, I'm just another dancer, but anyone will help you if you ask them. What's your name?"

"Everybody calls me Neon."

"Nice to meet you, Neon. My name's Don, but a lot of people call me Dancin' Don."

"Dancin' Don, Uh?" Neon enjoyed the name as a wide grin spread across his face. "I can see why."

The group class had officially come to an end and Rita was onstage reminding everyone about the dance that evening and that the second day of the workshop would start tomorrow at 9:00 am sharp. Neon and Don stood next to each other listening to Rita's updates.

When Rita was finished people were walking around in all different directions. Some of the group walked off the dance floor, some returned to the partners they had come in with, and still others stayed where they were, going over the steps they had just learned.

"Ok, Neon, good luck on your swing dancing." Don noticed Michelle walking in their direction as he shook Neon's hand.

Michelle made her way through the dancers and across the large floor. She was looking from Neon to Dancin' Don as she approached the two. "Neon, what a surprise. I didn't think you were going to make it here today."

"You know each other?" A noticeable degree of surprise was all over Dancin' Don's face.

"We met Wednesday night during the group class." Michelle checked herself. "But not... really in the group class. It was actually upstairs where we were watching the group class." She looked at Neon and the two of them laughed at her explanation. "Anyway, I suggested he come to the party tonight."

"Oh, yea, you should come to the party, yea," Don was repeating himself. "There will be a lot of people swing dancing and a lot of ladies for you to dance with."

"Yea, and Michelle will be there, too." Neon had been silently taking in the awkward situation.

"Yea, and Michelle will be there, too," Dancin Don confirmed and the two turned their attention to Michelle, who seemed to enjoy the whole thing.

"So," she said.

"So," Don repeated.

"I guess I'll see you both there," she said with her hands clasped behind her back which gave her an Alice in Wonderland kind of look; a very shapely Alice at that.

"I'll be there," Dancin' Don pledged.

"I'll be there too," Neon said, as if taking up a challenge.

"Great," Michelle rocked back on her heels and, when after several awkward moments it was apparent that there was nothing more to be said, Michelle left the two men. "Well, bye for now," she said, waving to them.

Either of the two men or both could have asked Michelle to give them a ride to the party, for it had been each of their plans from the beginning, but it was pride that kept their tongues silent; pride and fear. Both of them were afraid to ask and be turned down in front of the other, not knowing Michelle's true feelings.

"Bye," the two waved back.

"Say, Dancin' Don?" Neon said as they watched Michelle walk away.

"Yea, Neon."

"You got any wheels?"

"Nope."

"So how are we gettin' to that dance tonight?"

"We........." Dancin Don hesitated long enough for his Christian morals to check in, "are going to have to find a ride."

Don's first reaction was to exclude this black newcomer and challenger to his potential love interest. Don, however, held himself up to a higher standard. Whether one can maintain that perfect standard in an imperfect world is not really the question, since we all know you can't. The question is, how do you deal with that failure when the realities of this world and the people in it, knock you down.

"Michelle seems to be a really good person," Don asserted.

"She's fine, and that's for sure."

"Yes, she is. Yes, she is."

CHAPTER TWENTY

I was keeping my distance from Detectives Towning and Sails. I wasn't ready for any kind of token 'How are ya' or 'How ya doin' transparent greetings we might exchange, as if we really cared, which we both knew we didn't. I'd save that for people I actually did care about. When they left the office, they stopped for only a few minutes to talk to Pat, presumably to fill him in on how their investigation was going. I could see Detective Sails give the room one long, panoramic sweep, and when he decided he had seen enough swing dancers for one day, he left with Detective Towning.

"Don't you think we should we have said something to Detective Towning while he was here?" Ann had reached me from the other end of the ballroom.

"No, I'm sure the detective understands our reticence. He's got your statement from yesterday morning; he shouldn't need anything more from us. Hey, did you know Vanessa's father was State Senator Allen Billings? That is, before he died of a heart attack a few years ago?"

"Really," Ann recognized the name and title. "Wow, I remember seeing him on television more than a few times. I guess that's why they showed up in force today."

"Yea, and did you get a chance to see Detective Towning's new partner?"

"Wasn't that the detective who questioned us, back during the.....you know?"

"It sure was."

Sheila came over and stuck her head in between us. "Hey, I don't know what went on in Pat's office today but Bob is in a terrible mood."

"Well, Bob seems to be in a terrible mood a lot lately." I was losing sympathy for Bob by the minute.

"Tell me about it," Sheila agreed. "I don't know if we'll even be going to the dance tonight. He just came up to me and said 'get your things, we're going'."

"What a jerk," Ann was unsympathetic as well. "What could they have said to him? I mean, we saw him when Vanessa's car drove off. He's not guilty of anything, is he?"

I didn't answer Ann. I was remembering what Detective Towning told me on the phone about Vanessa's stalker, ex-boyfriends.

"Anyway, I can see him standing over there fuming," Sheila went on. "But I didn't want to leave without saying goodbye."

Ann gave her friend a hug. "Listen, just give him some time to settle down and if he still doesn't want to go, you give me a call and you can go with me and Jerry."

"Yea, no problem, Sheila," I told her.

"Thanks, you guys. I'll call you later, Ann."

We were watching Sheila and Bob walk out when I spotted Klaus, Rita, and Monica. They were on the other side of the tables from the dance floor, just in front of the coat check area in a thick huddle. I would have completely missed their little cabal were it not for the gesture I saw Klaus make in the direction of where Bob and Sheila must have been walking down the stairs. There was something very wrong about the three of them standing there together and I got a sudden interest in what Vanessa might have written about Monica in that diary of hers. Of one thing I was certain, by the end of the night the rumors and gossip about some of the details of Vanessa's life and untimely death would spread through the scene's grapevine as fast as bad news can travel.

"What is it, Jerry?" Ann noticed me staring at something, and following my line of sight, wanted to know more.

"I haven't told you about Vanessa's diary yet, have I?"

"Diary? Vanessa had a diary?"

"Com' on, I'll fill you in."

There was a common area under the church of Our Lady of Good Hope at the 3300 block of Washington Ave. where the dance was held. The church, school, and playground, was one of the last Catholic holdings remaining in an inner city that had a decreasing number of active Catholics and an increasing number of theft's and vandalisms. With each advancing year these old buildings got more and more expensive to maintain and the cost of repair and maintenance loomed over these ancient structures like the draped figure of death, holding its scythe. The building was more gothic in its appearance than the vintage look of the big band era that we were celebrating. The black stained mortar and stone added to the already morbid feeling of an inquisition.

I parked the car in a lot surrounded by a twelve foot high, chain link fence, and felt secure because of it until, duh! I remembered the wide open space that we entered through and there was no one to watch the lot.

Ann and I were passing under the nearly adequate lighting that acted as security for the parked cars when Marty drove past us in his white Ford pick-up. Marty was at the wheel, Dancin' Don at shot gun, and in between the two men was Neon, George Waterman's assistant, whom I had met at Casa Loma earlier that week. Were it another time and place, and if not for Dancin' Don riding in the cab with them, I'd have worried for Neon's safety. I stopped in my tracks for a second at the sight as I waved curiously to them.

We entered from under the church steps, heading down and through very old, double doors, and into an open foyer. The ladies room was set off to the left, and a hallway lead to the men's room on the right. The narrow corridors that lead to the men's room went around the outside of the downstairs and to the extreme other end of the space in an apparent effort to further separate the sexes. Across the small foyer there was another set of four steps that led down to the music and dancing.

If the death of one of our own had cast a shadow over the proceedings, a newcomer would not have noticed. In a strange way it was like a festive New Orleans wake with the crowd dancing away whatever sorrow or sadness they were feeling over the loss of a friend or loved one. We walked past the dancers who were spread out around the room. The walls were lined with folding chairs and there was a table of soft drinks and several pitchers of water with plastic cups that the Federation had set up with the volunteer help of eager members.

I could see Klaus and Rita not far from that table, dancing with the others, and enjoying the rhythms of Fat's Waller's 'Your Feet's

Too Big', an almost too slow beat for swing. They were purposely finishing their 'swing out' just a second early and holding in place like statues until the downbeat signaled them to come back to life and repeat the pantomime once again. It looked good, and it looked like fun. I wanted to do that, too.

We got on the floor and finished up the last 30 seconds of Waller's piano excursions then stayed up for the next tune which turned out to be Lionel Hampton's 'Flyin' Home', a much more energetic tempo. We knew we were challenged at that speed and tried some of the Charleston steps Frankie had taught earlier that day which proved to be a sane alternative to any of the triple rhythm moves we were used to doing. When the music ended, I looked at Ann and we gave each other a 'high five' at having kept up with the pace and also at having remembered the Charleston step patterns.

Bob and Sheila were waiting for us on the sidelines and as we went in their direction they acted as an impromptu audience, clapping for our performance. I recognized Bob's change of attitude and responded with an enthusiastic handshake. I figured if Sheila was going to stay with him, we all would have to get used to his up and down mood swings.

"Hey, listen," he shouted over the sound of the music.

"Yea," I shouted back.

"Those two detectives kind of raked me over the coals today and I guess I didn't handle it very well."

I shrugged my shoulders as if the whole thing was nothing and kept watching the dancers.

"Sheila says I need to check my attitude when I get stressed. What do you think?"

"I think she is probably getting to know you better than me," I told him.

"Yea," he admitted.

"You knew they were coming today, didn't you?"

"Yep," I answered.

"I figured."

"So," I asked. "How did it go?"

"Like I said, they raked me over the coals."

Bob went on to admit that he knew Vanessa and Klaus had been intimate as well as Vanessa and Rita. He explained it all in more detail than I wanted to hear, possibly in hopes of gaining some sympathy from me. I figured I'd given him more than he deserved but it probably wasn't near as much as he wanted. I left it at that. We were listening to the girls go back and forth about the dancing, the outfits, and who was there and who wasn't when Rita walked right up to me and asked me to dance.

I was surprised and hesitated at first. "Of course," I said, feeling all eyes on me.

I thought she might want more than just an opportunity to do underarm turns in the basement of the old church. As we danced together through various swing moves, I was distracted from the normally enjoyable experience, wondering what exactly she wanted. During the whole Keb Mo' song that was playing, we said little to each other, and when the music ended and I opened my mouth to say 'thank you', she brought up the subject that I was hoping we had avoided.

"Jerry, I'm guessing you know about the detectives who were at Casa Loma today questioning some of us about Vanesssa's death?"

"In fact, I was just talking to Bob about it."

Just as I answered Rita, the next song came on. Whatever came out of her mouth was unintelligible to me.

"What," I said, and put my hand to my ear, to which Rita took me by the arm and lead me off the dance floor and away from Ann, Sheila, and Bob. I dutifully followed her lead and looked helplessly over my shoulder to my friends who watched the curious maneuver.

"I was hoping you could help me," she started.

I bent down to hear what Rita was saying. "How can I help?" I asked, suspiciously.

"It's Klaus. I think it's just a lot of stress," she said. I wasn't sure what she was talking about but I guessed it had something to do with the questioning Klaus got from the police.

"I don't think I know anymore than you do, Rita. The police are waiting for the autopsy report to see if Vanessa's death was accidental or not."

"What do you know about anyone in a broad brimmed fedora hat?" she got right to the point.

"I know that someone who was described as being very tall and thin and wearing a broad brimmed fedora hat got into Vanessa's car Wednesday night at Casa Loma, and that was the last time anyone saw Vanessa alive…that we know of." I wasn't sure why I added that part. Maybe I was unconsciously thinking about what Detective Towning had said about how some of her ex-boyfriends were stalking her, according to her diary. I knew I might be implicating Bob by saying so, but it was too late to take anything back.

"So the police think this guy with the hat may have murdered Vanessa, is that it?"

"I think they are looking at it as a possibility," I told her, "but like I said, they're waiting for the results of the autopsy."

"Well, of course we are concerned about the safety of everybody, especially the girls, if this turns out to be a male predator. At the same time we don't want to create a panic if this does turn out to be no more than just an accident."

Rita was getting all official on me, but I felt there was something else that she wanted to say. "It's going to be hard to keep a lid on this for very long," she continued. "You know once people start talking, all sorts or rumors will fly."

"I'm sure you're right about that," I told her. "Listen, don't get me wrong, I appreciate you're talking to me like this but why didn't Klaus come to me?"

"Klaus is a little embarrassed about this whole thing; about our involvement. In fact he doesn't even know I'm talking to you about this….and well, I don't know how much you know, Jerry."

I could see how difficult this was for her. "I know enough, and as far as I'm concerned most of it is none of my business."

"Thank you for that," she put her hand on mine. "I'm just worried about Klaus. These last few weeks have been such a strain for him."

"Why?" I wasn't sure what Rita was referring to.

"It's really nothing, but it would bother Klaus if he knew I told you. I haven't even mentioned it to Monica. For some reason I just think I can trust you."

"Look, if this is something the police should hear…."

"Oh no, it's nothing like that. It's these dreams he's been having."

"Really," I thought it strange that she would choose me to confide in.

"I keep telling him it's only a dream," she told me. "It's about a man whose being chased along an old country road by a black man playing a saxophone. It's always the same dream, and always the same music, 'Blue and Sentimental', from the Count Basie Band."

"That is odd." I remembered our drive home that fateful night and how we couldn't get that music off the radio.

"No, what's odd is the man who is being chased by the black man, is tall and thin and wearing a broad brimmed fedora hat."

It was peculiar hearing that Klaus's dream had the same man in a fedora hat that Ann had seen getting into Vanessa's car, and was punctuated by seeing Michelle walk through a sea of dancers and right up to me. Our serious faces made her hesitate once she approached us.

"I'm not interrupting anything, am I?" she addressed Rita.

"No, you're fine, Michele. Jerry and I were just talking that's all."

"Would you mind? I wanted to steal Jerry from you and get a dance in with him while it's still early."

"Of course," Rita stepped back. "I should be dancing as well." It looked like Rita didn't see any need to say anything else. "Thank you for the dance, Jerry, and I enjoyed our talk."

"Sure, Rita," I said, walking away with Michelle.

We found an open space on the floor and when I started to get into closed dance position with Michelle, she stopped.

"I'm sorry, I haven't asked you yet. I mean maybe you don't want to dance."

"No, that's fine," I shook my head. "I'd love to dance with you, Michelle, really."

A smile spread across her face as it went from concern to relief and my ego got a warm belly rub at the idea that I may not want to dance with this incredible beauty.

We finished our dance and I walked her off the floor to meet Ann.

"Ann, this is Michelle, Michelle, this is my girlfriend, Ann." I reached around Ann and pointed to Sheila, "and this is our friend, Sheila."

The girls exchanged hellos and I could see Bob straining his head in our direction from the dance floor being otherwise occupied with his current dance partner. I knew he would be almost as anxious to be there for these introductions as he was to find out what went on with Rita and me. I, on the other hand, enjoyed the good fortune of not having to deal with his 20 questions and drooling over Michelle in front of the girls. I couldn't resist giving him a taunting wave from the sidelines.

"How long have you been dancing, Michelle"? Ann asked.

"Only about a month so," She answered. "I'm still a real beginner, not like you two. You look like you've been dancing for years."

Ann and Sheila liked Michelle right away. "Oh, we've only been dancing about as long as you have, maybe less for me," Sheila told her, laughing with Ann as she said it.

"I had a few ballroom lessons from Jerry. You know he use to be a dance teacher, but it's not like the dancing you see here."

"You were a ballroom dance teacher? Well, you didn't tell me that. No wonder you're so good."

"Yea, well, like Ann says, it's a little different from the vintage dancing you see here, but we work at it together. I think the practice is what makes the difference."

"I'd just be happy to look like you two when you do that step Frankie calls the 'swing out'. I just love the way you twist your hips like that, it looks so cool and retro at that same time."

This girl could sell Bibles to the Pope, I thought, watching her giggle with Ann and Sheila as if they suddenly had inherited a sister.

The music ended and I wasn't ready for Bob's interrogation just yet, so instead, I asked Ann to dance, leaving Sheila to Michelle and the two of them to Bob who was walking off the floor.

"I really like her, Jerry."

"She's a better dancer than she thinks," I mentioned.

"Well, she sure looks good in those clothes of hers. How do you think I would look in that outfit?"

"You'd look great, and you'd look great dancing in them, too."

"I think I'll ask her where she gets them. They don't look like they come from a used clothes store."

"So I won't get any 'death eyes' from you if I dance with her from time to time?"

"Of course not, you can dance with whoever you want to, you know that. It's just dancing after all."

We finished our dance and right away the next song, 'My Baby Just Cares For Me', by Indigo Swing, started. It was a favorite of ours and many of the other dancers as was evidenced by the surge of couples filling up the floor. We stayed for the song but moved to the other end of the basement to find more space.

When we left the dance floor and walked back to the other side of the room, I could see Michelle, Dancin' Don, Marty and Neon, all working together on Neon's dancing. Michelle and Dancin' Don were teaching some basic steps to Neon. Marty was standing off on the side, interjecting a comment or a suggestion at irregular intervals, much to the consternation of Dancin' Don, who was trying to do some teaching of his own. I could tell Michelle didn't care too much for Marty's comments either, or for Marty in general, by the look she gave him whenever he would feel the need to speak up. Marty would stand there with his arms folded across his chest like some kind of inspector, releasing one hand long enough to illustrate whatever instruction he was giving, then fold it back across his chest. Neon looked totally confused. He was trying to listen to everyone at the same time as he went from Marty, to Dancin' Don, and sometimes Michelle, who would offer an occasional suggestion of her own.

The normally even tempered and Christian minded Dancin' Don had such a stressed look on his face that I imagined he might explode at any second. He was dealing with way too much at one time. First there was Vanessa, a recent love in his life, who had just died, and may have even been murdered. Then there was Michelle, who was the current object of his affections, who was now paired up with Neon, his potential competition for the beautiful woman's attentions. Even worse, Dancin' Don was now helping this newcomer by teaching him to swing dance with, the beautiful Michelle. On top of all that, he was doing this over the distractions of Marty's totally inaccurate and unsolicited remarks which nobody believed Marty should be giving. Through it all Don looked like a man who was trying to focus on one thing but was being pulled apart by too many others.

Rather than try and come to his aid, I decided not to add another voice to the choir and headed to different part of the basement.

I told Ann about the dreams Klaus was having and how it was a dead ringer for the man she saw in the parking lot that evening with Vanessa's car.

"Do you think he might be making his whole 'dream thing' up?" she asked me. "After all we never heard any of this until after the detectives questioned him about someone in a fedora hat."

"That thought did cross my mind. But Rita mentioned that the man was tall and thin, and then there was the music that was playing in Klaus dreams….and can you guess what music that was?"

Ann thought a moment then looked at me incredulously, "Blue and Sentimental?" she posited.

"Bingo," I acknowledged, "and I know we didn't tell the detective that part."

Ann's thoughts began to darken, "Well, either this is really getting weird or Klaus is involved in this somehow. Do you think he might have one of those split personalities, like someone else we've known, and his dreams are punishing him for the actions of his 'other side'?"

"I don't know. It all seems a little too coincidental that every bad guy has a split personality. And then there's that black man playing the saxophone and chasing the fedora hat guy. What's that all about?"

"You're asking me?" Ann had as many answers as I did. "Have you talked to Bob about this?"

"I don't think this is something we can tell Bob or Sheila," I emphasized, "especially since I'm already breaking a trust by telling you."

"Oh," Ann didn't like my suggestion. "Sheila is my best friend. I don't want to keep secrets from her."

"I know, and I'm sorry, but if we tell Sheila then she's most likely going to tell Bob, and to be honest, I'm not sure how Bob would use this information."

Ann was in total agreement, "I wouldn't put it past him to go straight to the police if he thought he could get at Klaus and Rita and the Federation."

"Maybe that's who we should be talking to right now," I suggested.

"No," Ann rejected the idea right away. "I don't know who it was that got into Vanessa's car that night but I'm very sure it wasn't Klaus. Besides, if Klaus and Rita are involved in this then that witch Monica has got to be in on it too, and I just think that's very unlikely."

"Ok then, for now we'll just tell Bob and Sheila that Rita was trying to get me to join the Federation."

"I hope I don't lose a good friend in Sheila over this."

Ann and I danced the next two songs in a row when someone tapped Ann's shoulder to dance. Her new partner was not very tall, with a thin build and square shoulders, and was nice enough to ask me, after asking Ann first, if he could dance with my partner.

Couples like Ann and me had the opportunity to dance regularly together and got better faster than those without a steady partner. With Ann, I knew how much energy I needed to use to lead her on a step so there wouldn't be any pulling or pushing. As long as I led with my body and not my arms, our moves were smooth and effortless. We were able to ascend to faster beats of music because of it.

The vintage swing dance scene for singles was the same as any other dance scene. Singles danced with ever changing partners who had varying levels of ability, demanding the lead adjust the steps he could attempt with each partner. With all these variables a single dancer may go a long time without a dance partner who could help them improve and get to another level.

I watched Ann and her partner dance for a short time, and then decided to look for a partner of my own. As I moved along the periphery of the room, I allowed myself to make some physical assessments of the single ladies that were potential dance partner options. I was looking for someone who was close to my height and body type, someone who was cute, and most of all, someone who looked like they wanted to dance. If I took the time to consider my criteria I would have to admit to being a bit vain and superficial. But there it was, and when it came down to it, I had to admit these were my instinctive priorities. But now that there was only about two more minutes of the Duke Ellington's music left to play, I didn't have time for any moral redress. As it happened I ran out of time and asked the next free girl I could find. She was much shorter than me and had trouble following, but we did the best we could together and, if the margins of success were registered by our degree of fun, we did very well. I then thanked the young lady and she thanked me, and we were better for having met.

While I was looking for Ann, I passed Dancin' Don partnering with Michelle and Neon and Marty standing in the background. It looked like Don had given up trying to breakdown the step into individual parts and was just demonstrating the swing out over and over. Neon stood close to them, anxiously holding out an empty hand in hope of getting a turn with the lovely young partner.

"It'll take a while before you get this step down," Dancin Don told Neon. It was obvious Dancin' Don was indulging himself with his partner, Michelle. "Stay with the basic steps tonight and we'll work on the swing out the next time."

I had made the same mistake in the past that Dancin' Don was making now. Sometimes as a teacher you just want to dance the darn thing, even though you know you're only dangling that brass ring at someone who is not ready to attain it. It's like saying to someone, 'here's a hundred dollar bill, but you shouldn't reach for it, you should be happy reaching for ten dollar bills'. People won't listen to that; we covet what we see, and Neon had seen the brass ring in the form of the swing out step and as sure as God's in Heaven, the first chance he got, he was going to try that swing out step.

A young girl from the workshop came up to Don and asked him to dance, and as soon as he relinquished control of Michelle, Neon was eager to take over.

And there they were, Michelle and Neon, arm in arm in the middle of the dance floor with the music playing.

It was amazing how a young man, distracted by the knowledge of swing dancing, can forget that he has a beautiful woman in his arms. But that was what had happened to Neon, and I almost wanted to turn away from watching him ignore his lovely partner.

Leading is a learned thing and it usually happens in stages. First you think about what you have to do, then you think about what your partner has to do, then you think about both you and your partner dancing together. Once you have these three concepts, it usually happens all at once on the dance floor. Most people learn it one stage at a time.

That is where Neon was, at the first stage. His mind was totally occupied with his part and Michelle would have to be a mind reader to know what steps she was supposed to be following. Had he stayed with simple moves, like Dancin' Don had suggested, it would have gone a lot easier, but these are emotional decisions and his emotions were telling him to swing out, swing out, swing out.

Watching the two of them struggle was like watching any other couple in similar distress. After a few missed steps I just looked away.

"Was that a turn, Neon?" Michelle could have been on the other side of the room with the direction she was getting.

"Uh, yea, but that wasn't what I was doing just now. I was doing that swing out step…and you just stopped." He gave her a big smile, half of it was out of forgiveness for her lack of following and half of it was for his lack of leading.

"Well I didn't pick up on that," she explained, not understanding the side of his smile that was directed at her lack of following. "But that's Ok, let's try it again."

Neon tried to mentally gather together his accumulated knowledge on swing dancing in one breath, and with Michelle in his hands, gave it another try. Their combined and determined efforts allowed them to plow through a few other additional, tortured moves, before having to stop.

"Maybe we should try staying away from that swing out step?" Michelle counseled. "I think it's throwing you off."

"Yea, I think you're right." Neon felt like a spot light was on them standing in the middle of the dance floor. Everyone else was dancing all around them and he just wanted get through the song.

Nothing succeeds like success, and nothing fails faster when it follows what failed first. Had they started with basic turns and steps that were meant for beginners, they would have had a foundation to work from, as it was, they had not established any connection with any step. The only thing they had established was that they had no connection at all, and now those simple steps, that should have been easy, had become difficult.

"I just can't do this swing stuff, that's all," Neon made no attempt to hide his frustration. His mood had changed, like a light.

"Oh, that's not true. I know you can do this, you just need to be patient." Being a cheerleader for desperate causes came naturally for Michelle and Neon's current swing dancing skills filled that description perfectly.

"Look, I know you think I can do this because I'm black, but I can't. I think this swing stuff is for white people," Neon turned his back on Michelle and headed off the floor. "Anyway, it's not for me," he called over his shoulder.

Neon went over to where Marty was because he had been his ride and Michelle followed because of Neon. He stood there next to Michelle who was rubbing her hand across his back in an attempt to sooth his battered ego and bruised pride. He was in a room full of people and anyone of them would have willingly stopped what they were doing and come to his aid had he asked. Instead he stood alone. His temper and frustration were dictating his actions. He was the only black man there, the only one who lived near the Casa Loma ballroom, and the only one who couldn't swing dance. What did these people know about him? They visit his neighborhood for a few hours a week, never leaving the security of that one building, and talk about black people like they know them. The more he let his anger rage inside of him, the angrier he got. Neon thought about leaving without his ride in Marty's white, cracker, pick-up truck, no matter how long it took to walk back home.

Dancin' Don finished his dance and as soon as he got close enough to see Neon, he understood immediately the reason for his poor disposition.

"Don't let it get to you, buddy, it takes time," Don slapped him on his back on the other side of where Michelle was. "You'll get it as long as you don't give up."

Dancin' Don appeared gracious in his support, but Neon could see through his veiled encouragements. He knew Don was secretly cheering for him to fail and hoping he would give up and go back to the ghetto so Don could romance Michelle, uncontested.

"It's not as easy as you thought, is it?" Marty's snide comment was the last thing Neon needed and the last thing he was going to put up with.

"Fuck this," he declared and stormed toward the exit.

Michelle reached to stop Neon but he shrugged her hand off his shoulder. She turned for help from her friends and saw what looked like relief in Dancin' Don's face and downright laughter in Marty's. Disgusted at their reactions, she chased after the young black man to the dismay and surprise of her less than hospitable friends.

"Man, I guess she digs black guys," Marty declared. "Can ya believe it, a hot chick like that?"

Michelle caught up with Neon out on the parking lot.

"Neon, wait. Where are you going? You're not going to walk all the way back to Casa Loma, are you?"

"Sure, I'm used to walking in neighborhoods like this. These homie's won't bother me, but you're another story. You stand out like a black man at a white people's party."

"You'll protect me, won't you?" Michelle was skipping to keep up with him.

"Protect you?" Neon stopped in his tracks. "Why would you put yourself in a situation where you would need my protection? Because of me? What do you know about me? You don't know anything about me, do you?"

"I know you have a temper."

"Yea, I got a temper, and it's gotten me in trouble before."

"And I know you tried to learn something and when that temper got in the way, you gave up." Michelle's calming influence was affecting Neon.

Neon put his hands on his hips and looked up at the towering church steeple piercing the night sky.

"And I think you were probably feeling pretty alone being the only black man at that party," she added.

"Yea, that's pretty true…I guess." He was almost mumbling as the last vestiges of anger and pride were falling away.

"Look, if you don't want to go back to the party, then why don't you let me give you a ride back to Casa Loma? It really too far to walk," Michelle asserted.

Neon looked down the almost empty road along Washington Ave., "Won't you miss the party?"

"I'll miss some, but that's Ok. I'll still have time to dance when I come back after I drop you off."

"You'd do that for me?" Neon was thinking that maybe he still had a chance with this sweet thing.

"I'd do that for you…or any of my friends," she added coyly.

"Ok, where's your ride?" he asked.

They re-entered the parking lot and passed the first line of cars to get to the cars that were backed up against the link fence where her Chevy Lumina was parked.

"My dad bought this for me to use." She fumbled through four or five keys in the dark until she held one up to the half light and tried to use it in the door lock. When Michelle turned the key in the lock, she heard a scurrying sound like someone stepping hurriedly across gravel behind her. Before she could turn around to see what it was, she heard a thud, and then felt the weight of Neon fall against her. She tried to hold the dead weight of his body as it slumped against her, then let if fall, limply to the ground, and let out a shrill 'Ahhh'. Michelle looked from the still body of Neon to the feet of their attacker. As her gaze rose from the pavement, she recognized more of a vintage outfit.

"Why?" was all she had a chance ask before a hand reached down and grabbed her by her hair. Michelle winced as she was pulled to her feet.

Her assailant got behind her and put a knife to her throat. "Bloody murder is what you'll get if you don't do what I tell you. Do you understand me?"

Wide eyed and infused with fear, Michelle nodded.

A handkerchief was then stuffed in her mouth and another handkerchief was put in her hands and she was told to tie it around her mouth. A strong forearm shoved her against her car and her hands were tied behind her back. The next thing Michelle knew, she was marched to the back of her car and thrown in the trunk.

Michelle could hear one of the car doors open and then felt the vehicle bounce slightly when Neon was dragged into the back seat. She heard and felt the engine start and soon after felt the swing and roll of the Chevy as it left the lot and pulled onto the street. The ride was rough and uncomfortable and lasted about 20 minutes.

Neon woke up in the alley of an old furniture store on Cherokee that was down the street from the Casa Loma Ballroom. He was terribly nauseated and was ready to vomit at any second. He reached up and felt a large knot and open wound on top of his head as he pulled himself up to a sitting position. He looked at the little bit of grass that pushed up through the white rock that paved the alley surface.

What had happened, he asked himself? Bits of memory came back to him like the waves of pain that were hammering inside his brain. Michelle? The parking lot at Our Lady of Good Hope; but how did he get here? The nausea finally got the better of him and his gut let go of what he had had for dinner, spilling all around the corners of the brick building.

A couple leaving Casa Loma were getting into the car they parked on Cherokee to save the three dollar parking fee in the secured lot on Ohio Street. They looked away in disgust at the sight and sound of the young black man, certain he was drunk or drugged or both.

Realizing he had been dumped by whoever clubbed him, Neon began to put pieces of a puzzle together. He lay there a long time waiting for his head to clear both mentally and physically. Slowly he began to remember the events leading up to the stinging thud that left him unconscious.

He sat there a while longer waiting to get his legs back, only to fall back asleep, then awaken yet again to the dismal realities that ached him. After what could have been an hour or more, Neon decided he wasn't going to feel any better staying where he was propped up against the side of the untenanted building. While struggling to get to his feet, Neon disgorged what little remained inside of him. He knew he was hurt, maybe seriously. He could barely walk and wasn't ready for the inevitable series of questions that would accompany the accounting of how he had gotten to be in such a terrible condition. And what story did he have? That he had been hit over the head while getting a ride from a white girl then dumped in this alley? And where was the girl now? And what did the man look like? And the thought of question, after question, after question, sent his head spinning. Neon leaned against the cold brick façade and retched at the thought. Slowly, with one foot in front of the other, he made his way home, and what normally would have been a ten minute walk, took forty five minutes of dizzying and agonizing effort.

The party in the basement of the church of Our Lady of Good Hope continued to entertain all who were attending. Almost everyone who had been at the workshop showed up for the party with as many more who hadn't attended. The burgeoning crowd filled the downstairs basement but the large dance floor continued to have areas for more dancers.

Roger, who had volunteered as DJ, announced that there would be a 'snowball' dance and everyone dancing backed out of the middle of the floor, creating a large empty circle.

A snowball dance is where one couple starts dancing in the center of the room until the word 'snowball' is announced, at which time the couple dancing stops and picks new partners from the crowd. The two newly paired couples continue to dance until they again hear the word 'snowball' and they in turn find all new partners. The process continues until everyone in the room, who is willing to participate, is finally up on the floor dancing. The process allows everyone to meet and dance with many new and different partners. Not surprisingly, Klaus and Rita were the couple to start the snowball.

From where I was standing next to Ann, I could see just about everyone we knew. Amazingly, I had been able to avoid Bob the whole night, but being exposed as I was, I doubted that would last for very long. I could see him on the opposite side of the circle with Sheila. Further down to the left of them was Marty and about 20 feet down the line was Dancin Don standing next to Monica. I could see Michelle's friend, Elizabeth, about a quarter turn of the circle, but I did not see Michelle or her friend, Neon, anywhere.

We all stood clapping to a version of 'Jersey Bounce' admiring the smooth, coordinated moves Klaus and Rita were performing.

"**Snowball**," came over the microphone and Klaus went to the outside of the circle picking Monica as his next dance partner and, much to my surprise and dismay, Rita came right over and reached for me.

"There's something else I'd like to talk to you about when you get a chance." Rita kept her head turned away from Klaus.

"Sure, of course now's not the best time." I lead her in a tuck n' turn and as soon as she came out of it, she moved herself into closed position. Her back-leading caught me off guard.

"There is one thing," she was not more than six inches from my ear. "I don't want Klaus or Monica to know about our conversation. You'll have to find me later and ask me to dance."

"Ok," I acquiesced with a certain amount of reservation.

'Snowball'

And I went right out and retrieved Ann.

"What's going on with you two?" Ann asked once we got in dance position.

"Nothing that I know of," I professed my innocence. "Except that she wants to tell me something else and she doesn't want Klaus or Monica around when she does."

"That doesn't sound good. Why you? Why tell you anything knowing how close we are to Bob and Sheila?" Ann stated the obvious.

"Unless she doesn't care if they know," I suggested.

'Snowball'

I left Ann and reached for an anonymous partner out of the crowd.

Ann had selected someone from the crowd at random and since he had his back to me, I was not able to recognize him. By the time the next 'snowball' was announced, the center of the room was filling up quickly. Almost everyone reached for the closest person to them instead of looking for a partner they knew.

I released my current partner and thanked her at the sound of the next 'snowball' and when I turned to find a new one, I found myself face to face with Michelle's friend, Elizabeth. Even before I was able to lead her through a basic step, she was asking me about Michelle.

"You know my roommate, Michelle, don't you?"

"Yes, I saw her dancing earlier."

"Have you seen her recently? I'm beginning to worry about her."

"The last time I saw her, she and Dancin' Don were working with Neon. Do you know Neon?"

"Barely, but yes, I know him," she told me.

"Well, they were working with Neon and then Neon and Michelle were dancing on their own and that's the last I saw of them. Have you asked Dancin' Don if he's seen them?"

"Yes, I did," she seemed genuinely concerned about her friend. "He said the two of them left together about an hour ago and never came back."

"Well, I'd say that's your answer there." I did my best 'nod and a wink' expression.

"No, I know what you're thinking and that's not like Michelle at all," she shook her head.

"She's a sucker for charity cases and anyone in need, but she wouldn't just leave with someone, especially someone she barely knew."

"Yea, well, I can keep an eye out for them and I'll tell her you are looking for her if I see them."

"Snowball"

"Thanks, I'd appreciate that," she said, with guarded enthusiasm, and we went to find other partners.

Concern over what might have become of Michelle transferred to my interest of where Ann was and who she was dancing with. I caught just a glimpse of her through the tangle of bodies of the crowd, saying thank you to someone for her dance.

"Thank you, Klaus. You are a very good lead."

"No, thank you, Ann. You are a very good follow."

After exchanging mutually gratuitous compliments, both Klaus and Ann disappeared into the mass of dancers looking for their next partner. It was at that moment Ann felt a tap on her shoulder and a voice that had a distinctive southern accent asked.

"Excuse me, ma'am. May I have this dance?"

When Ann turned around to see who was asking her to dance, a chill ran down through to her spine and the blood ran from her face. The towering young man that she was looking at was well over six foot and wearing dark pants. He had a long sleeve, black and red striped shirt with a long black tie that was loosened at the neck. The telling item in his ensemble was the broad brimmed fedora hat that Ann recognized immediately. It was the man she had seen that night in front of Casa Loma getting into Vanessa's car.

Without any further communication from the tall southerner, or even any verbal acceptance from Ann, he took her into closed position and began dancing with her. Ann was shocked into silence. She was wrapped in his arms, and so close to him she could smell the musky scent of his old clothes. She went through the motions of dancing, missing steps and leads in an almost catatonic state, like a mouse caught in a maze. Her heart pounded louder than the drum beat of the music, and her eyes darted to others who surrounded her on the floor in desperate hope that someone would come to her aid; but no help came to her. She thought of screaming or pulling away but didn't. She knew that this man was capable of anything and as long as she was within an arm's reach of him, she didn't want to force his hand. Her look of fear was interpreted as just another swing dancer struggling with her dancing. Ann bided her time, praying the ordeal would end soon. She knew that at any second she would hear the sound of 'snowball' and would be released from this nightmare, but what then? Would she just let him get away to do whatever harm he might to another victim? What could she do?

"Snowball"

"Thank you, ma'am," and tipping his hat forward he began to move away.

"Thank you," Ann responded, and in a rash instant reached for his arm. "Excuse me, but I didn't get your name?"

If he had not taken any notice of Ann before, he did now. His steel gaze first bore down on her hand that was holding him by his arm, which she quickly released, then he turned his focus directly into Ann's eyes and said, "The name's Hatcher, ma'am. Orville Hatcher." Again he tipped his big fedora, then moved past several couples and offered his hand to another dance partner.

A boy of about twenty one was holding out his hand and asking Ann to dance but she was frozen in place. She felt a chill race through her bones and burrow deep within her body. What was she thinking, grabbing him like that? With the difference in their height he had barely even seen her face until she made a point of making herself known to him.

"Do you want to dance?" the young man repeated, his voice finally registering in Ann's ears.

"What? No, I'm sorry, not now," she told him, and began to weave through the dancers as she searched for Jerry, or Bob, or for anyone who would help her.

Ann came at me in a rush, speaking very fast, in gulps of quick breaths.

"I found him….or maybe he found me; I'm not sure….the tall thin guy…with the fedora."

She was frantic but I understood what she was talking about and I went from fun and frolic to serious and dire in that instant.

"He's just over here. Excuse me," she said to my very confused partner and took me away by my wrist, dragging me back through the crowd. "Com' on," she said.

It was no more than a few seconds before we got back to the spot where Ann had last seen the man. Those few seconds were enough time for me to reassess my plan of action which was no real plan at all other than to confront the potential murderer with nothing more than blusterous accusations. When we found that he was nowhere in sight, I felt a tinge of guilt that accompanied a greater sensation of relief.

"What's going on?" Bob broke through with Sheila in tow and Dancin' Don behind her.

"Ann saw the guy with the fedora here just a minute ago," I answered Bob, happy to see him for the first time tonight. "It's the guy she saw getting into Vanessa's car the night she went missing," I explained to Don.

"Are you sure it was that guy?" Bob asked the question I hadn't had time to ask.

"Yes, I'm sure. I danced with him," she answered, a little upset at the suggestion that she may have been creating such a disturbance on mistaken identity. "His name is Orville Hatcher."

"You danced with him?" I was incredulous.

"Yes," she said firmly.

"And he told you his name?" Bob was equally surprised at how close her encounter had been.

"Yes, I told you. He said his name was, Hatcher, Orville Hatcher. And he had a real, backwoods, kind of southern accent, like he was from Appalachia or somewhere. He had on dark pants and a red and black striped shirt, a long black tie, and that fedora hat."

"Wow, you got all that, just dancing with him?" Sheila credited her friend. "You go, girl."

"All right," I got us in a loose huddle. "Bob, Ann and I will go to the right and you guys go to the left. We'll circle around to the back and return here. If we see him, either Bob or I will stay back at a safe distance until one of the girls can bring the rest of us back."

"Then what"? Bob asked a very pertinent question.

"I don't know. I'm making this up as we go. Let's just find him first and then we'll take it from there."

"Well, he shouldn't be hard to find," Bob stated.

We searched the basement from one end to the other then met back where we started without any sign of the lanky figure that Ann had described. I got my cell phone out and reported the incident to Detective Towning. Ann had been the only one to have seen the phantom suspect and now that it looked like her testimony would go unverified once again, she was becoming sullen and depressed.

"I swear to you, I did not make any of this up," she was addressing our collected group. "It happened exactly as I told you."

"Oh, honey, we believe you," Sheila consoled her friend.

"Of course we believe you," I added support. "This Orville Hatcher guy must have caught on that we were looking for him and left."

"Did you call your detective friend?" There was an unmistakable note of sarcasm in Bob's voice.

"As a matter of fact I did. He said he'd check it out and get back with me."

"Doesn't sound like he's in too much of a hurry," Bob wouldn't let it go.

"He knows what he's doing and he's a lot better at it than any of us." I didn't like the way my words sounded but it was too late to take them back.

"Oh, yea, sorry for gettin' in the way here," Bob's reaction was almost predictable.

"I'm sorry, that's not what I mean. Look, I appreciate your help, all of you, but there's just so much we can do on our own. I think the only thing for us to do now is for me to take Ann home and wait to hear from the detective."

Reluctantly everyone agreed to give up the chase for our recently identified suspect and leave the police work to the police.

Inside the Taylor home on Utah and California Gloria Taylor was watching television with her mother when she heard someone slowly walk up the porch stairs. Thinking it was her son, Neon, she waited for the door to open, but when the door didn't open she got up from the couch to further investigate. When she looked through the front living room window, she saw Neon. Immediately she opened the door and gasped at the sight of her son.

Neon stood in the light of the outside porch, blood was pasted on the side of his face from the wound on his head. His lower lip hung loosely and he was teetering back and forward as some inherent function of his equilibrium operated reflexively to keep him from falling on his face.

"Neon"! Gloria screamed, and reached out to grab him before he lost consciousness and collapsed right there in front of her. **"My son, Oh my god, my poor son,"** she cried.

Holding him with his arm draped over her shoulder and her arm around his waist, Gloria carried Neon inside. Gloria's mother, responding to Gloria's screams, met her half way into the living room.

"What happened to you, Neon? Who did this to you?"

"You haven't been messin' with those gangbanger punks again, have you, Neon?" Neon's mother and grandmother took turns hammering questions at him. Gloria poured her damaged son's body onto the couch and raced into the kitchen to get a wet cloth for his head.

By the time Neon's mother had gotten back, Neon could hear the sound of his young brother's feet scurrying down the stairs. "Neon, Neon! What's wrong with Neon, Mama?"

Through it all Neon let the questions wash over him like white noise. He was safe at home and grateful for the solace of having a family that cared for him.

"Thanks, Mom, I'll be all right," he said.

"Who did this to you, baby?"

"Don't know, didn't see him….need to sleep now."

"We got to get him to a hospital," Neon's grandmother counseled.

"**No**," he protested adamantly. "I just need sleep. Just let me sleep, please."

"Alright, son, you get some sleep. You're home now and your mama's with you." Gloria decided she would find out more about what had happened to Neon before alerting the authorities about his injury.

Two hours later Neon woke up on the living room couch. His head throbbed but his stomach had settled and he felt a lot better for having rested. His mother was asleep in the big chair across the room, waiting for Neon to wake and be there when he did. Family, you can always count on your family. If not for them, you are truly alone.

He propped himself up on one arm and reached for the glass of water and aspirin that was set out on the table.

The sound of the glass setting back down on the wood table woke his mother. "How are you feeling, son?"

"Better, Mom, thanks."

Gloria threw the afghan cover off and went to her son, kneeling on the floor next to him.

"Neon, what happened to you?"

"A girl," he answered.

"A girl did this to you?"

"No, Mom. But it was about a girl, I think."

Neon started to get up off the couch and his mother held up one hand stopping him from moving. "You are in no condition to do anything but get yourself better, son. Just tell me what happened. Who is this girl?"

"Her name's, Michelle, and I met her at that Casa Loma place. She's a white girl, Mom."

Gloria let her concern show on her face but restrained herself from lecturing him. "Oh, son," she exhaled in frustration.

"I went to this church on Washington Ave. for a dance she invited me to. It was nothin' but white people there, and I wasn't havin' any fun, so I decided to leave and walk home. Well, she stopped me and convinced me it was too far to walk that late at night and said she'd give me a ride home, so we went to where her car was parked. That's when someone hit me over the head when my back was turned and that's all I remember. I woke up in the alley next to where that old furniture store used to be on Cherokee."

"You think this girl set you up? Check your wallet, baby."

Neon checked his pockets. "Nobody robbed me." He lay back on the couch. "Probably just some racist, white guy, upset about a black man being with a white girl."

"That still ain't right," Gloria got upset at her son's casual acceptance of a racial attack. "I'm calling the police about this and I want you to tell them exactly what you told me." She got up to get the phone from the kitchen.

"**No**, Mom, **don't call the police.**" Neon bolted up to a sitting position and, feeling his headache, he stopped from moving any further. He grimaced in pain and put his hand to his head.

Seeing her son in such distress was enough to halt Gloria who was half way down the hall.

"Now don't try to get up yet, son. You're still in a bad way." She went to sit on the couch next to him. "Tell me why I shouldn't go to the police. You know for sure they'd already be knockin' on our door if it was you who'd done this to some white boy?"

"Cause all they'll say is what I already know. That I shouldn't be hanging with a bunch a white folks I don't know. Besides, I'd have to tell them I didn't see who hit me. Then they'd say it could have been anybody who done this, even another black man for all I know. I'd rather just let it alone. Please?"

Gloria stroked her son's head. "All right, baby, if that's what you want. But if you change your mind, you know you've got your family to stand behind you."

"I know, Mom."

"I'm going to bed now. You can stay here on this couch or go to your bed, whatever you want. I'll wake you in the morning and see if you want to go to services. I love you, son."

"Thanks, Mom. I love you, too."

Gloria went upstairs to her bed but it was a long time before sleep took her. She had her doubts about not going to the police and doubts about whether her son was telling her everything, but she would wait before pressing these questions to him.

CHAPTER TWENTY ONE

That Sunday morning at Casa Loma was much like the previous morning with sunlight bouncing off the hardwood flooring, reminding tired bodies that in a very short time they would be moving on that wooden dance space again.

Rita was scurrying from one end of the room to the other playing host one minute, then answering questions about dance steps the next, then working with Monica setting up the Federation's literature table at the entrance of the ballroom.

I was relating to Bob the best I could what information, or lack of information, I had gotten from Detective Towning earlier that morning.

"There is no one listed in the phone book or in any of the police records by the name of 'Orville Hatcher'. Detective Towning did a nationwide search and the youngest man by that name is 66 years old."

"So that means what?" Bob's eyes glanced at Ann for a split second then back to me.

Ann and Sheila were staying out of the discussion. It was obvious that Bob was ready to cast doubt on Ann's story. His questions about what Rita and I discussed the night before, was the other shoe waiting to drop.

"I can only guess that he made up the name," I told him. "The detective wants Ann to come down to headquarters Monday morning and look through some pictures to see if she recognizes any of them as the man she saw last night."

Bob knew that if he attacked Ann or her story, he would do so without any support from the rest of us. He stretched his neck from one side to the other while measuring the words he was about to use.

"Ok, so this guy, who is taller than me and wearing a hat, comes from nowhere and disappears into nowhere, and he does so just to dance with Ann. Then he lets her get a good look at him, and when she asks, he tells her his name?"

"What are you saying, Bob?" I asked.

"I'm saying either this guy is acting like he's not guilty of anything or...."

"Or...?" Ann spoke up.

"Or somebody is playing a real sick game."

We all spoke at once.

"Ok, wait minute, Bob," Ann cautioned.

"I'm sure he's not referring to you, Ann," Sheila defended.

"If you don't trust us, Bob, just say so," was my answer. We had all reacted pretty much at the same time, but it was my words that hung in the air.

"Ok," he said directly to me. "Let's talk about trust."

"Ok...," I accepted his challenge.

"What's up with you and Rita?"

"Bob," Sheila blushed and held on to Bob's arm with one hand and put her arm around the back of his waist with the other. "What Jerry and Rita talk about is none of our business."

"Look, if we're going to run around looking for some 'tall, dangerous guy with a fedora hat' at a moment's notice, then I think we're entitled to ask a personal question or two." Bob was answering Sheila but he was talking to us at the time.

Sheila had reached the limit of what she was willing to put up with from Bob. She dropped her arms from him and took half a step back. "We do those things out of friendship; without conditions."

"That's Ok, Sheila." I didn't want to be the reason for their break-up. "I think you're both right. I think Bob is entitled to ask a personal question if he wants. But all I can tell you is this, it was a private conversation and it had nothing to do with you."

Bob took a deep breath and looked away from all of us. He knew a lot of people in the swing scene but he didn't have a lot of friends, and he knew it. He enjoyed the unique profile of a man apart, an outsider who thought outside the box, but his independent attitude also alienated him from the group as a whole, losing the confidence and close friendship of many. He had let go of Vanessa and felt her loss as a result of his radical behavior, now he was dangerously close to losing Sheila.

"Yea, Ok, I'm sorry for doubting you, Ann. I guess I was out of line…again," he said humbly and turned to Sheila. "You need to let me know when I get like that so I don't make a fool of myself."

Sheila was perplexed that he needed a signal for something he should realize on his own. "I don't know how I could be more obvious. Maybe I could pull on your sleeve and shout 'jerk alert'. Do you think that would get your attention?"

"I think that would be like trying to put a fire out with gasoline," I joked.

We were all about to welcome Bob back into the fold when Dancin' Don, who had been standing back from our small circle the last few minutes, decided to speak up. "Hey, you guys, I'm sorry to interrupt, but I need to ask you all something."

"Yea, you're fine, Don," Bob was thankful for the interruption. "What's up?"

"Well, you know, Michelle's friend, Liz?" he looked to any one of us for recognition and I nodded. "Anyway, they're roommates."

"Well, if we didn't, we do now. What's up?" Sheila answered.

"Liz is worried about Michelle because she didn't come home last night and she's been asking around, as discreetly as possible, if any of us knows anything."

"The last time I think any of us saw Michelle," I looked to each of us, "she was dancing with that guy, Neon."

"Yea, the last time anyone saw her was when they left the party last night," Don reported.

"I thought Neon was your friend?" Ann directed her question to Don. "Didn't you guys ride together with Marty?"

"I just met him here last night," Don explained. "He mentioned he needed a ride so I asked Marty if he could come with us. When he left with Michelle, we figured they left together." Don let his eyes lower to the floor with his final admission.

My concern for Michelle overrode my sympathy for Don. "Doesn't anybody know anything about this guy?"

"I saw him talking to Pat Brannon yesterday afternoon," Bob remembered.

"I saw him talking to Pat too, last Wednesday night," I confirmed. "I don't have Pat's number but I'm sure Klaus or Rita does." I took Don by his arm, "Com' on, Don."

We caught Rita at the table by the entrance with Monica.

"Listen, Rita," I looked over at Monica. "Can you give us a minute?"

"Sure," Monica agreed.

"I'll be right back," Rita told her. Monica nodded, confident that she would get all the gossip once we left the two of them alone together.

"What is it? Is there a problem?"

"Maybe, anyway, I hope not. I don't know if anyone has asked you yet but it looks like Michelle didn't come home last night. You know who I'm talking about; Michelle, the really cute blonde who wears all the vintage dresses?"

"Yes, I know her, but it's like I told her friend, Elizabeth, I haven't seen her."

"That's fine, but we're trying to locate the guy she was last seen with. His name is Neon and we think Pat might know something about him. Do you have Pat's phone number?"

"Yes, I have it right here."

"Thanks," I told her.

When I dialed Pat's number, I could see Rita and Monica exchanging notes several feet behind me. I figured it wouldn't be more than five minutes before the whole room knew that another girl had gone missing and we were now looking for a young black man as the possible suspect.

As I waited for Pat to answer, I asked Dancin Don to go find Michelle's roommate, Liz. She arrived just as I got off the phone with Pat.

The news of another missing girl alarmed Pat enough that he decided to come down to the ballroom.

"I just talked to Pat," I told her. "It looks like Neon met Michelle here Wednesday night. That must have been when she invited him to last night's dance."

"That's right," Don said. "They told me that yesterday evening after the workshop."

"What else did Pat say?" Liz was being less than patient. "Does he know anything else about him, like where he lives, or a phone number?"

"He said Neon works for the guy who cleans the floors here and he lives a couple of blocks away. Pat's on his way down here now. He's going to call the guy Neon works for and see if he can get an address and phone number."

Klaus approached us from the direction of the table where Rita and Monica were. "Hey, did you guys find out anything else about that Michelle girl? I heard she didn't come home last night."

"Oh, god," Liz exclaimed. "I hope I didn't blab this all over for nothing….actually, I take that back."

"We're trying to find the phone number or address of that guy she was with last night," I told Klaus.

Ann, Sheila, and Bob got tired of waiting for my report and joined us. The area in between the bar and the entrance was becoming crowded with curious onlookers and eves droppers who wanted to know what was going on.

"Does this have anything to do with all that running around you guys were doing at the party last night?" Klaus asked.

"Yea, I saw that too." Marty had come up the stairs and stopped to see what was up. "You guys were bolting around the floor like you were chasing somebody. What was that all about?"

"It was nothing," I said, trying to diffuse any further questions about Ann's sightings. "Ann just thought she saw somebody she knew and we were looking for him. It had nothing to do with Michelle being missing."

"Michelle's not missing, she's here," someone almost shouted from outside the large crowd that was assembling. "At least her car's here," they reported. "It's parked on the upper parking lot near that other street."

"Yea, I saw it there, too," someone else said. "Are you sure she's not here somewhere?"

"I'm sure," Liz pleaded. "Jerry, we need to find out where that Neon guy lives."

"Shouldn't we call the police?" someone suggested.

I spoke to Liz in answer. "The police may already be involved. Have you talked to her parents yet?"

"Oh, I don't want to do that unless I have to. Let's find out what we can from that Neon guy first." She spoke quietly as if it was only her and me standing there but in fact we were surrounded by an ever burgeoning crowd.

"Who's Neon?" a voice asked.

"He was the last person to see Michele last night," Bob spoke up.

"Does anybody know this Neon guy?" Another onlooker spoke to our little cluster of people that was getting bigger and bigger.

"He'll be hard to miss in this crowd," Marty's snicker was not well received.

"Why is that?" a young girl who was not at the party did not understand Marty's inappropriate joke.

"Because he's black," it was Ann who answered.

A half minute went by before Monica spoke what many were thinking. "Do you think this has anything to do with Vanessa?"

"Don't even say it," Liz jumped all over her.

"I was just thinking out loud. I didn't mean anything by it," Monica back peddled.

"It's a terrible thing to say, even to think. And it would take a venomous old bitch like you to speak such a terrible thing. You're no help to anybody with that foul mouth of yours," Liz said, tears streaming.

"Ok, Ok, we're all a little charged up about this," I put my arm around Liz to comfort her. The real damage, however, was not to Liz, but to Monica. That mirror that Liz had held up to her in front of everyone had turned the ice queen into a slowly melting puddle of remorse. Her normally unfazed countenance was shriveling into wrinkles and rivulets where tears were streaking across a very guilty face. Monica dipped her head low and turned to cry on Rita's shoulder.

"Look, just because the guy's black, doesn't mean he's guilty. I think we all know that." All eyes were on me but the look from Frankie Manning being escorted up the entrance to the stage by Erin Stevens stopped me cold. I could feel the blood rush to my face from the embarrassment I felt for all of us and for the defense I was making. They had arrived to hear only what I had just said, and it was obvious that racism was rearing its ugly head. I could see it in their faces and especially in Frankie's eyes. Suddenly, I felt like a part of a lynch mob, a sorry reminder of a different time.

All I could do was try to disperse the crowd. "Hey, don't we have a workshop to get to? I think we've got enough people working on finding Michelle."

Ann and Sheila helped me console Liz while the collection of concerned friends and fellow swing dancers slowly dispersed back onto the dance floor. Their conversations were hushed in private exchanges of rumors about a girl gone missing and another girl found dead. These were people they knew, friends and members of their own swing community. They were concerned about the safety of the neighborhood and a young black man who may be responsible for at least one missing girl.

Pat Brannon came up out of the entrance stairs with dark eyes and furrowed worry lines on his forehead.

He came directly to me. "I've got some information. Where is the one who is this girl's roommate?"

"That's me. I'm her roommate," Liz sniffed and blew her nose into her handkerchief.

"You're Liz, right?"

"That's right."

"Ok, Liz, does Michelle's parents live close?"

"Not close, but not too far. I didn't want to call them unless I had to."

"Well, I think it's time we called them and let the police get involved. I can make the call if you want, or we can let this detective we know talk to them."

"No, I'll talk to them. I just don't know what to say." Liz was still sniffling and looking very distraught.

Out of sympathy for Michelle's parents as well as for Liz, Pat offered to relieve her of that burden. "Why don't you let me talk to them?"

"Would you?" she said.

"Sure, what's their number?"

Pat took a few steps away from us for his call. When he finished, he dialed another number for Detective Towning before coming back to us. I don't know what he said but it couldn't have been easy. Behind us Erin Stevens had started the workshop.

"All right, I talked to Michelle's parents, Ron and Marion. They sound like very nice people," Pat said solemnly.

"They really are," Liz attested.

"Yea, then I called Detective Towning. He and his partner are the ones who are investigating Vanessa's death," he explained to Liz, who became even more agitated at the information. "They are going to get in touch with Ron and Marian and fill them in on what they know."

"Which is?" I asked.

"Which is not meant for everybody," Pat warned us. "The detectives are going to go over to Neon's home and talk to him." Pat set a level stare at each of us. He took a heavy breath and continued. "Now understand that these details can get really twisted and changed around once they spread from one person to another. I don't want to cause any hysteria or panic."

"Sure, Pat. What's up?"

"Well, it doesn't look good for Neon, I hate to say. I thought he was a pretty good kid when I met him, but the story I've been getting doesn't give us many answers."

"What does he say?"

"I talked to his mother and she says he came home last night with a head wound and blood all over his face. Neon told her that someone hit him over the head when he was getting into Michelle's car after she offered him a ride home. He says he woke up in that empty lot next to the vacant furniture store on Cherokee and walked the rest of the way home. I asked if he went to the hospital or reported it to the police and his mother said he didn't want to."

"That sounds really suspicious," Bob declared. "He gets knocked out and dumped across town, and when he wakes up, he doesn't go to the police, even when he doesn't know what happened to Michelle? I'd say we got our man."

"Let's wait and see what the detectives find out before passing judgment," I said.

"I think that's a good idea," Pat agreed. "You guys should get back to your dance lessons and let the police handle the rest of this."

We started to head back to the group and find a spot in the rotation when Dancin' Don, who was sitting at a table, sprang up and grabbed my arm.

"Is there any news about Michelle?"

"No, I'm sorry, Don, there isn't."

"How about Neon, do they know where Neon is?"

"Yea, they know," I assured him. "The police are involved now, they'll handle it. Com' on Don, we still have a Frankie Manning workshop going on here."

"You go ahead," he told me. "I'm going to wait here for a while," he sat back down at the table, determined and resolute.

"Don," I tried to reason with him. "Sitting here waiting for Michelle is just crazy." I sat down across the table from him. "To be honest you're freaking people out a little. I mean you're Dancin' Don, and you're sitting out on a Frankie Manning lesson. You owe it to Frankie to be involved, and you owe it to yourself."

I could have been talking to the wall. If he heard anything of what I had said, it didn't register in his face.

"You go ahead, I'm just going to wait here a while. I'll join you when I'm ready."

I looked over my shoulder at the group. Some of them facing us were clearly spooked by the events of the day, and Don and I were becoming a further distraction. But, I had done all I could.

"Ok, sit here as long as you want. When you're ready, Bob and I will make a space for you. Cool?"

"Sure, cool," he responded, stone faced, and I got up and joined the group.

Gloria Taylor went up to her sons' room to get more answers from Neon after talking to Mr. Brannon, the owner of Casa Loma Ballroom.

"The girl you were with last night is missing, Neon. She never went home."

"Michelle?" Neon woke up with a different kind of head ache than he had when he went to sleep. "You were right, Mom. I should have gone to the police. Whoever hit me over the head took Michelle and dumped me in that alley, and did it all to frame me."

"Well, you can bet the police are gonna be here real soon. Is there anything else you remember about last night? Who do you think might have done this to you? Who do you know that was at that party?"

Neon shook his head, "I don't think they needed to know anything more about me than I was a black man with a white girl, but if I had to guess, I'd say it was that Marty guy."

"Marty?" Gloria repeated.

"Yea, a real cracker if you ever saw one," Neon stated. "He'd be big enough to knock my head that hard and strong enough to toss me in that alley."

"You tell that to the police, and you can show em' that bump on your head when they get here."

"Did you tell Mr. Brannon I was here?"

"I told him you were asleep and not feeling well after that blow you got on your head."

"Listen, Mama, I can't talk to the police. I'm a black man with a record and on probation, and I was the last one to be seen leaving the party with that white girl….and there's somethin' else. We had an argument before we left that place."

"Oh, Neon, you didn't tell me that before. What else haven't you told me?"

"That another white girl went missing only a couple of weeks ago and then she showed up dead in the Mississippi river."

"Oh, my Lord, son, what have you got yourself mixed up in?"

"I can't let them take me in. I'm seventeen now and I can be tried as an adult. Once they got my black ass in hand cuffs, they gonna through away the key."

"What else can you do? You can't run, not for long. Where would you go? You'll just make yourself look guilty. You got to trust in the Lord, son."

"I'm not gonna run, but I am gonna hide," Neon jumped up and started getting dressed quickly.

"If they take me in now, they'll stop looking for anyone else or for any other evidence. As long as they don't have me to throw in front of a judge and jury, they'll keep working all those special investigative sciences that they have and eventually they'll find the one who really did this thing."

"I don't know, honey. This doesn't feel right, not at all. What am I supposed to tell the police when they get here?"

"You tell them I went to the church, and you won't be lyin' neither." He finished stuffing his wallet in his pocket but left his cell phone on his dresser. He could see his mother had real concerns about his plan.

"Look, Mama, I trust in the Lord, really I do, but we both know how the system works and I don't intend to get caught up in it. I'll keep in touch with you and let you know how I am. When you let the police see my room, and you know they're gonna want to, you make sure you let them see I left my cell phone here. Don't turn it off either."

"Son, are sure you know what you're doin?"

"I think so, Moms."

We were making a mess of the rotation with Bob, Ann, Sheila, and myself entering at different times, but given what was happening, everyone made allowances. From my place in line I could see Don sitting at the table and facing the direction of the entrance with his back to the group. I also noticed Monica sitting at the table they had set up with the Federation's literature. Her head was turned away from the group, staring in deep reflection and she held a handkerchief to her nose. It would obviously take some time before she was ready to join us, if ever. When Liz rotated to me, I found her decisively unsympathetic.

"Don't even ask me to apologize, because I won't. I meant what I said and I'm glad I said it."

The workshop went on without any further problems. Frankie and Erin were full of enthusiasm even though there was an obvious undercurrent of apprehension throughout the room. I kept an eye on Dancin' Don but he never did re-enter the group. He sat there for about thirty minutes then just got up and left without even looking back.

At noon we got a lunch break and we all went to Big Mac land. Bob called Don, and Don told him he was fine, but that he didn't feel like dancing today which worried us even more.

When we finished the workshop at four o'clock, Rita brought Frankie and Erin up onstage for an appreciative round of applause. Pat was standing off to the side of the stage when Rita announced that all of the ladies should be escorted to their cars for the time being and that our safety was everyone's primary concern.

Most of the dancers left at the same time and only a few pertinent players remained. Klaus was carrying out the last boxes of equipment and literature that belonged to the Federation. In spite of the cautious warning that she had delivered to everyone else, Rita told him that she and Monica would be along in just a moment and to wait for her in the car that was parked on the curb across the street. It was still daylight, she pointed out, and she wanted to sit with Monica for a minute before leaving the keys with Pat and they would be down in a little while.

Pat was busy talking to Detective Towning and Detective Sails which caught my attention and the attention of our little private group. I told Bob and the girls that the detectives were more likely to talk to me alone than the four of us together and suggested he take girls to the car and wait for me there. Bob surprised all of us when he agreed without any protest. His compliance was met with laudable praises from both Sheila and Ann. I thought it odd that when somebody, who usually reacts the wrong way, suddenly becomes a really nice guy just by acting the way he should have in the first place.

I approached the three men standing at the far end of the main bar.

"Jerry Russell," it was the unmistakable sound of Detective Sails. "How are you doin', my man?" He reached out with his hand and I responded solely out of reflex by putting my hand in his. The next thing I knew Sails had his arm around my shoulder as if we were old army buddies.

"I'm good Detective, thanks," my voice shook with his vigorous hand shake.

Detective Towning ran interference for me. "Detective Sails and I were just telling Mr. Brannon that the forensics department went over the missing girl's car."

"Did they find anything?" I asked.

"Some hair and fibers," he answered. "And some blood in the trunk, but no fingerprints. It looks like somebody tried to wipe it clean but missed a little in the dark," he said solemnly. "We won't be able to identify the blood for another day or two yet."

"Did you get a chance to talk to Neon?"

"We talked to his mother but the boy wasn't there," Towning said.

"Do you think he's running from you?"

Detective Sails shunned the idea, "He's got a record but we don't think he's running."

"Why not," I asked?

"What do you always take with you wherever you go?"

I gave his pop quiz a quick moment of consideration. "My wallet, my keys, my money…and my cell phone," I answered.

"We called him on his cell phone and got a voice message. We could hear his phone go off upstairs in his room."

"But he's got a record?" I reminded him.

"The kid got caught up in the local gangs two years ago and was picked up carrying drugs," Detective Sails recounted Neon's past in a dismissive tone. "He was convicted in juvenile court and put on three year's probation. His proby says he's been clean ever since and his pastor at the church says he's been a regular member for the past two years. And he's got a two year old son."

"A son?" I repeated, surprised at hearing the details of Neon's life.

"Not exactly the profile of a serial abductor, is it?" Detective Towning added. "This kid wasn't seen around here until after Vanessa's body was found. If you ask me it looks like somebody might be trying to frame the only black swing dancer in the group to cover their tracks."

"Or," Detective Sails offered. "Somebody didn't like the idea of a black man being with a white girl and used the opportunity to rid themselves of some uppity nigger."

"Does that mean the swing dancers you questioned yesterday are cleared?" I asked.

"For now," Detective Sails left the idea open. "The girl president said she was with the boyfriend all night, which gives them both an alibi. The other two we're still not sure of yet."

"We're still looking into this 'Orville Hatcher' that Ann saw last night," Detective Towning added. "He was spotted both times just before a girl went missing."

"Both times by your Ann," Sails pointed out.

I didn't want to address his implication so, I said nothing.

"We thought it unlikely that he would use his real name, given that the police might be looking for someone so recognizable."

"That's why we'd like Ann to come down to the station and look at some police photos," Detective Towning reminded me.

"You know the routine, don't you, Jerry?" Sails mentioned.

"We know the routine," I said to Detective Towning ignoring Detective Sails. "Ann is downstairs right now, waiting me now."

Kluas was also downstairs sitting in his car across the street from the entrance of Casa Loma Ballroom.

Klaus Tiegmier was a second generation German whose parents traveled from Hamburg Germany 30 years ago when Klaus's father, Karl, got a promotion at IBM and relocated to the United States. Klaus had picked up the German language from his parents, but having been born and raised in this country, spoke English as well, if not better than, any of his American counterparts. His father had gone over to Microsoft in 1985 and his influence on his son and his association with that company allowed for Klaus to land a much better than entry level position. Klaus's family had always been financially secure, and at 24 years of age, after obtaining a substantial income, plus benefits, Klaus had established a solid and secure future for himself.

He had never been much of a joiner, even in his teen years. The public schools he started out in were rife with confrontations and fights, and after his first year in middle school, his parents sent him to a private catholic school. Chaminade was a Catholic College Preparatory High School, where violent actions were limited to the sports fields, which for Klaus, was soccer.

Klaus didn't show interest in girls until his first year of college at Washington University. It wasn't that he lacked an interest in girls; it was the awkward, nervous chatter that was an inevitable part of the dating ritual. So, in 1996, Klaus joined an on campus swing dance club as a way to meet girls. His motivations were based on practicality with the intentions of having an actual purpose for interacting with females both physically and verbally.

The swing club turned out to be a mixture of socially and gracefully challenged misfits as well as some talented dance enthusiasts. With Klaus's athletic background, he excelled in getting the steps well before anyone else, and found instant popularity among the group. Something else happened too; he found a love of dance, specifically, swing dance.

He stayed with the swing club through his college years but looked for other avenues to expand the limitations that the little swing group put on him. By his senior year he began to notice a growing movement, through the internet, of vintage swing dancers in San Francisco, Los Angeles, and other parts of the country and around the world. When he went to his first vintage swing workshop in L.A. in 1998, he met fellow St. Louisan and swing dance enthusiast, Rita Beltman. Rita was a perfect partner for Klaus and the two hit it off right away. When they went back to St. Louis, they decided to do what they could to promote Lindy Hop in their city as it was being promoted all across the world.

Rita, a strong and willful young woman, became the catalyst that motivated Klaus. She pushed him to help her create The Vintage Swing Federation, and even though the name needed work, the organization began to grow. The dance, and their love for it was always there for them, but the Federation was something else. It evolved into more than they had hoped, taking on a life of its own. People all over the city, and other cities as well, knew or had heard of the Federation. Local news media did articles on them, and there were television spots highlighting their accomplishments and talents to illustrate the new vintage swing craze that was sweeping the country. They were regularly asked to perform, and only those chosen by Rita, Klaus, and sometimes Monica, were allowed to participate. They had a growing membership and the membership fees paid for lunches at restaurants, trips out of town, lessons, and equipment. Rita and Monica reveled in the attention and the perks that came with it and saw it as one long party that might never end. Klaus, on the other hand, had reservations. He could see the effect it was having on Rita and feared the runaway train they were riding would eventually have to end, and he didn't want it to end badly. He didn't like the idea that their relationship was linked to the Federation. He just wanted to dance socially, with the girl he loved.

Klaus was sitting in his six month old Chevy Malibu parked on the other side of Iowa St., only 30 yards from the entrance of the

Casa Loma Ballroom. He hadn't been sleeping well lately because of a recurring dream he'd been having. He had trouble making sense of it, with the music, and the tall, skinny man in the broad brimmed Fedora hat running down some old country road trying to get away from a black man playing the saxophone. He'd gone over it in his mind so many times after waking up in the middle of the night. Was it his subconscious trying to tell him something? And what message could it be?

He turned the car stereo off and listened to the silence and felt the gentle breeze outside his window. Maybe some peace and quiet were what he needed most. It was nearing the middle of October and he could smell the grass and the changing color of the leaves that gave off a dry, crisp scent, almost like the smell of wheat. There was a slight chill in the air and as Klaus reached for the electric window control, he saw someone across the street. He thought he recognized him when he saw him turn the corner from Cherokee onto Iowa, heading straight for the Casa Loma Ballroom. The tall young man with the broad brimmed fedora hat moved quickly down the side walk with his long legs stretching out in front of him. Klaus sat up in his seat and thought to call to him, but stopped. What would he say? Was this the one the police were asking about when they had questioned him about Vanessa's death? Was this the man he was seeing in his dream? By the time Klaus got himself together, the tall man had disappeared into the entrance of the ballroom. Klaus knew Rita and some others were up there. He got out of his car and crossed the street, following the man up the cement staircase and into the ballroom. Once inside he walked around the entrance to face the dance floor. Klaus saw no one inside except the tall man who was on the other side of the floor entering under the 'Employee's Only' sign that lead to Pat's office. Klaus looked around the empty room. Where had they all gone? There had to be at least twelve people left in the building, surely they would not all end up in that office. Klaus crossed the floor and stopped at the door that lead to Pat's office and knocked.

"Anybody here? Rita, Pat, Monica, are you there?" he called into the dark space. He had been in the office before and slowly made his way in touching the sides of the walls so he wouldn't run into anything. The door was closed and he opened it cautiously feeling for a light switch as he entered. Once he got fully inside, he felt a hand at his back.

"Klaus?" the sound of Ann's voice jolted him up in his car seat parked across the street of the Casa Loma Ballroom.

"Oh, Jesus!" Klaus called out, clutching the steering wheel with both hands.

"Oh," Ann jumped back into the street at his sudden shock. "I'm sorry," she started to laugh. "I didn't mean to scare you."

"Where?" Klaus turned from the steering wheel to Ann. "How did I… did you see him?" Klaus rambled.

"Who? See who?" Ann was beginning to understand how upset she had made Klaus, waking him from an apparently sound sleep. "Are you all right, Klaus?"

"I'm fine," he answered, and immediately opened the door and got out of the car. He started to cross the street, then stopped and looked at Ann with the wild eyes of a hunted animal.

"Have you been watching the front here?"

"Yes, I saw you sitting in your car and I wanted to talk to you," she explained.

"You're the one who saw him, that night when Vanessa went missing?" he said excitedly, "the tall man with the fedora hat."

Ann visibly sank back into herself, not wanting to admit to it, "Yes, I saw him."

"Well, did you see him just now? Walking down the street there and into the Casa Loma?"

Her eyes now widened with fear, fear and at the same time recognition, realizing what Klaus was referring to.

"You saw him?" she reached out then drew her hand back.

"I'm not sure what I saw. Maybe I was dreaming, I've been dreaming a lot lately," he said, drawing his fingers across his forehead and through his hair.

"Maybe you see him in your dreams," Ann stated, "but I see him in real life. I saw him that night getting into Vanessa's car, and again last night at the party. He said his name was Orville Hatcher."

Ann had found a kindred spirit in Klaus and she could no longer contain her excitement. "It's the same guy. We're seeing the same guy."

"Yea, but for me it's just a nightmare," Klaus scratched his head.

"Yea, well it's a nightmare for me, too. Only for me, the nightmare is real."

Rita and Monica came through the double glass door entrance, looking quizzically at the two standing in the street next to Klaus's car.

"We should talk about this, Klaus," Ann suggested.

"Yea, maybe we should, but not here," Klaus said, looking at Rita and Monica

"I'll tell Jerry to call you tonight," Ann said backing away.

"Ann?" Rita addressed Ann cautiously, hearing only the last few things that were said.

"Hello, Rita," Ann acknowledged the two women approaching them. "Tonight, Klaus, he'll call you tonight."

"What's going on?" Rita asked.

"Get in," Klaus said without answering. "I'll tell you on the way."

CHAPTER TWENTY TWO

When I got close to Bob's car, I noticed something was wrong right away. He was backed up against the cement embankment in the parking lot and I could see all their faces. There was no music and no conversation. Everyone was looking straight at me, stone faced and silent. Ann got out of the back seat when I got close.

"What," I said, glancing at Bob. "What's wrong now?"

"Nothing," she answered. "I'll tell you in the car."

"Jerry," Bob called out from his window.

I went over while keeping an eye on Ann.

"Look, you know I don't think much of Klaus and Rita, but I do think a lot of you and Ann. So whatever you guys do, I hope you'll include me."

"Sure, no problem," I told him, not sure of what I was committing to. "Listen, did you get hold of Don?"

"I just called him, but no answer, again. I'm going over to his place and knock on his door."

"Good, we'll come with."

"That's not really a good idea," Bob warned. "He's a little self conscious about his cheap digs. You know what I mean."

"That's cool," I said. "Just let me know how he's doing, Ok?"

"Cool," Bob fist bumped me, and I questioned why he was getting so chummy all of a sudden.

Once we got into my car and left the parking lot, Ann started getting real vocal and real excited. She told me about what happened to Klaus and how she woke him up from his nightmare only minutes earlier. She also told me she promised him that I would call him tonight with the intention of getting together and comparing notes.

"And as soon as Bob found out he went ballistic?" I tried to fill in the blanks.

"Only a little at first," she defended him. "He said they are not to be trusted, and we shouldn't even let them into our house, and blah, blah blah, blah blah."

"Yea, I got it."

"Then I told him that he was invited, and that if he didn't want to come, that was fine, too. That's when he settled down, real quick."

"I'm betting Sheila's getting an earful about you right about now," I said.

"Well, if she is, I'll find out later and it will be just too bad for Bobby in the long run."

"You're tough girl."

"Bet your ass," she confirmed. "Now what did Detective Towning tell you? Did they find Neon?"

"No, and the detectives, mostly Detective Sails I think, are more interested in your Orville Hatcher then Neon."

"Really," the vindication about Ann's accounting of Orville Hatcher was quickly replaced by the attention she would get because of it. "What else did they say?"

"They still want you to come in and look at some police photos."

"Did they say when?" Her voice was trailing off as her enthusiasm began to wane.

"I told them we'd do it tomorrow."

Ann looked out her passenger window. "I'll have to take time off from work."

"I know, honey, but it is the next step."

She looked at the back of her hand and wrinkled her forehead. "I have to wonder, are we just looking for a ghost?" She shook her head free of the doubt she was feeling and looked back out the passenger's side window. "I did see him," she said emphatically. "I danced with him, touched him, and I heard him tell me his name, 'Orville Hatcher'. But when I think about him, I feel as though there's a distance there I can't explain."

I reached across and put my hand on hers. "We'll look at the pictures tomorrow, and we'll take it from there."

Bob and Sheila were already at Ann's house when Klaus, Rita, and Monica arrived. They were civil enough to each other trading obligatory 'Hi's' and 'How are you's'. Bob even offered a 'How have you been?' to Rita and it would have gone a lot further had he not realized how pretentious it actually sounded and let his expression betray his real feelings. I was explaining how the police were just as interested in our 'friend' Orville Hatcher as they were in finding Neon.

"They found blood and fibers…I think that means hair fibers, in the trunk, and some hair fibers in the back seat," I told them, "but no fingerprints anywhere."

Klaus was sitting on the couch next to Rita. "So someone must have deliberately wiped certain places clean, like the steering wheel and the door handles. Places where there should have been finger prints."

"That's the way I see it," I acknowledged. I looked over at Bob to see if he would wade into the discussion but he wasn't saying anything. He was leaning against the fake fireplace mantel on the wall and looking into the Kaleidoscope Ann had purchased in St. Charles several months earlier. He was purposely ignoring Klaus.

Rita did some deducing on her own. "Was anyone missing at the party after Neon and Michelle left?"

There were shrugs and expressions of indecision leaving it unanimous that no one knew.

"When did you see this, what's his name?" Rita paused to ask.

"Orville Hatcher," Ann told her," and it was during the snow-ball dance. Then he left right after."

"So it had to have been Neon, or this Orville Hatcher, or the two of them together," Rita tried to narrow down the possible suspects, "Because everyone else was at the party, right. So it had to be one of those two." Then she said decisively, "and my money is on Neon. He was seen arguing with Michelle just before they left. All he had to do was walk home after leaving the car in the parking lot."

"Doesn't that seem kinda stupid?" Bob interjected. "I mean, for him to incriminate himself like that, by leaving the car only a couple of blocks from where he lives."

"And from what I hear, he'd been hit on the head," Sheila added.

"That's what his mother says, anyway," Rita argued, "but there's no Neon around to prove anything, and if he was really hurt, why didn't he go to a hospital or to the police?"

"Wait a minute," I thought we were getting ahead of ourselves. "Just because everyone was there for the snowball dance doesn't necessarily mean they couldn't have hijacked both Neon and Michelle then come back to the dance to throw off suspicion. They could have tied and gagged both of them; Neon would have been knocked out, and then parked the car around the block. They made sure they were seen at the dance and left when no one was noticing." If nothing else, this was getting everyone thinking beyond the limits of what was obvious. "In fact, they would have had time to dump Neon off in that alley and make it back for the snowball with Michelle all tied up in the trunk. Once the snowball was over, they could have gone to the car where they had it parked out of eyesight."

Ann supported the idea, "People were coming and going all night. Anybody could have left without being noticed."

"So," Bob proceeded with the next obvious question, "Was anyone missing before the snowball dance?"

"Well, a lot of us could have been missing," I realized, and made a checklist of the people in the room. "You, for example, Bob. I didn't see you after the first time I danced with Rita. Or Klaus, I didn't see you after that first time I saw you and Rita dance earlier...."

"I was there," Bob's defenses were up before I could finish my sentence. "I thought you were avoiding me. And now that you mention it, where were you all night?"

"He was with me, Bob," Ann testified. "I danced with him most of the night.

I picked up where Ann left off. "As I'm sure Bob was dancing with Sheila and Rita was dancing with Klaus, not that anyone in this room needs a witness. The point is, just because we saw someone at the snowball dance, it doesn't necessarily give them an alibi."

My point was well taken and all eyes roamed from one person to another, assessing each possibility.

"If you're saying it could have been anybody, then what about this Orville Hatcher guy? Isn't that why we're here?" Bob redirected suspicion from those of us in the room.

"That's true," I agreed, "and the question is, how did this guy get from Klaus's dreams to getting into Vanessa's car, and then dancing with Ann during the snowball last night?"

Rita did not want to go ghost hunting. "It sounds like the police think this mystery man is as much a suspect as Neon? It seems to me they'd have a lot more answers if they'd find the last person who was seen with Michelle."

"I think they're following up on all possibilities," I wanted to get back to the real reason we had gotten together. "I don't think they've given up on Neon, not by a long shot. Which leads us back to why we're here in the first place?"

I decided to get right to it. "I think we are all here to discuss, Orville Hatcher, if that really is his name. Anyway, that's what we'll call him for now. Agreed?" Everyone nodded.

I continued to act as moderator for the moment. "Ann."

She looked up from the floor.

"Why don't you get everyone up to speed and review what you know?"

"Ok, well," she began reluctantly. "It started in the parking lot that Wednesday night after we all left Casa Loma……" Ann related her experiences about the tall thin, young man we were now calling Orville Hatcher. She told us all about him getting into Vanessa's car and driving away. She told us about the vision she had of the woman whose face was beaten in with a star shaped, glass ash tray by Orville Hatcher as he left her laying on a couch, and she told us of when she saw him in the flesh, just the other night, and of dancing with him during the snowball dance and asking him his name. She talked in a detached manner, as only her eyes could see the images she was describing.

"But you were the only one to have seen this, 'Orville Hatcher' person in all these instances? Isn't that right?" Rita voiced the one glaring inconsistency, and it weighed heavily against Ann's accountings.

"Yes, just me," she admitted, letting her shoulders drop as her eyes found the floor again.

"But, as we know, she's not the only one to have seen this tall stranger with a broad brimmed, fedora hat. Isn't that right?" I indicated Klaus.

Klaus took his hand off Rita's shoulder. He hesitated before recounting his experiences. "I've had these dreams," he started slowly, "the same dream actually, and I keep having it with more and more regularity. That's when I see him, your, Orville Hatcher," Klaus looked at Ann, "if that is his name. I've never really seen him like you have, Ann, although I thought I had today."

"Why don't you tell us about the dream you keep having?" I thought he needed some prompting.

"It's like most dreams. It doesn't make a lot of sense." It was clear Klaus didn't want to take the chance of looking foolish, especially in front of Bob.

Bob, who was a therapist by profession and understood Klaus's reticence, surprised us all by encouraging him. "Go ahead, Klaus, there's nothing to be afraid of. Dreams can mean a lot of different things, and there are different theories about dream interpretation as I'm sure you may know. I'd be the last one to criticize you or anyone because of their dreams."

Klaus was both encouraged and apprehensive at the same time. After all, it was a very subjective topic, as Bob had testified, and the door was now open to him to either accept or reject any interpretation he might get.

"My dream always happens on some old, backcountry road," he started. "It's dark out, but it's not night, with big black clouds in the background. This Orville guy is running. He's tall, and he's dressed like you described him, Ann, with those black pants and long sleeve shirt, and that broad brimmed fedora hat. He's running from - and this is the part I really don't understand - a black man playing a saxophone. The black man is very well dressed, with a pinstriped, double breasted suit, and he's wearing what I think they called a pork pie hat. His head is turned to the side at a 45 degree angle, like he's looking away from anyone who might be watching. I know what he's playing even though I don't ever remember hearing any music in my dreams...."

"Blue and Sentimental," I interjected.

"Yea," Klaus pointed at me in amazement. "That's the one, 'Blue and Sentimental'. Who told you?"

"No one told me," I assured him. "We," I indicated Sheila, Ann, and myself, "had a pretty strange incident on the night Vanessa went missing, when we couldn't get that tune to stop playing on my car stereo."

"Don't you know who you are describing?" Bob's mouth was hanging open. He had a slight twinkle in his eye like he knew something no one else knew; something he thought we all should have known. At least it was something he thought Klaus should have known.

"It's Lester Young, one of the two tenor saxophone players with the Count Basie Band," Bob expected that would be enough information for the rest of us to respond in a chorus of 'Oh, yea's', but, we didn't. The name Lester Young was still as foreign to us as the neighborhood around Casa Loma.

"I'm guessing that it was Count Basie who recorded this 'Blue and Sentimental'?" Monica wasn't afraid to guess.

"You're right there," Bob added. "They were called the 'Greatest American Rhythm Section' back then. I mean the saxophone and clarinet players were like lead guitarists in their day and Lester Young was one of the wildest, and one of the best. He was real superstitious and had some kind of close friendship with Billy Holliday. Some people say he quit the Basie band because they scheduled a practice on Friday the thirteenth. That was in 1940, the same year Casa Loma burned almost to the ground."

"So that's Lester Young playing the saxophone on 'Blue and Sentimental'?" Ann asked.

"Nope," Bob corrected her. "Herschel Evans played 'Blue and Sentimental'."

Monica, like most of us, was getting confused. "Ok, now, who the hell is Herschel Evans and what does he have to do with any of this?"

"He was the other tenor saxophone player with Count Basie," Bob said, enjoying the whole thing more than he should have. "The two of them had this competition between them, Lester Young and Herschel Evans, where they would trade off solos spots, but off the stage they were actually very close friends. Lester was devastated when Herschel died. It wasn't long after that that Lester quit the band." Bob directed his attention back at Klaus. "You have to have seen him somewhere, man. I mean you described him to a tee."

Klaus was almost dumb struck. "I didn't know the man existed until I just heard you talk about him tonight. What I want to know is, why is he in my dreams, and what does he have to do with this Orville Hatcher?" Klaus shot back at Bob.

"Good question," Bob responded. "Standard dream interpretation doesn't explain how this Orville Hatcher guy keeps popping up in front of Ann, or how this same guy gets in your dreams, or, how any of this relates to those missing girls. I mean, no one has seen this guy but Ann. And that name, it's like from the sticks, and from a long time ago." Bob was getting into unraveling the whole thing. "Jerry, you said one of the detectives did a nationwide search on that name and out of all the matches the youngest was 66 years old?"

"Yea, that's right," I said.

"Well, the name, it's vintage, like swing dancing," Bob pointed out. "It's a name somebody would have given a child born around that time, like Lester Young."

"So?" Klaus questioned.

He didn't see where Bob was going, but I did. "So, it's all related to this vintage thing we're all into," I said, picking up on Bob's line of reasoning.

"Ok, sure, but if this guy I keep seeing in my dream is all that old, then how is it that Ann keeps seeing him in the present, as a young man in his twenties?"

"That's a tough one all right," Bob scratched his head, "unless what Ann saw was some kind of hallucination, or a daydream, maybe?"

"It wasn't any hallucination or day dream," she emphasized.

"It sure didn't seem like a dream today," Klaus argued, "or at least not till you woke me up. I mean, it felt so real. I was already out of the car and almost on my way upstairs when I realized you had just awakened me."

"Well **I** - wasn't – dreaming," Ann restated decidedly. "I touched him, and he touched me, and he spoke to me. 'Orville, Orville Hatcher' he said, as clearly as I'm talking to you now."

This back and forth was destined to become an outright argument. There was one other possibility that none of us was willing to discuss, or even suggest, but it was the real reason all of us were here. It was the 800 pound Gorilla in the room that nobody wanted to admit to and we weren't going to get anywhere until someone did.

"If we believe Ann, which I think all of us do, then we have to accept that she did in fact see this Orville Hatcher. So the next thing to do is to look a little closer at Klaus's dream…" As soon as I spoke, I suddenly remembered what I had seen under the bar at the Casa Loma Ballroom. It was odd that I hadn't even thought of it until just now, and I stood there in a daze as everyone else stared at me, waiting for me to go on.

"What is it, Jerry?" Rita sat across the room on the couch facing me. "What aren't you telling us?"

"It's something I saw written on the wall behind the bar at Casa Loma the first night I worked there. It was a poignant little poem about people dancing, and clapping hands, and may the Lord keep and protect everyone, or something. And I was thinking, just now, how the thing ended. '*Jack Buckmueller and the Book of Dreams 11/5/41*'."

"Did you ask Pat about it?" Klaus asked.

"That's the weird part, because as hard as he tried to find it, he couldn't. And when I tried to find it again, I couldn't either. A couple of days later Pat showed me a photo of a guy who he said was this Jack Buckmueller. He used to be a bartender at Casa Loma right around the time of the fire." There was that awkward silence in the room again when everyone had something on their minds but no one willing to speak up.

I was tired of beating around the bush and decided to take a walk on the wild side regardless of how I might look. "It's like these people are reaching out to us from the past, and they get closer to some of us than others. For me it's just some scribbling on a wall, for Klaus it's a recurring dream, and for Ann it's the real thing. Maybe the closer the encounter, the stronger the message, I don't know. I know it sounds strange, but I'll bet some of you are thinking something just like it?"

"OOOOO-Kaaaaaay…" Bob expressed his opinion, and his doubt.

No one else spoke; instead they shifted uneasily in their seats. Had they laughed, or just passed it off with some comical whimsy, like Bob, I might have dropped it right there. But they said nothing, no one was laughing and no one offered any contradictory opinions. They were silent, still afraid of jumping in and getting wet.

Rita was the first to test the water. "So what's the message?"

"I think the message is to be afraid," I told her. "I think the messages tell us to watch out for this Orville Hatcher."

"Well, yea!" Sheila stated loudly. "Aren't we already doing that?"

"We are," I agreed. "And I'm only saying it as a basis for getting deeper into the dream."

"Well, if we are going down that path," Bob got a little more serious, "and I'm not sure I want to, I think we should look a little closer at the aspect that Klaus's dream is a recurring one."

"What's the importance of them being recurring," I asked?

"Because most people consider recurring dreams especially important," Bob explained.

"You mean my subconscious mind is yelling at me?" Klaus surmised Bob's point.

"Yea, that's about it," Bob went on. "But if we're going to use terms like a 'Book of Dreams' or people sending messages to us from the past, maybe we should consider a more Biblical interpretation about your dream."

"You're talking prophesies." I had no idea where Bob was going with this, but I remembered our conversation at the bar.

"That's right. And what are these dreams predicting?" Bob's question was for anyone.

Sheila decided to get her feet wet next. "Haven't we already decided they are warning us about this Orville Hatcher?"

"That's only the Orville Hatcher part of it. There's more to Klaus's dream than just Orville. What about the storm and Lester Young? And don't forget the dark old road that Orville's running down. What parts do they play?"

"Is there anything else about Lester Young that you haven't told us?" Monica spoke up.

"Well, he was married three times and each time it was a white woman." Bob informed us.

"Which, you're saying, looks bad for Neon," I stated what I thought Bob was inferring. "But Neon looks nothing like Lester Young." I countered, "The only thing they have in common is that they are black."

"And they both have an affinity for good looking white women," Bob re-emphasized.

"We all have an affinity for good looking white women," Klaus noted.

"That's not what I mean," Bob was trying to be subtle. "Lester Young may not look like Neon, but he could represent him in the dream."

"Because they're both black, you mean?" I said, dismissing his premise. "But you make an interesting point, although you and I arrive at different conclusions. Just because we see someone who looks like Orville Hatcher in a dream doesn't mean he can't represent something else. And, maybe," I turned to Ann, "just because we see someone who calls himself Orville Hatcher in life, doesn't mean you're seeing him as he actually is."

"You're losing me there somewhere, honey," Ann shook her head.

"Orville Hatcher could be a 'perceived reality'…your perceived reality. You see him a certain way, and the rest of us see's something else. That's why nobody else has seen him but you. The person you see as Orville Hatcher could be anyone."

"But why do I see him as Orville Hatcher?" Ann questioned.

"Maybe this person is more like the real Orville Hatcher than he wants to be or even realizes, and only you see him for who he really is. Maybe this guy has so much in common with Orville Hatcher that he's bringing the memory of him back. Things like swing dancing and vintage clothes. And swing music, especially Count Basie music, and girls who look like Vanessa and Michelle."

"Young, shapely blondes," Bob profiled the victims, looking at Sheila and Ann.

Ann wasn't convinced, "But I saw him. I looked into his face."

"With a hat on," I argued, "and only for a few seconds, isn't that what you said? You said most of what you saw was the side of his body."

"Well, if we're not looking for Orville Hatcher, who are we looking for?" Klaus asked.

"Someone with an obsession for Count Basie and Lester Young music," I tried to complete the profile. "Someone who is deep in the vintage scene, and probably had a close association with both Vanessa and Michelle."

I suddenly realized I was describing Bob and Klaus, and in that moment, tried to both hide my realization and consider them at the same time. "I know this could describe a lot of people," I said without turning to face anyone in particular, "so we need to look for more information about this Orville Hatcher. I think we should pay close attention to the details in Klaus's dreams and Ann's sightings."

Bob had been supportive up until that moment, "Aren't we taking a lot for granted here? I mean it's one thing to entertain these ideas at parties and these get-togethers for fun, but to act on them as if they were anything other than superstitious nonsense? None of this has any foundation in scientific fact. This is more like fairy tales and folk lore crap."

"It's all we have to go on," I tried to justify. "The police are better equipped than any of us to deal with anything scientific and factual."

"You'd look at it differently if any of these things were happening to you," Ann turned to Bob.

I wanted to avoid any arguments. "I think we actually made progress here tonight. It may sound a little out there, I'll give you that, but I'm willing to give it a try."

Bob didn't like the idea at all. "You can't be serious. Getting your answers from ghosts? Looking for a killer based on dreams?"

"Ok, Bob," Rita was willing to entertain a more reasonable approach. "Let's talk about the more accepted theory of dream interpretation that you mentioned earlier. What would a rational analysis of Klaus's dreams be?"

Bob gave the question a moment of thought and addressed Klaus. "Let's start with the two guys in your dream. We know at least one, Lester Young, who is real, but has been dead a long time, the other we're not sure of," Bob gave a nod to Ann then hesitated a moment before continuing. "The storm probably means you're heading for trouble and Lester Young could represent your involvement with the vintage swing. Now this Orville person could be you, Klaus, running from something that your involvement in the vintage scene is causing, and you're running, trying to get away, but you can't."

"All right, that's enough," Klaus interrupted and starting reaching for his jacket. "I came here in friendship. I trust you with my dreams, and you turn it into some kind of witch hunt."

"Isn't it obvious?" Bob defended. "I mean, how else could they be interpreted?"

Klaus was headed out the door with Rita in one hand then turned on his heel. "The police told me you accused me of lying and stealing and that wasn't enough for you. You had to act like you wanted to help me and take advantage of my honesty."

"Did I lie?" Bob was shouting after him. "Tell me then, did I lie? Well, did I?"

"Oh, Bob," Sheila said, exasperated yet not surprised.

"Wait a minute, Klaus," I caught them at the door. "I'm sorry about that. You don't have to go."

Rita was out the door and stuck her head back around to answer Bob. "Yes, you are a liar, Bob, and a very, mediocre dancer, and that's all you'll ever be."

"Oh yea, well, that's only when I'm dancing with a mediocre partner like you," Bob shouted back.

"I'm sorry, Jerry, sorry, Ann." Klaus shook my hand. "We can do this again, but not with, Mr. Wonderful there."

"I'll call you, Klaus. Again, I'm sorry. Goodnight Rita, Monica."

"How would she know what kind of dancer I am?" Bob ranted. " We haven't danced together in months. If anyone is mediocre it's her."

Sheila took Bob's shirt sleeve and gave it a gentle pull, "Bob, remember that signal we talked about?"

"Forget that," he denied being culpable for any wrongdoing, "I've done nothing wrong."

"**Bob,**" I had raised my voice without knowing it. "Wasn't it just this morning that you apologized to all of us for being a jerk? And wasn't it just last night that you apologized for the same thing, and

Friday afternoon to Sheila for the same thing…again? What's with you, man?"

"**He** lost his temper first," Bob argued, sounding more like a nine year old than a grown man.

"Because you harassed him," I answered back.

"Oh, no," Bob was standing his ground, "not this time. I only told him the truth and I'm not about to apologize for that."

"Oh, we're talking truth here, are we?" I wasn't backing down either. "Can you 'handle the truth', Bob?" I used my best Jack Nicholson voice that I could muster, dripping with sarcasm. If Bob was ready for a fight, then so was I.

"Bring it," Bob said simply.

"Did you try to contact Vanessa after she left the parking lot that Wednesday night when she went missing?" I asked him.

"You think I did it, don't you," Bob got in my face. "It was me you were describing a few minutes ago, wasn't it? I'm somebody who's heavily involved in the vintage experience, somebody who has an interest in Count Basie music, and somebody who knew both Vanessa and Michelle. Well, that description could match a lot of guys in the swing scene, including Klaus." He looked to Sheila and Ann who looked back with questioning faces. Why didn't Bob just answer the question?

"Do you deny stalking her after you broke up?" I was angry. Bob had pushed my buttons and I wasn't going to let him off easy.

"I didn't stalk her," he shot back. "I followed her home a couple of times because I was worried about her. **Klaus** was the one stalking her; he was the one calling her all the time. Anyway, that's what she told me. She caught me parked across the street from her apartment one night and went all crazy on me. That was the last time I followed her – **the last time I followed her**," he shouted his answer at us.

I decided I would let my temper subside before speaking again but as far as I was concerned, Bob was still on the hot seat.

Sheila had not said much the whole night. She'd been listening to us all and waiting to hear what each had to say before voicing her opinion. "I don't think Bob's guilty of anything, except speaking his mind, maybe." She reached up and took his hand, "It wasn't Bob who lost his temper tonight and ran off when the going got tough. Bob's answered all your questions truthfully. He's hasn't tried to hide anything. He wasn't anywhere near Vanessa's car when it drove away that night, we all know that, and he danced with me most of last night. He couldn't have had anything to do with Michelle being missing. I believe him, and I think you should, too."

"Sheila's right," Ann said in support of her friend. "At the time, I thought Bob's interpretation of Klaus's dream was pretty reasonable; he laid it on a little thick, but it made sense to me. I mean, why didn't Klaus just deny it if he wasn't stealing from the Federation. Bob stood here and took it, why didn't Klaus?"

It made sense, what Ann and Sheila was saying. It just took me a little longer to cool down.

Bob had gotten my temper up, like he did with Klaus, and probably on purpose. I had been thinking what an inept therapist he must be, but maybe he was better equipped to deal with his emotions than I was with mine.

"All right, look, I'm sorry," I threw up my arms. "This thing's just got us all on edge," I held out my hand to him. "Maybe I was the jerk this time. Am I forgiven?"

Bob shook my hand, "No problem. I'd rather you ask me and get it all out instead of suspecting that I might be some kind of killer." He dropped my hand and gave me a level stare. I felt the full force of the tension that had been circling over all our heads, realizing I had just accused a friend of murder.

Bob was cool and composed, "Only don't think that I buy into all that hocus pocus about someone coming back from the dead. I'm sticking to a guilty Klaus running from his own crimes."

"How guilty do you think Klaus is?" Ann asked Bob.

"I don't think it's too farfetched to think of him as a suspect. After all, you thought I was."

Bob and Sheila left in a volley of apologies and acceptances. We parted as friends but with a few unresolved feelings. Bob still had it out for Klaus and continued to be a ticking time bomb ready to go off at any minute. And the existence of Orville Hatcher continued to be a mystery.

Ann and I were scheduled to go into the police dept. the next morning and look at photos for a man who may have been dead for many years. We would have to go through the motions and dreaded the trip that much more.

CHAPTER TWENTY THREE

Neon dragged his head up from the sleeping bag that he was wrapped in as he lay in the back seat of Janeakwa's 85' Nissan parked on the street just around the corner from Neon's mother's and grandmother's house. He was only half awake when the sound of a police radio's squawking instructions and information on changing lines alerted him that they had arrived in the early morning hours armed with an official search warrant.

He dropped his head back down behind the seat thinking they would have enough evidence in the drug stained car upholstery he had slept on to send him off to jail for a long while. The car had broken down sev`eral months earlier and had been sitting there on the street and would probably continue to do so. The Missouri license plates that were on the vehicle came due in January and would force Janeakwa to either repair the car and renew the license plates or get the car off the street by having it towed to the junk yard. Either way it was an expense she was willing to put off for as long as necessary.

Neon dug a power bar out of his pocket. He had not asked Janeakwa for permission to use her auto for an improvised B&B, knowing the grueling interrogation would be as bad as, or worse than, that of the police he was hiding from. The car had become a part of the many other unofficial landmarks that dotted the streets of the neighborhood, and as long as Noen stayed quiet and still, he was unlikely to be bothered by anyone.

Bob Trentway lived alone in a two bedroom apartment at Heather Ridge, situated behind a stylish seafood restaurant. It was centrally located and was not more than twenty minutes from just about anywhere in St. Louis.

Like most nine-to-fivers, Bob had a tried and true routine of getting ready for work each day that operated with a consistency of a Swiss watch. It started this Monday morning with his alarm clock playing 'One O'clock Jump' a random selection on KDHX radio station from the campus of SIUE in Edwardsville, Illinois, waking Bob at exactly 7:15 am. Giving no more thought to the Count Basie piano runs at the beginning of the music, Bob pulled himself out from under the covers of his double bed. He went directly to the kitchen to brew two cups of black coffee, taking time to look out at the clear blue sky of the October morning. He proceeded, with coffee in hand, to the bathroom to shower and shave. He put on his striped shirt, tie, and black dress pants. Having finished his bathroom duties and gotten dressed, Bob retrieved his morning paper from the entrance of his building and went back to his apartment. He headed to the kitchen to eat his toast and cereal and finish his second cup of freshly brewed coffee while reading the current issue of the St. Louis Post Dispatch; front page, sports, and editorials; all in that order.

It was when Bob finished his breakfast and began to put the dirty dishes in the sink that he noticed the fast approaching clouds just over the neighbor's roofs. Fearing that he might get caught in a downpour, Bob quickly retrieved his briefcase and made his way out the door, down the hall and out the entrance on his way to his 95' Audi that was parked under an overhang on the other side of the lot.

As soon as Bob opened the entrance door to his apartment complex, he was buffeted by a blustering, 40 mile per hour wind coming out of the southwest. His clothes wrapped tightly across his body and his jacket was almost blown off him. Dust particles from the pavement were getting into his eyes and he had to squint to see the overhang where his car was parked. Shielding his face with his forearm, he took one step at a time, fighting to keep his balance against the onslaught of the increasing wind. It took several minutes for Bob to cover the fifty yards of pavement to get to his car, and with great effort, he pried open the driver side door and squeezed his body inside.

His relief at having gotten shelter in his Audi was almost immediately interrupted by the sight he saw ahead of him through the windshield of his car. The sky was totally covered in gray and in the background there was a line of coal black clouds reaching out to pull a shroud over the entire St. Louis area. Frozen as much by fear as he was amazed by the meteorological display, Bob watched the thick fog of dust that the dark cloud carried with it which was now almost on top of him.

He made a second's decision to try to drive somewhere to safety, away from the ominous dust storm. In a frenzy of hurried motions he jammed his car keys into the ignition and tried to power up the car but with no luck. He could barely hear the turning of the engine over the loud cry of the wind. He continued to try to start the vehicle while stealing glimpses of the buildings in front of him as they became engulfed in what looked like a merciless cloud of dirt. It was a second later that the car was rocked by tiny pellets from the dangerous clouds. Even though he was protected from the storm by the car, Bob threw up his hands in front of him as if the storm might find its way inside. The wind thrashed and howled all about him and he let his arms relax by his sides to watch the fury of the wind wreak havoc. It was then that Bob felt something begin to collect around his shoes. Dust from the storm had somehow found a way into his car from under the dash board and began to fill up inside his car. He looked down in shocked disbelief at his feet as he watched the dust build up with increasing speed as it was now around his ankles.

That was enough, he decided, and reached for the handle of his driver's side door and pushed with his shoulder, but it would not budge. With building panic bolstering his urgency and strength, he managed to break the seal of the door only enough to let more dust inside. The dirt was filling up the backseat as well as the front and was now around his knees. Bob began to yell in horror at what would eventually claim him if he did not find a way out but his voice was lost in the wind and he was spitting out the dirt that was flying all around on the outside and inside of his car.

He could see the parking lot where the dirt only blew across the pavement and only slightly collected in the corners and doorway of the buildings. He looked at the empty cars around him, sealed safe and tight. Why was this happening to him and on the inside of only his car? The dirt was at waist level, and as hard as he tried to push the dirt off his lap with both hands, it had little effect, and kept filling up the car. He pulled his knees up to his chest, cradling himself on the driver's side seat. The dirt had gotten up to the dash board almost covering the speedometer gauge and the sound of the wind seemed to increase with the degree of dirt that filled up inside. He was pressed against his car seat from the weight of the dirt and he was coughing ferociously as it found its way into his mouth, down his throat, and into his lungs. The last thing Bob remembered was trying to keep his head and mouth above the dirt. His eyes and lungs were burning and he couldn't breathe……then the alarm went off.

Bob jolted up in bed coughing out dirt that wasn't there and gasping for breath when he didn't need to. The radio/alarm that sat next to his bed read 7:15 a.m. and Count Basie's 'One O'clock Jump' was being broadcast out of SIUE Edwardsville, Illinois. Bob's heart was pounding so hard he put his hand to his chest to keep it from bursting through his body….and the room smelled of wheat.

Ann had gotten up at her usual 6:30 am time, and as usual, I stayed in bed. She pushed me once and suggested I get up and have breakfast with her and as soon as I said 'OK' I rolled back over and went right back to sleep. I thought of asking Ann about her dreams in that instant of consciousness but the thought morphed into seeing my car with me in it, driving itself around the dance floor at the Casa Loma Ballroom before stopping in front of Ann and asking her to dance. I turned to take a look at the main bar and saw Bob and Neon dressed as sailors and waving to everyone as if they had just come back from WWII. Then Ann woke me.

"Jerry, its 9:30," she said softly. "I think we should be heading out pretty soon, don't you?"

Scratching my nose and elbow, I rolled over and peered at the clock on the table. "Heading out where?" my voice catching some gravel.

Ann stayed sitting on the edge of the bed. "I'm supposed to look at those photographs at the police department and you said you'd go with me. Remember?" she shook my shoulder rolling me across the bed sheet like bread dough. "Don't you remember, honey?"

"Yea, that's right, it's all coming back to me…damn," I rolled onto my face and pulled the pillow back on top of me.

Ann persisted and got me out of bed. I was finishing my cup of coffee when she told me about Bob's call an hour and a half earlier.

"He was frantic and going on and on about a dream he had of a big black storm cloud and being drowned in its dirt while sitting in his car outside his apartment."

"What?" I said in disbelief.

"Yea, and it took about twenty minutes before I could put all that together from all his gasping for breath over the phone. I had to tell him three times to slow down and catch his breath."

"Why did he call us?"

"He said he believes now, and he's totally on board with the Orville Hatcher thing. And…he said he, 'smelled wheat'."

"Wheat?" my ears picked up.

"That's what he said. He said he smelled wheat."

"Wow."

Ann and I went to look at the police mug shots but it was more formality than function. Ann picked out a couple pictures of men who shared certain characteristics with our slippery Orville Hatcher but none of them were a 100% match. It was clear from the beginning that the hat would make any identification practically impossible. That, plus the distinct possibility that Orville Hatcher was a conjured spirit from the past and could only be seen through Ann's eyes. We kept that part to ourselves. Detectives Towning and Sails were there to assist us, but after an hour of going through police photos with no luck, we gave up and said our good-byes.

By 'noon thirty' I was well into a nap that was induced by the magazine article I was reading on the 'The Current Rebels and Radicals of Wall Street Who Are Changing our World'. The magazine itself was open and lay across my chest and I was stretched out on Ann's sofa in the living room. When my cell phone, which I had balanced on the back of the sofa, rang sparking me from my slumber, the magazine slid off me going in one direction and the cell phone fell behind the sofa in the opposite direction after the hand that flew up to grab it, missed. Scurrying off my resting place in an effort to retrieve my mobile phone before the pre-arranged, 5 rings that I had programmed into it elapsed, I succeeded at banging my knee on the coffee table, crashing my elbow on the hardwood floor, and scraping the back of my hand across the textured wall before finally grabbing the devise as it sounded the fifth and final ring. I caught my breath and rubbed the various parts of my bruised and battered body as I hit redial to return Bob's call from his job at the State Correctional Institution.

"Jerry, did you get my messages?" Bob was whispering, but with a distinct urgency in his voice.

"Ann told me you called this morning," I answered. Bob sounded urgent, I didn't.

"Did she tell you what happened to me?"

"Yea, and why are you whispering?"

"I'm at work and I don't want anyone to hear what we're talking about."

I pictured Bob in his cubicle office space with his hand around the mouth piece of the phone. I was glad to hear he was on board with us but the image of him trying to hide a call from his fellow counselors tickled me to no end.

His words were breathy and insistent. "Listen, I've been thinking all morning about what you said and it's beginning to make sense, in a strange sort of way. There are case studies where victims have given completely different descriptions of the same criminal, even after seeing them up close. Fear and adrenaline, Jerry, fear and adrenaline, it can alter your perception. Do you know what I'm saying?"

"Fear and adrenaline, yea," I repeated. "So you think I might be right?"

"Yea, yea, that's what I'm trying to tell you. I've made a list of all the guys in the swing scene that have a strong knowledge of dance history and big band music, and who are heavily into the vintage scene. Guess who comes up number two behind Klaus?"

"Uh, I don't know."

"Dancin' Don," Bob was almost full voice.

"Dancin' Don? I thought you guys were good friends?"

"We are, and Don's a good guy, all right, but his name's way up on the list. Nobody's more into the scene than Dancin' Don, I mean, nobody. You haven't talked to him when he starts throwin' out all those Bible quotes of his. I deal with some career criminals who do the same thing and some of these guys are guilty of terrible things."

"Ok, I'll go along with you on that first part but I don't think having knowledge of the Bible should incriminate anyone, should it?"

"Of course not," Bob quickly corrected himself. "I didn't mean to imply anything like that. I'm just saying it sets him apart from everyone."

"So, what's your plan?" I asked.

"I think we can get this thing straightened out ourselves. I'll get out of work early and we can go over to Don's apartment this afternoon."

I didn't like the idea of showing up at Dancin' Don's doorway unannounced like bill collectors. I liked Don, almost everybody liked Don, and in spite of Bob's list, I truly felt we were barking up the wrong tree. I was going along with Bob for no other reason than to prove that Dancin' Don wasn't guilty of anything.

We parked Bob's car on the street outside the coffee house that was below the little apartment where Don lived. The coffee house looked like the brave little engine that could, with an old man smoking a cigarette at a table and a young girl wearing an apron, also smoking a cigarette, leaning against the end of the counter. The walls were painted dark red and black in what appeared to be an effort to hide the cracks in the plaster. The glass display case that held assorted sandwiches, bottled drinks, and pastries wasn't long enough to cover the work area behind it so there was a small table with a fake plant on it to cover the open space. We walked past the front of the business to a door that was so unnoticeable and narrow I would have missed it entirely had Bob not stopped me. The street was deserted with the exception of a mongrel dog sniffing a trash can and two semi-curious locals sharing a bottle of something that was wrapped in a brown paper bag. The door was locked so we went around back and came up from the exposed wooden stairs that led up to a shared balcony. Bob stuck his head in the window of Don's kitchen, peering unashamedly into the confines of Don's home.

"Hey," I cupped his shoulder with an open hand, "he's a friend, remember."

"Yea, right," Bob pulled his head back.

I knocked on the door and the glass rattled as the wooden door shook against the frame that held it. It made enough noise to get the attention of the entire neighborhood. Bob and I turned around to see who might respond.

A minute later the door in opened maybe three or four inches and I could see a nose and a mouth in the small opening. "Hey, Bob….Jerry. Did they find Michelle?"

"Don, is that you?" I wasn't really sure.

"It's me," the door opened a little wider and we could see Don scrunch his face because of the invading daylight. "Is there any news?"

"No, I'm sorry, Don, there isn't," I told him.

"How ya doin', Don," Bob asked? "Can we come in?"

Then the door opened up enough to expose all of Dancin' Don. He was wearing a plaid pair of white, red, and black, baggy pants and a white, short sleeve undershirt. There was a chain on his belt that went round to the back pocket and clipped to his wallet. I felt like I was in an old James Dean movie.

"The place is kind of a mess. I didn't know anybody was comin' over."

"That's Ok, Don," Bob smiled. "We don't care about that. We just want to talk."

Finally Don stepped back and opened the door all the way to allow us entrance. Once we got through the door and past the daylight we were engulfed by the darkness from within. There was a short hall with a small kitchen on our left and closet doors on our right. We followed Don to the living room. There was a couch that was backed up to the edge of an iffy railing. The railing was tied by a string to the back of the couch. On the other side of the railing that the couch was backed up to was a staircase that went down to the street. I could see the legs of the couch had been nailed to the floor to keep the couch from sliding through the railing and into the stairwell.

"You can sit over there if you want to," Dancin' Don sat on the couch and pointed to a chair next to the television. "I know it doesn't look it but the couch is plenty safe." He pushed against the back of the couch to prove it wouldn't move and topple over the edge.

"That's Ok," I stopped him with wide open palms. "Really, I'm fine just standing."

I took a position over by the window which was covered by blinds and thick curtains.

"Like I said, I didn't know you guys were coming over." He looked a little embarrassed. "It's not the nicest place to live, is it?"

"Don't worry about it, Don. It's no big deal," I tried to let him feel at ease.

Bob took a seat next to the television shoving some of the VHS tapes that were strewn on the floor with his foot.

"Yea, just move those things out of your way," Don said, and got up off the couch to collect a few of the misplaced tapes. He gathered five or six of them in his arms but couldn't find an empty shelf so he stacked them up against the wall on the floor on the other side of the television from where Bob was sitting.

The walls were painted a dark maroon, like the coffee house beneath them and the dull finish of the hard wood floor was mostly, but not completely covered, by an old dark green rug that was frayed on the edges.

Don explained that the building was almost 100 years old and that there had originally been 5 apartments with one communal bathroom at the end of a hall. He recited the history of the old building with the same kind of aesthetic interest he used when he talked about vintage swing. He said that Margaret and her husband, Carl, who was a bricklayer by trade, had purchased and refurbished the entire structure. They put kitchens and full baths in each of the apartments and reduced the number down to three.

I don't know what I had expected. I thought maybe old mahogany furniture with maybe an imitation Tiffany lamp somewhere. I had thought that Dancin' Don and all his vintage clothes would be more…organized.

Then there was the smell. The old decaying smell that was outside permeated the whole building and I had begun to smell it as soon as we got out of the car. This couldn't be the smell of nostalgia, I reasoned. That would be a fragrance of cinnamon and spice, of warm bread and the essence of home, hearth, and safety. It would reflect those times when things were easier and less complicated; when the world lived with open doors and security was defined by your faith in your fellow man. If I had never been inside of Dancin Don's apartment I would have imagined it to be that way, warm and safe. Maybe we remember the past in a nostalgic rapture because we can, since it's too far away to see it the way it really was.

"So, what's up? What did you want to talk to me about?" Don got us started.

"Well, it's about these sightings Ann has been having. You know, the guy in the hat we were chasing the other night during the snowball dance," I began to explain. It wasn't until just then that I realized we didn't have any more of a plan than to just confront Don. We hadn't rehearsed anything.

"I remember. Did you get any help from that detective?" Don asked.

"No, he looked his name up on a national data base but only found a few around the whole country." I was stalling for time.

"So maybe that wasn't his name?" Don tried to help.

"We thought of that, and it's a possibility," Bob told him. "But we've been thinking a little bit out of the box."

"Oh," Don was looking from Bob to me.

I looked up at Don and did my best to get him up to speed. "We think that this Orville Hatcher is a visual interpretation, in Ann's mind that is, of the actual person who is committing these crimes."

"So you think she imagined this guy?" Don replied.

"No, we think this guy is real. Actually, no," I corrected myself. "We think this guy was real; that he was born back in the vintage times, during the big band days. We also think he was a murderer, when he was alive."

"We think," Bob continued the explanation, "that whoever is abducting these girls is very much like the way this guy, Orville Hatcher, was when he was alive. So much so that that's the way Ann sees him, when she does see him, I mean."

Don just looked at us without reaction and I could clearly see that Bob needed some help. "So since she only sees this guy as the manifestation of Orville Hatcher, then we don't know the real identity of the one who's been doing these terrible things."

"I am the vine; you are the branches," Don responded.

"What?" I thought we lost him.

"John 15," he said, as if his answer explained anything. "*You did not choose me but I chose you, and appointed you that you would go and bear fruit, and that your fruit would remain, so that whatever you ask of the Father in My name He may give to you.*"

"Don," Bob bent over more in Don's direction. "I know you're reciting the Bible but what does that have to do with what we're talking about?"

"If a man…"

"**Don**," Bob interrupted with a louder voice than he needed. "Look, I mean no disrespect, but can you please speak in language that we can all understand."

"We are all one; one in the same. Where God sits there are no yesterdays or tomorrows, there is only the now, where God always was, always is, and always shall be. If a man or woman lives today, then they are living in the past, and the future, for we are all living with God and God in us. It would not only be possible for us to channel someone from the past but we are, in fact, doing it right now, right here. It is nothing to God, for he knows all things, and see's all things from the beginning of time to the end of time."

We weren't sure exactly what Dancin' Don was saying but it sounded like he not only believed us but understood what we were saying, maybe even better than we did.

"That's cool, Don," Bob said carefully. "But what we came here to tell you," Bob checked with me and I nodded, "is that we think we have a way to identifying the guilty son-of-a…the guy."

"Really, how?"

"We think he's someone who is heavy into the vintage scene, someone who has a strong knowledge of dance and big band music history. And someone who knew both Vanessa and Michelle," Bob laid it out for him.

"That sounds like you and me," Don said candidly.

"Yea," Bob continued to return Don's questioning stare without further comment.

Don was beginning to understand why we had barged in on him like we did.

"You think **I** am the one who did that to Vanessa….and whatever terrible things are happening to Michelle?"

"It wouldn't be you, really," I tried to sugar coat it. "You would have been possessed by this spirit. You wouldn't have been able to control yourself."

"Do I look like I'm possessed?"

This was the first time either of us had seen Dancin' Don get upset enough to raise his voice.

Bob attempted to justify our crude behavior. "Don, like you said, about the past and the present, and all that. You know, God being in us and we are in him….right? Don? I thought you understood."

"I didn't think you were talking about me. What about you, Bob. You're all those things you mentioned, as much as me, anyway. How do we know it isn't you?"

"I was on the hot seat just like you are," Bob declared proudly. "And I proved that I'm not guilty."

"How?" Don was cooling down but only a little. "How did you prove you aren't guilty, and how am I supposed to prove that I'm not 'possessed'?" Don was sitting on the edge of the sofa. Bob and I were both equally perplexed as to how we could answer Don.

"I guess it was easier for me to account for my actions than it will be for you, Don, since Sheila was with me most of the time."

"Your girlfriend stood up for you, was that it? That's convenient," Don shot back. It looked like Don had run out of patience. "This has gone on long enough," he stood up. "I'm not going to sit around here with you two while you decide whether I'm guilty of something. It's time for you to leave."

"Wait a minute, Don," Bob held his hand up, "just work with us a minute. Look, you're not the only one we thought of. We came to you first because you're a friend."

I knew Bob was lying but I didn't say anything. I wanted to see how far his deception would go.

"If you throw us out, then there's no use asking anyone else," Bob argued.

Don started listening again. "Who else?" he demanded.

"Marty….and Klaus," Bob reported.

"You're going to confront Klaus with this?" Don sounded interested.

"You can come with us if you want," Bob tempted.

Don's mood lightened as he considered the prospect. Then his face changed when he remembered it was his turn to answer unwarranted accusations.

"So what do you want from me, an alibi? What can I tell you that you don't know already?"

"Well, I don't know," Bob looked at me but I had nothing to add. It looked like Bob might be letting go of any real suspicion he had against Don. "Something that proves your innocence; some show of faith that you took this thing seriously."

"Like what?" Don asked suspiciously.

"How about your bedroom," Bob indicated the only room in the apartment we had not seen.

"Let us see what's in your bedroom and inside the closet doors."

Don looked at me, and although I didn't like forcing our way into more of Don's home, it sounded like a way to be done with this awkward visit.

"You want to see my bedroom and look through my closets?" Don asked both of us. Bob nodded eagerly and I shrugged.

"So you can tell other people how I went along with this?"

"That's right," Bob answered.

"Well, you can't," Dancin' Don answered defiantly.

Bob was dumbfounded, "Why not?

"Because this is my home," he was resolved. "It may not look like much to you but it's still my home and you're not going to tell me what to do in it."

"But if it clears you from being a killer, isn't it worth a little loss of privacy?" Bob argued.

"**I am clear**," Don shouted. "And I don't have to show you my bedroom to prove anything."

I was feeling more and more uncomfortable with the way we had presented ourselves and more sympathetic to Don. We were guests in his home and were acting like Gestapo agents.

Don had clearly reached the end of 'Mr. Nice Guy'. "Did you let people into your home to see if you had any missing bodies lying around?" Don's face was only a few feet away from Bob's.

"I didn't have to. Sheila was with me the whole time during the party. She can tell you where I was."

"You didn't, did you? I didn't think so. You're so quick to point your finger at everybody else, you don't care who you slander. You say you were with Sheila the whole night but does that mean every dance? Because I know I saw you dancing with a couple other girls. And how long does it take to go outside and overpower a teenager and a girl? Three minutes….four? What about that Count Basie song they played, 'Swingin' at Newport'? That song is eight minutes long. Who did you dance with then?"

I could see that Don was making a point, and a good one.

Bob got defensive and lashed back at Don. "Oh no, I see what you're doing. You're trying to turn the attention from yourself to me. Why won't you just open your bedroom door, let us see inside, and we'll be out a' here? What have you got to hide?" Bob was really getting into Don's face. I was watching what had been two good friend only a day ago accusing each other of despicable acts and I had had enough.

"Forget it, Bob. Don's right, this is his home and he doesn't have to show us anything."

Bob did not want to give up so easily, "All he has to do is show us his bedroom."

"He doesn't have to show us anything," I repeated, a little stronger. "The only reason he opened the door in the first place is because he thought he was letting in friends. This whole thing was a bad idea in the first place. We're turning against each other like hungry wolves. You guys used to be friends and look at you. Don, I'm sorry about all this. Com' on, Bob, let's get out of here."

"But if we," Bob started to protest.

"We're going, both of us." I wanted to make it clear that if push came to shove, I would be on Dancin' Don's side.

The ride back was tense. Bob argued that Michelle might have been locked up only a few feet away and I told him that was crazy. We went back and forth like that until we got to Ann's.

Ann and Sheila were sitting at the dining room table playing gin rummy when we walked in. They continued to play cards with very little reaction while we told them what happened at Dancin' Don's.

"You mean he didn't let you see his dead body collection? God, the nerve of him," Ann could be very sarcastic when she wanted.

"Yea, and I'm sure you told him in a very nice way that his home was about to be searched," Sheila had some fun with it as well. "I'll bet they knocked first," she turned to Ann.

"I'll bet they did," Ann answered and looked up at me. "Big mistake, Jerry, they always know you're coming when you knock first."

"Did you knock first, Bob?" It was Sheila's turn at sarcasm.

"Very funny, ha, ha, ha…" Of course Bob didn't like it when the entertainment was at his expense. "If Michelle was in there and she was alive, we may have just blown our only chance to save her. Have any of you thought of that?"

Bob and I had argued this all the way back from Don's and I was ready to go again. "If Michelle was in there, do you think Don would have opened the door in the first place? Besides, this is Dancin' Don we're talking about; Bible quoting Don, giver of free dance lessons and ambassador to swing at the Casa Loma Ballroom. Do we really think that he had anything to do with these crimes?"

"Well we'll never know, will we?" Bob became indignant. He didn't like to admit he could be wrong. "Unless his taste for blood gets so bad that if forces him to kill again and someone catches him in the act."

"Oh, come on, Bob," I pleaded. His rhetoric was more than I could take, "'*taste for blood*', isn't that being a little dramatic."

"I don't think those words and Dancin' Don should be in the same sentence," Sheila agreed with me. Ann was the only one who did not speak out against Bob's hyperbole.

"How about you, Ann," Bob noticed her silence. "You think I could be right, don't you?"

"No," she said simply. "But what you said about 'catching him in the act' gave me an idea."

"What?" I wondered what Ann might be suggesting.

"Now before you get all negative on me, think about this. The chances of getting anyone to admit they are guilty of murder and kidnapping is slim to none. Your visit to Dancin Don's should tell you that, but if we catch this guy in the act, like Bob said, we've got him."

"How do we do that?" Bob asked.

"With bait," Ann answered. She put down the cards she was holding in more ways than one.

"No, no, no, no," I objected. "I know what you're thinking and it's out of the question. I'm not willing to let you use yourself as bait. It's too dangerous and there's no reason for it. We'll let the police set traps for suspected killers; it's their job, not ours."

Ann got up from the table and went over to me. She put one hand on my shoulder. "Listen, if all this talk about possession and spirits from the past is just superstitious nonsense; we'll have nothing to worry about. We'll be chasing after ghosts, the kind that don't exist, and we'll all have a good laugh when we're done. But if these strange things, which have been happening to all of us, have any meaning, then we'd be crazy, maybe even irresponsible, not to pay attention to them." Ann turned around to address Sheila and Bob as well. "If Jerry's interpretation about the dreams and what I've been seeing is correct and Orville Hatcher is coming after us, then maybe we can be ready for him when he makes his move. I can call Rita and find out where she gets her vintage clothes. Hopefully it will be the same place Vanessa and Michelle got theirs and I can be ready by Wednesday night."

"You mean, **we'll** be ready," Sheila said. "There are two blondes in this room, remember. And you know I'm not about to let you do this on your own."

Ann went over and hugged her friend, "Oh, it'll be fun. We'll wear more make-up than rodeo clowns."

"How do you know he'll show Wednesday night?" Bob and I were being left out of the plans and I didn't like that.

"Because these dreams and sightings seem to be escalating," Ann answered. "Besides, it's the 13th, and there's a full moon." Ann pointed out details which only worried me more.

"All the more reason we should lay low," I cautioned. "This is a job for the police."

"Maybe not," Bob challenged my assertion, to my surprise. "Chances are we won't see the police until after another girl is abducted just like Vanessa and Michelle. What we're talking about is a sting operation and there is no way any of us is going to convince any police official to set a trap for a man we think has been dead for 60 years. Ann's way is pro-active and I like it. The girls go in and we watch them from the side lines."

"Yea, but I'll be behind the bar," I protested.

"But you'll be off early," Ann reminded me. "And until you do, we'll stay close together and dance near the bar where you can see us."

I was the sole dissenter; even Sheila was against me. "It's a plan, Jerry. You and Bob tried yours, now it's our turn."

"I still don't like it, but I can see I'm outnumbered," I acquiesced.

"We've already got a list of possible suspects," Bob pulled out his infamous list.

"Ok, fine," I gave in. "I don't want to argue about that list of yours any more. Who else is on it?"

Bob handed the list over to me and Sheila leaned over my shoulder to read it along with me.

- Klaus Tiegmier
- Dancin' Don Bartowski
- Neon Taylor
- Marty Richardson

"Klaus Tiegmier," I read from the top of the list. "Why am I not surprised? Hey, what is it with you and Klaus? I mean you guys have so much in common, same music, same dancing, you know the same people; you even went out with the same girl. Is there something you haven't told us? I mean this can't all be about the questionable, misuse of funds."

I saw recognition in Bob's eye. There was something more to Bob's mistrust of Klaus and he was about to tell me.

"I've known Klaus longer than any of you. I remember when he first came onto the scene and he only knew a few basic steps. He was still a teenager in college but he picked it up fast, too fast if you ask me. Even the 'swing out' was easy for him. He was dancing almost every night after he met Rita and he still breezed through college. It was like he didn't have to work at anything; like he'd done it all before."

"Or like he'd been there before, isn't that what you're saying?" I suggested.

"That's exactly what I'm saying." Bob gave a look. "I've known a few other guys like him in my life and I don't trust them, any of them, and I trust Klaus even less after all of this."

"You sound a little frazzled, Bob," Ann asked out of concern, "everything, Ok?"

"Bob had a rough morning today, didn't you?" Sheila noted.

"You can say that again," Bob assured us. "I thought I was going to die. If the alarm hadn't gone off, I almost belief I would have."

Sheila took his hand, "Oh, baby, I'm sorry."

"It opened my eyes to other possibilities," Bob went on. "I've been thinking about the things Jerry said last night. I thought they were silly and superstitious at the time, but now I'm not so sure."

I did not appreciate how much Bob's dream had affected him until now. "There was something Dancin' Don said earlier," I told them. "I thought, at the time, it pretty much summed everything up. '*We are all one in the same. For God knows all things and sees all things from the beginning of time to the end of time*', remember?"

"I remember," Bob acknowledged. "And if that works for you, then fine. I just have a problem with all the Biblical references. It's just a little too touchy-feely for me."

"So how would you say it?" I asked.

Bob gave the question a moment's consideration before answering. "I think our lives are like that Kaleidoscope over there." He pointed to the mantel. "The casing is the world we live in, and the broken pieces of glass represent our lives. What we think of as dying is just someone shaking the pieces of the glass inside and what you get is a different, colorful, picture. It looks different, but it's always the same little pieces of glass."

"That's beautiful, honey." Sheila beamed.

"And maybe the light you hold the kaleidoscope up to, is God?" Ann attempted to invoke a deity in his analogy.

"Maybe," he answered.

Gloria Taylor kept getting up from watching the news and looking out the front window, half expecting her son Neon to walk through the front door. It was getting dark earlier and she hoped to see him when night fell. He called her earlier from a pay phone telling her he was alright, that he would see her soon and not to worry. But the temperatures were dropping and she didn't know where he was staying. She worried about him and didn't like the idea that he was hiding from the police.

She opened up the front door and called to her other son, "Jamal, you come inside now. It will be dark soon, com' on."

The young boy threw the football he was playing with near the porch and followed its path to the house, hiking his trousers up onto his waist. "Is Neon coming home tonight, Mom?" he called back to his mother, unconcerned what he might be announcing to the neighborhood.

His mother looked up and down both streets to see where an audience might be. "Get up in here, right now," she conveyed with no uncertainty that young Jamal was in trouble. "Do you have to let the whole world know about our problems?" She shook her head and lightly slapped the back of Jamal's head as he passed through the front door. "Sometimes I don't think you have a brain…."

"Neon," Jamal's voice was hushed once again after seeing his older brother standing in the front room. Neon had snuck in through the back door.

"Oh baby," Gloria rushed to her son and bear-hugged him. "Are you Ok? Did you eat? Go inside the kitchen and I'll fix you some dinner."

When Neon finished his dinner they were all sitting around the kitchen table; Neon, Jamal, Gloria, and their grandmother.

"Where you gonna stay tonight?" Neon's grandmother was asking. "You know it's supposed to git down ta 48 degrees. That old sleeping bag a' yours ain't gonna be warm enough for that kind of weather."

"Your grandmother's right, son," Gloria intoned. "And I wouldn't want to be anywhere within earshot if Janeakwa catches you sleepin' in that old car she's got parked in front of her folk's house."

Neon was listening to their warnings, especially the last. "I know. I know everything you are sayin' and I agree with you."

"So you're going to turn yourself into the police?" Gloria surmised.

"No, I can't do that, not just yet." Neon pushed away the empty plate in front of him. "I got another plan."

"What kind a plan are you talking about if you're not going to the police?" his mother asked.

"Tell us your plan, Neon. Tell us your plan," Little Jamal chanted.

"Hush now, young one," their grandmother grabbed him by the wrist. "And don't you be repeating anything you hear tonight. You understand me, boy?"

"I understand."

"Moma, remember that night when you told me about my father?" Neon's question had a sobering effect on the two women.

"Jamal, you come with me," their grandmother announced. "We're going to the living room and watch some television."

"But I want to hear. Why can't I hear about my father?"

"You'll hear when your mother is ready for you to hear and not before."

"Go with your grandmother," Gloria told him.

Gloria waited until Jamal and her mother were sitting in front of the television before continuing. "It's my guess you're thinkin' about goin' to your father for help; to stay with him. Is that right, son?"

"That's right," Neon nodded. "It would only be for a little while and since you already told the police that I don't know who my father is, then they won't be lookin' for me there. Did they ask you his name and address?"

"They did, and I told them."

Neon sat back and thought about how this news might affect his plans. "Well, that might work out just as well. They've probably already been there and asked him about me, and since I wasn't there, they won't be hangin' around lookin for me."

Gloria sat looking at her son with a very solemn face and Neon could tell there was bad news coming.

"What is it, Moma? What aren't you tellin' me?"

Gloria chose her words carefully. "Son, when I told you about your father and that he had deserted us, and wouldn't help us, that was true, then." Gloria could see the hope in her son's eyes. "You remember when you got back from your trial and they put you on probation, you remember how hard it was for you to get a job? How nobody would hire you because you had been a gang member?"

"I remember, Moms, if it wasn't for Mr. Waterman, I don't know what I woulda' done."

"George Waterman changed everything when he did that, son, and I made him a promise when he hired you, a promise I'm about to break."

"What are you tellin me, Momma? Are you sayin' George Waterman is my….father?"

"It was his way of making up for abandoning us years ago. He was going to tell you himself when you turned eighteen. He's helped us, Neon, more than you know. He's given me money to pay bills. He's a church goin' man now."

Neon was devastated. George Waterman, the man he'd been working for the past two years and had come to know as a friend, was his natural father. Neon felt relief, then shame, and then anger. George was a good man, anyone who knew him could tell you that, but if he was such a good man then why had he deserted him and his mother and brother. What did they do? What was wrong with them? What was so much better about this other family he had than the one he had right here.

"If this man is my father, and he really is a good, 'church goin' man', like you say, then I need his help now more than ever."

Gloria felt there was more to Neon's motivation, "I can't help but think you want some kind of revenge for him not admitting all this to you before." She looked deep into Neon's eyes and made a snap decision, "I'm going to call him first and tell him you're comin' to see him."

"No, don't do that. I don't want you to call him."

"That's it, isn't it? You want to shove yourself in his face and demand that he take you in?"

"That's not it at all. I don't want revenge. I just want help, if only for a few days."

"So you're gonna knock on his door at night and ask him if you can stay with him, without any warning? What do you expect him to say? How would he explain that to his wife and children?"

"How about my explanation?" Neon argued. "Don't I deserve an explanation, too?"

"Son, you can't go up there out of the blue and demand to be part of his family. You'd just be setting yourself up for rejection."

"I'll call him," Neon agreed. "I'll call him on the way and tell him I want to talk to him. I'll tell him I need help. He wouldn't turn me down. George wouldn't turn me away."

"Neon, I'm so sorry. I'm afraid I was wrong for sayin' anything."

"You don't have to tell me anything else, Momma. I already know where he lives. In fact, now I know all about George Waterman."

"Oh, baby, are you sure this is the right thing to do? George doesn't know you're comin' and he's got that family of his. This may not be the best time, with the trouble you're in…I just don't want you to get your feelings hurt, son."

"It'll be alright. If George won't help me, I'll come back home here, and take my chances with the police. Would that make you feel better?"

Gloria reached across the table and put her hand on her son's face. "Just remember, no matter what happens between you and George, you'll always have a family that loves ya' here."

"I know, Momma."

CHAPTER TWENTY FOUR

Ann and Sheila went to Pixie 9 Vintage dress shop Tuesday night to find dresses to wear for the dance on Wednesday at the Casa Loma Ballroom. I had just seen the two of them off when I got a call from Bob. He was working late but took a minute to find out if anything had changed.

Bob and I weren't friends as much as our girlfriends were friends. I imagine if I'd grown up living on the same street as Bob, or if we had gone to the same schools, I would have had time to get used to his strange mood swings and self absorbed attitude. Then again, maybe we wouldn't have been friends at all if I had time to get to know him.

I wondered if knowing your neighbor or school mate is a jerk made any difference to a child. Children are so accepting but are adults any different? Don't most relationships develop out of necessity by our associations as a result of those we spend time with? Generally your friends are the people you see every day, the people you work with and people you live next to, demanding that a living or working relationship be developed. Shouldn't we be more discerning with the people we call friends? After all, doesn't every thief, liar, and murderer all have to be somebody's neighbor? What if we learned to judge our friendships from an early age on the merits of each one's personality? Would that put a higher premium on who we call 'friend' or would that just mean a less friendly world? Maybe learning to get alone with each other is an important part of this big social experiment we call life. When people we know become difficult to be around, maybe that's how we define what the word 'friend' really means.

"Anything new today," Bob asked? It was an open ended question given the recent developments. His voice got increasingly agitated, "Any sightings, any contacts, any incredibly **terrifying, daydreams that don't allow you to sleep at night?"**

"Whoa there, Bob," I cautioned. "You need to keep your head on straight, buddy. You're a therapist, remember. I believe there are people who are counting on you to maintain a certain level of sanity over there at the State Correctional Institution? I'm just guessing here but isn't that a pre-requisite for that job of yours?"

"Yea, well, my sanity has severely come into question as of late, as well as my scientific objectivity." Bob's lack of sleep was having its effect. "The things we've been talking about are the kind of things that get you an extended stay here at the facility, and usually because of my recommendations."

"I guess when all this is over and done with, you're going to have to reopen some of those files of yours, huh?"

Bob didn't like that idea at all. "Don't even suggest that. I'd be backed up till doomsday and half the people in here would have a case for immediate release."

Bob quickly changed the subject. "Any news on Michelle?" he asked.

"No, nothing about her," I told him. "But there is some other news, although I'm wondering if you're ready for it." I started to second guess myself.

"What is it? Whatever it is, you got to tell me. Now that I know there is something, not telling me would be that much worse."

"Right, Ok, Ann works at the Chamber of Commerce in Clayton. I don't know if you knew that."

"I knew that," he said, impatiently.

"So she has access to some public records and access to people who have access to other public records," I explained.

"She's got access, I got that."

"She sent the word out for information on the name 'Hatcher' in St. Louis and someone found an obituary written in 1951 for a Warren Hatcher. The Obit read, 'God bless this good man who joins his wife, Sara, daughter, Claire, and long lost son, Orville. May they rest in peace,' It was signed…'Jack Buckmueller, Friend'."

"You mean your 'Jack Buckmueller'?"

"Gotta be," I said.

"So they probably knew each other, Orville Hatcher and Jack Buckmueller?"

"They may have known each other," I emphasized. "Jack Buckmueller was a bartender at Casa Loma Ballroom around the time they had the big fire that destroyed the place. This Warren Hatcher might have been related to Orville Hatcher and Jack Buckmueller could have known Orville as one of the swing dancers there."

"This get's stranger by the minute," Bob did not like having more evidence of the paranormal.

"And the police had no record of an Orville Hatcher. What about any unsolved crimes around that time?

"None," I was ready for him. "Ann thought of that too and checked. There were no unsolved murders during that time in St. Louis, but that doesn't mean one didn't happen and went unreported."

"That's kind of a leap, isn't it?"

"Maybe, but a lot of people were indigent in those days. There was a depression, remember. Being lost and missing was a way of life for a lot of folks. And then there's that southern accent of his that Ann told us about. He may have committed his crimes in other states as far as we know."

I had gone over all this, first with Ann, then with Sheila, and now it was Bob's turn to ask twenty questions.

"You said Pat Brannon had a picture of this bartender, didn't you?"

"I'm going to ask him if he has any other pictures, but I don't want to tell him too much. The only person who has seen Orville Hatcher is Ann, so I wouldn't know what to look for anyway, and the odds of him having a clear picture of this guy are slim at best. Besides, even if we find did find a picture of him in 1939 that would only confirm what we already know."

"So, how does that information help us?" Bob questioned.

"It tells us we are on the right track. I just hope we're not making a mistake, using the girls this way. If anything happens to either of them, I'll have only myself to blame."

"Don't worry about that," Bob sounded a bit over confident. "I'll be there until you get off work, then we can both watch the girls. Besides, there will be plenty of other people around if we need any help."

"Yea, well, this guy seems pretty resourceful. I don't want to underestimate him," I cautioned.

"Listen, I see guys like this, all day, every day, and I'm here to tell you there are no genius's among them."

"As long as he's flesh and blood and someone I can put my hands on," I said, giving more thought to Ann's safety than with dealing with a 6' 3" serial killer.

"Just be careful," Bob cautioned, "we don't want to alarm anyone before the trap's been sprung. I'm telling you, man, this guy is just some frustrated hillbilly taking his anger out on defenseless women. I guarantee you that once we confront this idiot he'll fold like old money."

We were dancing all around the subject without saying it aloud. The truth was we were setting a trap for a man who had been dead for 60 years. "But our guy isn't exactly like all those guys you see every day, is he?"

Bob had been feeling the same apprehensions that I had. "You know, I woke up this morning asking myself the same question. What are we doing? This is crazy, isn't it? I mean, we're frickin' ghost hunters, aren't we?"

"We are," I acknowledged.

"If you had asked me yesterday morning, as I was spitting out the dirt in my mouth – the dirt that wasn't in my mouth - all over the inside of my car, I would have agreed to almost anything. But in the clear light of day, and given time to put the whole crazy thing behind me, I have to ask myself, wasn't it really just a dream?"

"I know what you mean. It's always easier not to believe in a thing, isn't it? And given time, like you say, we could probably forget these wild dreams and sightings. I think human beings have an incredible capacity to forget their past and their history. I read somewhere there are white racists who are trying to deny that the Holocaust ever happened. So why should any other history be any different? As difficult as it may seem now, in time, we'll probably forget about Vanessa, and then Michelle."

"I won't forget Vanessa," Bob denied.

"You say that now, but wait another five years and see if you still have those same strong feelings. It only took a day to start doubting that dream you had. You remember that dream, don't you?

Remember calling Ann yesterday morning screaming about how a storm was sent to suffocate you in your car?"

"I remember, I remember." It was not Bob's finest hour and it was obvious he didn't like to be reminded of it. "But what if it was just a dream? Wouldn't that make more sense?"

"If all these things that seem to have relevance and are happening more and more often; if all of these things are just dreams and tricks of the imagination, then nothing will happen tomorrow. We'll all go to Casa Loma and dance and have a good time. And, God willing, that's how it will play out."

Bob waited to ask the only question he could ask, "And if it doesn't play out that way?"

"Then we'd better be keeping a close eye on the girls," I answered.

"Don't you worry; we'll be there for them," Bob said confidently.

"I hope you're right."

"Sure I'm right. The girls will be safe with us."

"Yea......." I let my thoughts wander.

"Yea, what, what does that 'yea...' mean?"

"I was just thinking about Michelle."

In a dark room somewhere in St. Louis was an over sized foot locker. The cherry red finish had long ago lost its mirror like shine, and the brass corner pieces, lock, and wrap around band, wore dents and scratches where a glass reflection had once been. The hinges on the top had been damaged from misuse over the years which kept the lid from closing all the way and allowed a small line of light of about six inches long and two inches wide to invade the darkened space. The narrow band of light on the inside of the trunk touched a face, illuminating the terrified eyes of Michelle Torence.

CHAPTER TWENTY FIVE

Wednesday's temperature turned decidedly cooler and the sky was a mix of continuously rolling gray clouds with an endless display of changing dark shapes that moved overhead like faces at a carnival. The temperatures at night had been dropping down into the lower 40's but during the day it warmed up to comfortable temps in the 50's and 60's. It had been sweater weather at most, but not today. Today it was blustery and chilly, with possible thundershowers predicted for the evening.

I talked to Ann on the phone that afternoon, expressing concern and a kind of anxious hope that all of this was only foolish nonsense. I described our efforts as ghost hunter antics and attempted to make light of the whole endeavor in hopes of setting both our minds at ease. I joked that our discussions on the afterlife were only melodrama and dismissed any chance we might have of entrapping anyone. I told her we were all going to have a good laugh when the night was over, but Ann only listened. Her experiences had been as real as the girls who were now dead and missing. She was resolute and serious and more than ready for the night to come.

I got off the phone scratching my head, wondering if our culprit really could be a spirit from the 1930's. Everything that had been happening pointed to it; all the evidence had lead us all to believe that, not only was it a possibility, but a probability.

There were too many hard realities to deny something terrible was at work. Vanessa was dead. Michelle had been missing now for almost four days. Some tangible, real person had to be responsible for these reprehensible acts and someone had to be accountable for them. At most, I could only allow myself to accept the possibility that our world might be influenced by memories from the past. But to see, hear, and touch a manifestation of someone who had been dead for 60 years, as it would appear to be happening to Ann, was more than I could wrap my mind around. Why was Ann able to see what eluded everyone else? We all perceive the world and the people in it through eyes that have been colored by life's hard realities and prejudiced by its injustices. At best, we are guessing when we look into the face of another human being. Maybe this was one of the few times that someone like Ann was seeing with eyes wide open and Orville Hatcher was more of a reality than any of us knew.

I left for work before Ann got home. Sheila and Bob would meet her there and, after the girls finished putting on the rest of their make-up, the three of them would leave together for the Casa Loma Ballroom.

"You just missed the film crews," Terry Strahan informed me after unlocking the front door and letting me in.

"I figured it was only a matter of time," I gave the news media a second's worth of consideration. "Does that mean Michelle is still missing?"

"Still missing, which means there's still hope." Terry held the door key which was held by a big, ten inch diameter key ring.

"I guess there's always hope," I said. "I'll bet Pat's not too happy about getting that kind of publicity?"

"Well, he's concerned," Terry said. We walked up the two flights of stairs to the ballroom while we talked. "He's worried about Michelle and everyone else's safety more than he is the business."

"Yea," was all that I needed to say. We both understood Pat would have his priorities in order.

The bar was easy to set up, just a few juices to get out from the coolers and unlock some cabinets and doors. The early bartender was there mainly for the few drink orders that might come in before the real rush that would follow in the later hours. Usually there was up to a half an hour of idle time before anyone came up the stairs and I always took the opportunity to lean against the back bar, take the time to relax, and imagine what the old ballroom was like when Harry James, Chick Webb, Count Basie, and the other big bands played here. I let the Benny Goodman CD I had brought from the car play through the house sound system and let the music take me back as I listened.

There were three lights from the stage shining on the wood floor and I could see the light flickering off the hardwood just on the other side of the tables.

I looked out on the empty floor visualizing the changing decades of dancers as my mind wandered back, back before the big fire at Casa Loma, before the attack on Pearl Harbor, before the world had changed forever. The CD switched from 'Air Mailed' to 'King Porter Stomp' and I had no problem letting my imagination settle on a time in the thirties, when swing dancing was big, really big, bigger than it ever would be again. I bounced my head ever so gently to the beat and fixed my eyes on a spot the light illuminated on the dance floor. I let my gaze stay on that one piece of wood and continued to bob my head to the music.

I found my gentle bounce produced a kind of stickman dancer, out of the marbled grain of the hardwood. If I moved my head in just the right way, the image danced with the help of the light and shadow. The music was really swinging and my head was bobbing up and down to its quick rhythm. By the time Benny Goodman and his clarinet came in on the middle of the tune, I had the shadow and light figure jumping on the floor like a yellow marionette. After a full minute of keeping up with the music my head began to tire so I let the motion subside, but somehow, the shadow/figure continued to bounce without my help.

I put one hand to my face to make sure my head was not moving but still the figure danced. I was no longer in control of its movements. It was the music and its subtle changes that controlled the dancing light. I wasn't sure what I was seeing but it looked like the thing had peeled itself off the wood grain design and had taken on a life of its own. It was growing in size and shape and was no longer limited to one spot, moving its own arms and legs but always in that marionette fashion, as a puppet on a string.

I thought I could make out a face. It was thin, gaunt, and laughing, laughing at me, and taunting me. In the music playing overhead Gene Krupa was pounding out a simple timing with the cymbals and the figure kept up the tempo, gesticulating with his knees and elbows. There could be no mistaking the outline of the image as it moved in my direction, and there could be no question that this dancing phantom with a fedora hat was the infamous Orville Hatcher.

I wanted to turn my head or close my eyes and be rid of the strange manifestation but the closer it got, the clearer I could see the details of his face, the face only Ann had seen until now. He had gotten to the edge of the dance floor, moving his limbs in that mocking fashion while the music was featuring a trombone solo. I could see some of the angles of his mouth and jaw as I heard the music repeat its final refrain, signaling the end of the tune and hopefully the end of the dancing menace. Members of the horn section split into two groups playing out a call and response to each other before they, and the rest of the band, were about to join in a tumultuous finish.

The vision of Orville Hatcher had now moved off the floor, and was hovering above a lighted candle that was set out on a table in front of me, his legs unmoving and his arms resting by his side. I could see him clearly now. He had stopped laughing, and with expressionless features, hung still in the air. It was then that the music stopped and the flame of the candle ignited the figure causing it to go up in a quick flash as someone's voice called to me.

"Hey, Jerry, you're girlfriend's here," it was Terry Strahan letting me know Ann had arrived.

I didn't know how long Terry had been standing at his spot at the top of the stairs. I hadn't been aware of anything but the dancing figure that played upon the light, but I didn't ask any questions. Ann was the one I wanted to see and she would be coming up the entrance stairs this very minute.

I went over to where Terry was standing and saw Ann. She and Sheila were taking off their jackets; I can only guess they wanted to show off their vintage dresses for me once they got inside the ballroom. Sheila had a red dress with a low collar, a bow at the waist, and short sleeves; her hair was wrapped up in a snood. Ann stood next to her.

I looked at her as though for the first time, so completely did her outfit and make-up transform her. She wore a white polka dot dress, and standing there, she caught the remaining light of the day from the door, which allowed the thin material of her dress to outline her figure. Flashes of an image I had seen weeks earlier in our bedroom went in and out of recognition as my eyes saw her as Ann - then someone different.

"There he is," Bob looked up the stairs and spotted me. "Hey, Jerry," he called.

Ann and Sheila were waiting at the middle landing of the staircase. They wanted to make an entrance together so I could see them both at the same time in full costume. They turned and posed, twirling their skirts and showing off their vintage clothes for my scrutiny.

"Wow," I said wide-eyed.

"Holy cow," Terry had been waiting for my response before adding his. "You two look like you walked out of a history book. You look great, both of you."

"Thanks, Terry," they both responded.

"Yea, you look good, alright."

My curiosity got the better of me and I spoke without thinking. "How much make-up are you wearing? I barely recognize you."

"All of it, you silly," Sheila admonished me.

"Is it too much?"Ann asked self-consciously. "Maybe I should take some off."

"NO, no, no," I tried to correct myself. "Don't change anything. It doesn't look bad; it's just so, different."

"Then remember the dress," Ann joked. "I don't want you going home with the wrong woman."

"Oh yea, I'll remember the dress. You can believe that."

"What's wrong with the dress?" she had that, 'what's wrong now' tone in her voice.

"Nothing," I did some quick back peddling. "You look great, believe me. Just don't let anybody dip you over their knee."

"Oh, that," she understood my concern. "This thing was so thin. So I put on some work-out pants underneath, just in case."

"Good idea," I said and we walked towards the bar. "You guys are the first ones in. You want something to drink?"

"Water for me," Ann answered.

"Yea, waters good," was the consensus.

"Nothing stronger," I questioned? "Considering tonight's activities?"

"Especially considering tonight's activities," Sheila answered.

"I'm guessing you missed the 6:00 clock news," Bob asked me.

"I didn't see it but Terry told me the news people had just left before I got here. What did they say?"

"Not much. It was really just a 10 second blurb about one girl dead and another gone missing at a south St. Louis ballroom," Bob explained. "They said there would be details at ten."

"We may be your only customers tonight, Jerry," Sheila warned.

"Don't bet on it," I argued. "In fact, with that little teaser the news gave, I'm betting we'll be packed with curious onlookers and inquiring minds."

"It's possible," Bob agreed, "but it's a hell of a way to get notoriety."

"You're not suggesting this whole thing could be good for business," Ann was perplexed by the idea.

I had my own opinion on the subject. "I think it will at first, but when they've found the one who is committing these crimes and we've had time for the dust to settle, we'll all go back to the way things always were. Casa Loma will survive the same way it always has, by its loyal customers who come here and dance each and every week."

The 'they' I was talking about, that were going to find the one committing these crimes, were very possibly going to be Ann and me, and Bob, and Sheila.

"So let's go over the plan," I directed. "When either of you girls dance with one of our chosen suspects, pay close attention to what he says. Look for leading questions, a southern drawl, and subtle hints, that kind of thing. Bob and/or the other girl who is not dancing will watch from the side just in case. If he puts a hand on you other than a dance move, you start screaming bloody murder."

The reality of the situation settled gloomily on us. Sheila rubbed her hands together as if a chill had crossed her. "Please don't take this wrong, everybody, but I hope we're being silly and nothing happens but a chance to wear these old dresses."

"I just want this thing to end," Ann said in response. "If I wake up tomorrow and it all turns out to be a dream, then I'll be more than fine with that."

"It's like Bob and I were talking last night," I said. "We're not looking for a ghost. We're looking for a real person. Whoever is doing these things is flesh and blood; someone real."

"Well, that doesn't make me feel any safer," Sheila rebuked.

"So we need to be watching each other's back and stay on our toes," I cautioned. "Remember, we're not alone out there. We'll have a room full of people who are friends and fellow dancers who will no doubt be there to help us if we need them."

Bob's silence did not go unnoticed by me. I guessed his belief in the supernatural was beginning to thin after a couple of days and a good night's sleep.

"What have we got to lose?" he broke his own silence. "If nothing else we'll get some great photo-ops in those vintage outfits."

"Then we're together in this, right?" I put my hand in the middle which was joined by Ann, then Sheila, and then Bob.

"Together," we chimed.

Neon got off the bus at the corner of Old Halls Ferry and Parker Roads in front of a brand new Walgreens drug store. After using the restroom in the Firestone Tire shop next door he took out a map in which he had circled the address of George Waterman, his employer and father. Neon did not take the advice of his mother to call George to let him know he was coming. He thought that this confrontation should be as uncomfortable for George as it would be for him. He was counting on George to do the right thing, as he saw it, without giving him too much time to think. Given time, George might come up with all kinds of reasons why he shouldn't take this one time gang banger and high school drop-out into his nice home and family.

It was getting dark and Neon would have a little over a mile to walk on a two lane road without a side walk before getting to George's suburban neighborhood. The shoulder of the road gradually disappeared after several hundred yards forcing Neon to walk in the gulley where water drained. He did his best to side step along the embankment but the few street lights were spaced far apart and offered little help. Occasionally he would step in wet areas where he muddied his shoes. Homes were set apart in distances of one or two acres or more and it was easy to see how the land had once been nothing but farms. He carried a brown grocery bag full of clothes but had neglected to bring any kind of jacket or overcoat and the cold wind easily breached the sweater he was wearing, chilling him to the bone.

Shivering, alone, and lost in the winding back roads of St. Louis County, Neon began to question the validity of his plan. Once the seed of doubt took root, he began to wonder what rights he really did have, and what his worth was to George Waterman and his family, or to anyone. He thought how lost he was, both figuratively and literally, on this cold, dark night. Hope was stripped away from him with each bracing gust and his determination lagged behind him every time he pulled his feet from the soggy earth. He was slowly moving across the county landscape underneath the cold October sky, and out of desperation, started to pray. He prayed for his son, and his mother, and the rest of his family and for George Waterman to accept him as his son.

After thirty minutes of walking in the chilling night Neon thought he could see a collection of small lights winking through the branches. Ten minutes later he entered a neighborhood with a sign that was labeled Sherwood Creek at its entrance. They were clean and well kept residences and the streets had names like Vanderwood, and Tally Wood, and other names all ending in 'woods'. It was only 8:30 but the streets were quiet and empty and the further Neon walked the more out of place he felt. He wished he were home. At the end of the street he found the house he was looking for.

Neon walked past the SUV parked in the driveway and onto the porch, his stride slowing with each step that he took. He could hear voices from inside; first a young, female voice, then an older male voice, then laughter. He reached for the doorbell then stopped. He did not want to be the spoiler, the fly in the ointment, and standing there with his grocery bag full of clothes and muddy shoes, he suddenly felt guilty. Guilty for being poor, guilty for being a suspect, guilty for having an illegitimate son, and now for being the illegitimate son of the man who lived inside. He could see shapes moving inside the house and backed away from the door. He backed away from the porch light, then off of the porch completely, with his feet gaining speed as he went. He was near the mailbox and just a few feet away from being free when he heard the front door behind him open and George's voice call,

"Neon, Neon, is that you out there? Where are you going, man? Come on back here now."

He was ready to run, to run away from these strangers and this tidy little neighborhood with big expensive homes. He wanted to run back to what he knew, to the streets in the city, to his home and family that loved him. Like a misbehaving school boy he turned at the edge of the drive way and walked back to the porch where George was standing.

"I'm sorry to bother you, George, this late in the evening, and everything," he cursed himself for the words he chose. Neon wanted to get an apology, not give one. He wanted acceptance but he had no words with which to make his case. Instead of demanding that this man who sired him be responsible and accountable for his actions, Neon fell back into his everyday roll of employee to his employer.

George walked out onto the porch and pulled the door closed behind him. "Don't worry about that. You've come a long way to see me. Now, what is it you want to say?"

Neon guessed that George was closing that door for more than one reason. "I'm not really sure. It took me most of the day to find your home and now that I'm here, I'm not sure what to say."

"We've known each other a long time now, Neon, almost two years. Isn't that right?"

"That's right."

"You should know by now that you can talk to me about anything you want. Just go ahead and tell me what you came here to say."

Never had Neon felt as alone as he did at that moment. He felt the chill of the wind deep in his bones. He felt as though the weight of the bag of clothes in his arms was a hundred pounds. His shoes were muddy and he was a stranger, a stranger at his father's home. He was tired, cold, and hungry, but worse than all of these things he had no words for his father. He started to sob and tears issued from his eyes. Embarrassed and ashamed, he turned his head away. "I'm sorry.....something got in my eye. I've got to go, got to go now, George."

Neon took two steps before George grabbed him by the shoulders and turned him around and hugged him. "You don't need to say you're sorry to me. It's me whose sorry, son. That's right, you're my son, and I'm sorry for not telling you sooner. I'm sorry for leaving you and your brother and your mother. I'm sorry for not bein' a father to you all these years. You go ahead and cry if you want to, God knows you got a right. God knows."

Customers entered from the stairs, shaking off the night's chill. There was an early fog that was beginning to roll in over the old homes and filter down the empty streets, and the occasional threatening thunder clap shuddered out of the night sky.

We watched the group class and commented on the ones who were getting it quicker than others. Some people just get it faster than others, frustrating those who took longer. Sooner or later though, as long as they keep trying, everybody gets it. The only ones who don't are the ones who give up. That is until you get to the point where steps aren't the issue anymore. Then, knowing step patterns isn't as important as knowing yourself. You can't teach improvisation and spontaneity, that's something that has to come from within a dancer. Playing the breaks in the music, and playing with the breaks, was just the start. There were all kinds of accents and changes in the music that allowed a dancer to really reach out.

Interpretation of the music with improvised steps was a very big part of swing dancing from the very beginning and still was among some of the more skilled dancers. Bob could do it, but his variations were a little too precise and careful. Dancin' Don had a couple of moves, but they were too limited and predictable. It was all too new to me and I seldom let myself get too inventive. Marty tried, but was obviously self-conscious and his partner had no idea what he was doing. Klaus however, was the undisputed master at the Casa Loma Ballroom when it came to leading and dancing improvised steps. He would take a simple move, take it apart, and put it back together, with holds and syncopations, and come up with something you had never seen before. And all to the delight and entertainment of his partner who was suddenly dancing something she had never danced before. He was good at assessing his partner's capabilities as to what she could or couldn't do. Sometimes it worked, sometimes it didn't, but he never let it bother him or his partner. As much as a lot of the other guys hated to admit it, they wanted to dance like Klaus.

The problem most guys had was how to lead their partner as they went off the beaten path of established moves. Their wild movements and radical departure of conventional rhythms was certainly expressive, but it generally left the lady confused and by herself while all the time linked to her partner by a handhold or two.

What it takes is work and practice. Dancers can become too easily satisfied or too easily frustrated and give up trying to get better.

When the group class finished and the house music started, I got busy filling water pitchers and selling them for $2.00 apiece. Bob and Sheila headed for the dance floor and when the music changed Bob came back and got Ann dancing as well. I was working with one eye focused on the girls, knowing my attention would be divided for the rest of the night until I got off work and could give them my full focus.

"Ann and Sheila wear those vintage clothes like they were made for them," Rita commented while getting her pitcher of water.

"Yea, she looks so different," I answered.

"I like her new look," she said.

"So, where's Klaus? I didn't see him come up the stairs with you."

"Klaus sometimes comes here straight from work. They let him take time off for weekend events like the Frankie Manning workshop and he makes it up staying late in the evenings. He'll meet me here later.

I stared blankly at the revelation. My next question must have been written all over my face although I didn't know how to phrase it.

Rita saw it in my expression and made the decision to speak up on her own. "You're wondering if Klaus worked late the night Vanessa went missing."

"That's what I was wondering, yea."

"Yes, he did," she told me outright. "Not that that should be incriminating since, according to what I heard, Vanessa's death was ruled accidental."

"But I thought you told the police that Klaus was with you all night?"

Rita looked at the pitcher of water in her hands and back at me. "Come down here a minute," she indicated the other end of the bar where no one was standing.

"I'm going to tell you something I wanted to tell you Saturday night at the party. I was lying when I told the police that I was with Klaus that night. I don't know why…wait, no, that's not true. I lied because he asked me to. I told the police that because I thought Klaus was innocent, and I still think he's innocent."

"Then why did he lie to the police in the first place?" I asked.

"He told me he got nervous when they mentioned the fedora hat, the one he'd been dreaming about. He was afraid if he didn't have an alibi for that night the police would have asked him all kinds of other questions and he was afraid of saying the wrong thing."

"So why tell me now?" I asked her.

"Because to tell you the truth I'm having doubts about what I did," she said plainly. "I still believe in Klaus. I still believe he's innocent, but I want to be sure."

"How can you do that?"

"Klaus trusts you. The only reason he came over to Ann's house Sunday was because he thinks you have a good head on your shoulders. He thinks you and Ann are as involved in this as much as he is, but he doesn't want to have anything to do with Bob. I think you can understand why."

"Ok, but what can I do?"

"Talk to him," she told me. "Find out what he did that night. Ask him if he saw Vanessa, or talked to her. You can tell him you talked to me and you discovered we both drove different cars that night. Maybe he'll tell you something, maybe he won't, but I'd sure like it if you'd try. He won't talk to me about it. Every time I bring up the subject he just ignores me."

Her idea sounded crazy but it wasn't any crazier than what our little group was attempting.

"I'll talk to him, if you want, but if he won't talk to you then I can't see why he would talk to me."

"I'm probably just being silly. If he tells you he just went home that night, then great. I just want to know."

"Ok, Rita, I'll do what I can," I told her. I agreed to confront Kluas with this new information but it wasn't only for Rita's sake I would be asking. There was a chance that maybe Bob was right about Klaus and I wanted to find out for myself.

Anna Schlemmer got behind the bar when she arrived without a minute to spare. The news spot on the television brought in almost every dancer that had ever been to Casa Loma and some people who had never been there before. I was making drinks and straining my neck around the crowd of four and five deep at the bar to see if I could spot Ann, Sheila, or Bob but saw only the faces of thirsty patrons. To say I was distracted was an understatement.

"Hey Jerry, how's it going?"

"Busy," I said without looking up, and when I did I saw that it was Dancin' Don standing at the end of the bar calling out to me.

"You look busy," he said in response.

I had not seen Don since Bob and I had confronted him Monday in his apartment and had not seen him out dancing since Michelle had gone missing. I stopped what I was doing and went right over to shake his hand.

"Good to see you out, Don. I'm sorry about the way things went Monday. I meant no disrespect. We had good intentions. Things just got out of hand."

"Don't worry about it. Anyway, that seemed more like Bob's tactics then yours." It seemed he had sized up the situation pretty well. "Bob's not a bad guy, but when you spend all your time with mentally disturbed people, it can rub off on you. You know what I mean?"

"Yea, thanks, Don. No hard feelings then?"

"No hard feelings," he said as he turned and disappeared into the crowd.

I took a minute to try and spot the girls and Bob before two voices called to me to get them drinks and I was jolted back to the onrush of the crowd at the bar. I wondered, in those few seconds, if there was any truth to what Don said about Bob. I also wondered if I had left the girls in the hands of someone who was mentally compromised.

It was an hour later that the flood of drink orders began to let up and the bar had only a couple standing at one end and a single guy standing at the other. It wasn't over, but it was manageable, and both Anna and I took a collective sigh of relief.

"You guys were pretty busy there for a while," Detective Towning's voice got my attention.

"Detective," I said, acknowledging him standing at the end of the bar. "Is there any news on Michelle or Neon?"

"None, but after they put Neon and Michelle's pictures all over the news tonight we should get a lot of help from the community; more help then we want, I'm sure."

"Did they talk to you at all?" I asked him.

"I talked to someone on the phone today," it was obvious the Detective was not completely satisfied that the media was now involved. "As you can see, being on television has its effects."

"So you're here for what, security?"

"Not exactly," he corrected me. "I think your boss has always had, and still has, plenty of security here. No, I was hoping to find a single male, over six feet tall, wearing a broad brimmed fedora hat."

"I've seen three guys wearing that kind of hat just from behind the bar."

"I've seen six so far, and three were over six feet." he countered.

"You don't sound encouraged."

"It's not that I doubt Ann's story, it's this crowd. They're contaminating the suspect pool. You'd have to be an idiot to try anything with this many people around. We may have lost the last chance we had at catching whoever abducted that poor girl."

I was reminded there was still hope for Michelle in all this and at the same time, a little bit relieved that we may not have any luck locating the one who was responsible. I was having more reservations about putting Ann and Sheila in danger even though we only had the slightest chance of encountering dangerous entities.

The next forty-five minutes were the longest in my life. There was a constant flow of patrons coming in with about the same number leaving after seeing nothing more than a bunch of swing dancers. The drink orders were manageable for one person but the threat of another rush remained until Pat came up and told me I could go. By then I had done all the clean-up that was needed and almost bolted from behind the bar to find the others.

When I got to the dance floor, I could see a circle dance going on in the center of the room. A couple had just gotten out on the dance floor ready to show their stuff. They started with a couple of sugar pushes, then a swing out and from that they did switches. It looked like they were having trouble keeping up with the brisk tempo of music being played before they were bumped by another couple. The music was quick and the next pair glided into the center with some smooth shag steps as they took their turn.

I was more interested in finding Ann, Sheila, and Bob than watching whoever was showing off on the floor, so when I squeezed through and spotted Sheila, I quickly made my way over to her.

"Hey?" I tried to speak above the music without yelling.

"Jerry, hi," Sheila was happy to see me.

"Where's Bob and Ann," I asked?

"I'm not sure where Bob is, but I saw Ann just a minute ago. Don't worry, she's fine. Everything's fine."

"I thought Bob was supposed to be watching you two?"

"I think we kind of gave up on our man hunt a while back," Sheila explained. "You're not disappointed are you?"

"Naw, of course not," I freely admitted. "I just think we should be a little more vigilant."

She looked at me sympathetically. "Ann and I danced with everyone on Bob's list and nothing; no visions, no voices with a southern twang, no overt acts of aggression, nothing."

"As far as I'm concerned, that's good news," I reassured her. "This has been the longest night of my life standing behind that bar and not being able to be out here with you and Ann."

"That's sweet of you," she smiled, while everyone standing around the circle clapped for the tricky move the couple in the center had just done.

"What was that?" I was almost shouting, trying to be heard over the music.

"I said that's very sweet of you."

"I still can't hear what you're saying."

"Never mind," she gave up.

"Where was it you saw Ann last?"

"Who," she asked?

"Ann, where did you see Ann?"

Sheila was not looking at me but in the center like everyone else was. "Ann's right there," she pointed to the couple in the circle who turned out to be Ann and Marty.

I was at once glad to have found Ann and at the same time concerned for her immediate safety at seeing her in the arms of Marty and the moves he was attempting in the circle. The music was Roy Brown's 'Boogie at Midnight', a manageable triple rhythm beat for Marty and most other swing dancers, as long as he didn't try the swing out step with all the Frankie Manning flair. As I watched, I became aware of a gleam in Marty's eye. I could tell what he was thinking and sure enough, by the next measure I could see the gesticulating leg move that was the beginnings of a Frankie Manning type swing out, all stretched out like an ironing board.

Before I knew it, Marty had Ann dangling from his left hand as he swung her wildly around the center of the circle. I was afraid for Ann, as much if not more than if Marty were the actual reincarnation of the serial killer's ghost we were supposed to be looking for. I would have to act quickly if I was going to save her from any physical harm. I couldn't wait for the right moment; I only hoped my timing would somehow come out right. I ran out, just as Marty was releasing Ann from a closed dance hold on counts 5 and 6 of the swing out, and slid in between him and Ann, stealing the lead. The transition worked smoothly enough that we were able to continue the dance without breaking our movement or rhythm. The crowd liked what they saw and clapped leaving a, none too happy Marty standing by himself looking foolish.

"My savior," Ann was happy to see me and be free of the train wreck she was destined to be a part of.

"Happy to be of service," I quipped.

I looked behind me at the hulking figure of Marty and gave him a shrug and friendly grin but instead of leaving the circle to let us dance, he just stood there. The moves Ann and I were doing demanded I turn my back on Marty and I could feel the hairs on the back of my head tingle knowing he was still there. Certainly Marty would not take his frustrations out on me right there in front of everyone. That would go way beyond any violation of dance etiquette and any excepted rules of the Casa Loma Ballroom. Still, in those seconds that I had my back to him, I couldn't help feeling like something was about to come crashing down upon me. It was then that I felt his hands grip my shoulders. The next instant I felt my whole body being flung into the air and came crashing down on the hard wood dance floor, shoulder first, with my arms and legs following like falling branches. Even though I half expected a retaliation from Marty, I was just as surprised seeing him try to continue his dance with Ann as I lay there looking up from the floor. He acted as if I had been appropriately removed from the picture and he was now Ann's legitimate partner. I started to pick myself off the floor as others were coming to my aid, not knowing how I would overcome such an opponent. I only knew that I had to get Ann from him one way or another. I felt someone's hands and arms pick me up and by the time I got to my feet, I could see Detective Towning and Terry Strahan take either side of Marty, effectively restraining him and removing him from the dance floor.

I went right to Ann as they were moving Marty away. Everyone was shocked at the outrageous incident that was happening in front of them. The clapping and cheering had stopped and gleeful expressions had changed to amazement. But the strangest thing about the occurrence was what came out of Marty's mouth as he was being dragged out of the circle.

"You take your black hands off me, you damned niggers."

Detective Towning, who was black, looked first at Marty then at Terry who was holding Marty's other shoulder, then back at Marty. You could see him mouth the words 'What did you just say'? It was the plurality of Marty's insult as well as the profanity of the 'n' word that made no sense to anyone. Maybe Marty couldn't see that it was Terry Strahan, a white man, who was the other one dragging him off the floor. Everyone knew Marty was racially biased but no one suspected him to be so overt with his declarations. His violent actions and disrespectful behavior had earned him a ride downtown and a possible warrant for resisting arrest. As yet, no one that evening had better demonstrated their potential for dangerous behavior more than Marty. Detective Towning would question him thoroughly before deciding on what to do with him.

"Are you alright, honey?" I asked once I got back to Ann.

"I'm fine, but what about you? Are you hurt?"

"I think I'm Ok," I did a mental check on my body. "My shoulder's a little bruised, but I'm Ok."

"What an asshole," Sheila declared.

"Well, that was pretty weird, even for Marty," Bob said, from just behind me. I figured it was he and Sheila who had helped me off the floor.

"Yea," I agreed. "Did you hear what he said? I think he said 'take your hands off me you damned'…" I didn't want to finish the sentence out loud.

"'Niggers.' He said the word 'niggers'," Bob was not afraid to say it aloud. "I couldn't believe it. He even shouted it."

"I was beginning to think we would get through the night without anything weird happening," Ann said.

"Do you think this is 'Orville Hatcher' related?" Sheila frowned.

"Well, I certainly do," I didn't wait for anyone else's answer. "I had a strange experience earlier tonight when a stage light coming off the floor took the shape of a tall thin man in a hat and danced all around the room. Then, just as his dance ended he went up in flash of flame."

"Why didn't you tell us this before?" Bob asked.

"I didn't want to scare anyone. We were all a little anxious when we first got here and I didn't see the need to alarm anyone any further. We've gotten a little lackadaisical and I think we just had a wake- up call."

"A wake-up call," Bob questioned?

"That's right, and I think we need to keep our eyes open and get back to watching each other's backs. Agreed?"

"Agreed," Ann and Sheila answered, with Bob giving a reserved nod.

Before I knew it, it was 11:30 pm, and the crowd had dwindled down to around seventy five, which, in a room as big as the Casa Loma, was such a small number of people that it made the place look empty. There were about ten or eleven couples out on the dance floor doing all they could to keep the night and the dancing from ending. Others were walking across the big dance space to say good bye to friends they had missed in the exchange of dancing partners through the evening. They were catching up on gossip that was acquired through the grapevine. Most of it was about Vanessa, Michelle, and Neon, and all of it being on television with little side bars about Marty's and my confrontation out on the dance floor.

Ann and I were sitting at a table by the center/right of the dance floor. I saw Klaus standing out on the floor talking to a couple not more than ten or twelve feet away.

"Remember I told you about what Rita said to me earlier, about Klaus lying to the police?"

"Yes, I remember," Ann answered, with only half interest. She had one of her shoes off and was massaging her foot under the table.

"Well, I'm going to go over there and ask him about it as soon as that couple leaves."

"Sure, go ahead, I'm fine." She reassured me. "I'll be sitting right here giving my feet a rest."

I was reluctant to leave her alone even if it was from such a short a distance. "Alright, but look, please stay right here where I can see you, Ok?"

"I will," she said impatiently. "Now go. I'll be fine."

Klaus saw me approaching and reached out his hand smiling. "Hey, Jerry, how's it going?"

"Good, everything's good," I smiled back. "Listen, Klaus, this maybe nothing at all but I wanted to ask you something about the night Vanessa….the night she died."

Klaus dropped his smile, "Ok," he said, as if taking up a challenge.

"Well, I noticed Rita came here by herself tonight and when I asked her where you were, she said that sometimes you stay late at work and you both drive different cars here."

He put his hands on his hips and looked first to the floor and then to me. "And you want to know if I drove by myself the night Vanessa died."

"Yea, that's what I want to know," I said.

Klaus looked at his foot and kicked the floor. We both knew I was acting on no authority whatsoever beyond my own self satisfaction and he could just as easily tell me to go screw myself.

"All right, I guess you could find out without my telling you anyway. We did drive different cars that night, so what?"

"So, were you with Rita that night?"

"Oh, for god's sake, who have you been talking to? This sounds more like the ravings of Bob Trentway than you. That crazy lunatic spends every day with deranged criminals. Don't tell me you're asking me these things on his advice?"

Bob and Sheila had just come up behind Klaus not having heard what we just said.

"I'm not asking you these things for anyone but myself," I tried to be civil. "Maybe we should finish this another time," I said indicating to Klaus that there was someone behind him.

Klaus turned around and saw that it was Bob and Sheila. "Oh, so this is an ambush, is it?"

"Nobody's ambushing you, Klaus," I tried to reassure him. "Bob and Sheila don't know what we're talking about or what we said. They just now walked over here."

"Just a coincidence, is that what I'm supposed to think, with all the sneaking around you guys are always doing, as thick as thieves. You think I'm going to trust you when you're hanging around with him?" Klaus was really venting his anger pointing his finger first at me and then at Bob.

"What's this all about, Jerry?" Bob jumped into the fray, armed with overblown suspicions.

"Why not say what you were going to say. Just because Sheila and I are standing here doesn't mean you can't talk about us."

"What I wanted to say to Klaus had nothing to do with you or Sheila," I argued.

We were shouting at each other and were drawing more attention then we wanted. Others began to gather around us. Dancin' Don tried to do what he could to calm the situation.

"I don't think name calling is going to get us anywhere," Don attempted to insert a little dignity into our ranting. "We all used to be friends once and I think it's important to remember that."

Ann watched the growing cluster gather around our heated discussion. Unimpressed by the displays of temperament, she preferred to sit out the blustery exchanges where she was, had she not felt the unrelenting call of nature. She made no effort to push through those who were gathered around Klaus and me and announce to me and everyone else that she was going to the ladies room. After all, she was a grown woman and was one of the few who weren't completely losing it.

She walked past the angry voices and across the ballroom to the stairs that led to the balcony. After she ascended the winding staircase, she noticed someone in a hat and long coat leaning over the railing looking down onto the ballroom below but gave them little notice. Moments later, when Ann exited the ladies room, that same person with the long coat and hat was still there at the railing. She didn't recognize who it was but for some reason she felt she knew them. She took two steps toward the stairs and hesitated, then one more step and stopped, her curiosity getting the better of her. Cautiously, almost on tip toe, she positioned herself just to the right and at a safe distance from whoever it was.

"Rita? Is that you, Rita?" Ann was still not sure who she was seeing.

The figure with the hat turned her head in Ann's direction. "Hello, Ann."

Downstairs on the dance floor, we had collected almost everyone who had not yet left.

"Go ahead," Klaus challenged. "Go ahead and tell everybody if that's what you want to do. You all think I'm responsible for Vanessa's death and Michelle's abduction. Go ahead, tell the world if you want to; you'll only make yourselves look as big a lunatic as this guy," Klaus indicated Bob.

"Oh, I'm the lunatic, is that it?" Bob started to get in Klaus's face.

Pat and Terry got into the argument trying to calm us and at the same time, get us to leave.

"If you have any reason to think that someone might be responsible for these missing girls you should be going to the police," Pat told us. "This is not the time or the place…"

"Why not now," Bob argued, "Why should we wait and let them get away, or go out there and harm other innocent victims?"

"Well, go ahead, Bob," Klaus answered him. "Why don't you tell everyone who you think is guilty? Go ahead, tell them."

Bob knew he did not have enough evidence to accuse Klaus directly; all he had was his suspicions.

"Ok, Jerry," Klaus felt he was ready for me, "how about you? Who do you think is guilty?"

Monica had found her voice and was more than ready to use it. "This is ridiculous. We know who did it and as soon as the police find that black guy this will all be over. You're all arguing for nothing."

Up on the railing Ann had realized it was Rita standing there. "What are you doing up here all by yourself?" she asked carefully, with an eerie sense that something was not quite right.

"I'm watching those idiots down there. Com' on over here and take a look," Rita smiled wryly.

Hesitantly Ann took the few steps that closed the distance between them that, until now, had been her safety net. She returned Rita's smile and looked at the scene below them. Just about everyone left was standing around Klaus and me. We were all shouting over each other, unwilling to listen and unable to understand.

"From up here they don' even look real," Rita's voice was not her own, it was changing as she spoke.

Ann felt a cold shiver go up and down her spine but rational thought told her not to jump to conclusions. She marshaled her courage and brought up a pertinent question.

"I've wanted to ask you something, and since it's just you and me up here…."

"Uh huh," Rita answered.

"Where were you the night Vanessa went missing?"

Rita had been leaning on the rail when Ann asked her about Vanessa. It was then that she straightened up and turned to face her. "Why ask me 'bout Vanessa? What's goin' on in that pretty little head a' yours? You think ah'm guilty a somethin' maybe?"

Her voice had unmistakably changed and when Ann looked into Rita's face she could see a shadowy image of someone else.

"NO, no, I don't know. I mean, I don't know you," Ann held up her arm to keep Rita away and as she backed up she tripped over a chair that was behind her. Rita lunged forward grabbing Ann with one arm around her waist and a razor at her throat. She had surprised Ann with her quickness and strength. Ann froze with the cold steel pressing against her neck.

"Hush, now, or you'll give me away," Rita said and dragged Ann away from the sight of anyone downstairs. Ann did not want to be taken anywhere near the dark corners that were all around the upstairs bar, but with the knife held to her throat, she had no choice.

Ann was thinking as fast as she could, "Rita, Rita, why are you doing this? I've done nothing to you."

"You were just at the wrong place, at the wrong time, that's all." Rita forced Ann to the edge of the upstairs bar. "Com' on over here now," she commanded, keeping an eye toward the stairs.

"We're gonna hide back here till everyone else leaves, then I'm takin' you home with me."

"Then it was you who took Michelle and….killed Vanessa?" Ann asked her.

"I didn't want to hurt Vanessa. It was her fault," Rita was talking in huffs of breath while forcefully escorting Ann to the other side of the bar. "We were meant to be together. She knew that it was God's will. She knew that and she fought against me anyway… fought against God's will. I'm truly sorry about Vanessa."

"And Michelle, what did you do with Michelle?"

"She's fine. That pretty little thing is safe and sound, you'll see. We'll all be together real soon. Just like a family; just like a real family." Rita held the knife to Ann's throat with one hand and turned to lift the hinged part of the bar allowing access. It took most of Rita's strength to lift that small part up and when she did, she inadvertently relaxed the razor she was holding to Ann's neck. Ann seized the opportunity and grabbed Rita's hand that was holding the razor. Rita abruptly dropped the end of the bar and it slammed back with a resounding bang.

The sound echoed about the walls of the ballroom, bringing our arguments to a dead stop. For the first time since I had approached Klaus, I looked over to Ann and saw that she was no longer sitting where I had left her.

The ballroom was so big that it was impossible to pinpoint exactly where the sound had originated as it reverberated about the room.

"Ann, where's Ann," I shouted to anyone. I pushed past Klaus and searched over the shoulders of Bob and Pat Brannon but could not find Ann.

"Where did that noise come from?" someone asked.

"Ann, can you hear me?" I shouted frantically moving in and out of those standing around me.

"Just relax, Jerry," Pat counseled me. "I'm sure she's here somewhere. She probably went to the ladies room. Can somebody…"

"I'll look," Sheila was on her way even as Pat was suggesting someone go.

"I'll go with her," Bob was already on the move and I could see that Dancin' Don and Klaus, were starting to wear the same concern on their faces as I was.

"I thought it came from upstairs," someone else said.

"Help, help," I heard a voice call out.

"Be quiet," I told everyone. "Did you hear that?"

"Help, help me," I heard Ann's voice come from somewhere.

Everyone else looked around the room for some sign of Ann or the source of the loud bang. I was doing pretty much the same thing as I took a halting step in one direction and then the other. I tried to focus on where the sound had most likely occurred. It was just then that I remembered the dancing image of light in the form of Orville Hatcher pointing up that I suddenly knew without doubt where the noise came from and that Ann was in trouble.

I heard Bob and Sheila cry out as I ran to the closest staircase to the upstairs balcony, everyone following close behind me. When I got to the top I could see Ann and the shadowy figure of someone in a dark overcoat struggling with each other. Bob was standing back holding his shoulder which had a deep slash and Sheila had her arms around Bob. I moved past the long upstairs bar faster than I could ever remember moving. It was then that I could clearly see Rita's face. She was wearing an overcoat and fighting with Ann to get her hand free; the hand that held a straight razor. Rita saw my face just as I saw hers. Behind me about twenty other people were about to converge on the scene. In a last desperate effort to get away, Rita reached for Ann's wrist and dropping the razor, took one step up on a chair, the next on a table, and then jumped over the railing of the balcony still holding onto Ann. Ann screamed with both terror and pain as her shoulder pulled from the weight of Rita's body. Most of us ran over to Ann as others went to the railing to see Rita swing precariously from the balcony.

By the time I got to Ann, she was about to be pulled over the edge. Rita dangled from Ann's outstretched arm, still too far from the floor for any kind of safe landing.

"Rita!" Klaus shouted, leaning over the rails with several others.

"We'll pull you up," I told her. My first impulse was to let her fall but, after hearing Klaus cry out, I had a change of heart. Rita was looking from the floor down below her then back up at us. Others were racing to get downstairs and she would have to make a decision quickly whether she would let us pull her to safety or take her chances letting go. Her face was calm and relaxed and I knew she had already made her decision.

"Can't stay," was her two word answer as she let go of Ann and dropped some fifteen feet to the floor below.

Those of us who were leaning over the railing let out a harsh gasp of breath as we watched Rita hit the hardwood floor. She let out another gasp of pain, and lay there reaching for her ankle which had just shattered in several places.

With the help of those around me I pulled Ann back up onto the safety of the balcony and held her for a long time in the solace of my embrace.

Klaus ran down to Rita as did most of the others. Someone suggested we call 911 which several were already doing. Pat was getting Anna to help Sheila tend to Bob's bleeding shoulder and get him to the office where there was a first aid kit. Down below Terry Strahan stood guard over Rita and kept everyone at a secure distance from where she lay. Klaus was able to break through Terry's protection and knelt down next to Rita holding her face in his hands.

"It'll be all right, baby, I promise. It'll be all right," he kept saying over and over. Rita just looked up at him with questioning eyes.

When Ann's shaking arms finally released me, she told me we had to call Detective Towning right away. She said Rita told her that she was keeping Michelle at her home. I called the detective who had just released Marty and was driving him back to his car at the Casa Loma Ballroom. I got Rita's address from some of the other swing dancers and gave it to the detective.

Later that night at Ann's home we got a call from the detective. He told us they found Michelle tied up in an old foot locker at the foot of Rita's bed. She was alive, but terrified and a little out of her mind. She was also malnourished and much in need of a shower.

CHAPTER TWENTY SIX

EPILOGUE

I woke up the next morning, slowly dragging my hands down over my face, allowing the dark to linger a moment longer as I recapped the bizarre outcome of the night before. Moments later Ann and I both sat up in bed and we looked at each other a long time before shaking our heads.

We made coffee and toast and watched the local news expanding on the story that had only been released the night before. The person arrested had been identified as one Rita Beltman and that Michelle Torence had been found locked up at the accused's home. With statements they had obtained from the police, the commentator also mentioned that another warrant had been issued for the accused in connection to the murder of Vanessa Billings, daughter of the late Senator Allen Billings. The reporter said they would try to follow up with statements from Casa Loma Ballroom's owner, Pat Brannon, later in the evening.

Ann and I were happy to be left out of all the press coverage. Pat told me I could take off that Friday night and that he would see me on the following Wednesday. We used our caller ID during the next few days in an effort to stay out of the news.

We called Bob and Sheila, mostly just to check in on them and on Bob's injured shoulder. Bob got twenty stitches and a scar he was all too happy to show off at family gatherings, or nights out with friends, or basically any time he got the chance. Through it all, no one brought up the name 'Orville Hatcher'. Rita Beltman was a real live citizen of the last part of the twentieth century. She was someone who could be held accountable for the crimes that were committed; the crimes she had committed. Rita's legal counsel based her defense on an insanity plea. Curiously, Rita's team of lawyers did not subpoena testimony of anyone from the swing group, even Klaus, in spite of Klaus's urgings. They instead used the expert testimony from several psychiatrists who unanimously attested to Rita's schizophrenic condition.

By the time Wednesday rolled around, we were remembering the entire incident as though it had happened in another age and at another time. When I went to work, I was greeted at the top of the stairs by Terry Strahan.

"Hey, Jerry, what's up?" He shook my hand and I heard the group class just finishing up.

"Looks like the same ol' same ol'," I told him.

"Some things never change."

"That's what I'm finding out."

"Hey, ya' gotta love it."

"Yea, ya' gotta love it," I repeated, but my heart wasn't really in it.

Most of the swing crowd had returned with a few obvious exceptions. Everyone was talking about who would replace Klaus and Rita in the Swing Federation. There were some who wondered aloud if anyone knew where the records were kept. Some were asking about Michelle. Neither Liz nor Michelle came back to the swing scene and everyone assumed they would probably never return.

Bob and Sheila got there about a half hour after I did. They attracted an ever changing crowd of three or four curious well-wishers as they walked around the outside of the dance floor. Ann had decided to stay home; it would be a couple more weeks, at least, before she would decide if she would continue her vintage swing dancing.

Everyone seemed to be adjusting to the tragic events of the previous weeks. That should have consoled me, but it didn't. Standing behind the bar and listening to the band start its first set I felt a strange sense of loss. I felt sympathy for poor Vanessa, Michelle, and Klaus, and even Rita, but there was something else. I felt like all of this, the vintage scene and everyone in it was slipping past me. I wanted to protect the memory of what had happened to us. To keep alive even the terrible moments of what we had endured during the previous weeks. Our obsession for the nostalgia of the swing era had given us a memory we were not likely to forget. But standing there, I felt like the whole thing was moving away from me. Maybe forgetting was a necessary part of the healing process and letting go was an intricate piece of its therapy. If that were true, then why did I feel as though we were in denial of the pain we should all be feeling?

I turned away from all the costumed dancers on the floor and the old swing steps they were performing. Out of some kind of perfunctory reflex, I looked down at the space behind the cabinets that had led me to see the scribbling that had once been underneath on the back wall. I wanted to crawl back there and see if I could find them again, as if not only to validate the existence of another time, but our time as well. Ultimately change would move mercilessly forward and everything that had happened would be nothing more than a memory, at best.

Did history repeat itself, and are we destined to repeat our mistakes, unable or unwilling to learn from them? Or, are our experiences unique, as we are unique ourselves? I existed in the here now and Ann was here with me and I wanted to hold on to that existence for as long as I could. I wanted to hold onto Ann.

We had embraced the nostalgia of the big band era with open arms, and at the same time, everyone in it as well, forgetting the danger of such naivety. Friendships involve us in more ways than we can imagine and we should look beyond someone's dance skills or position in the community before committing ourselves to anyone's cause.

Memories are fleeting and selective, but in the end, they are all we have to keep the past alive. Would nostalgia claim our story as we go on to live in the memory of what we think, used to be? I wanted what had happened to us to be remembered. I wanted everyone to know that we had written our own chapter in the Book of Dreams at the Casa Loma Ballroom.

The End

www.ingramcontent.com/pod-product-compliance
Lightning Source LLC
Chambersburg PA
CBHW061503050726
47593CB00002B/422